A VOW UNBROKEN

A Twist of Tobacco Series
Book Two

Rita Ownby Holcomb

Copyright 2016 Rita Holcomb

Published by Fountain Spring Publishing

ISBN-13:978-0692739198 (Fountain Spring Publishing)

ISBN-10:069273919X

Acknowledgments

To Darrell: For the photos taken; for the miles driven; for tolerating suppers thrown together and for fighting dust bunnies while I write; but most of all for being there for me constantly. Thank you, Darling.

To Stuart: For editing lousy first drafts; for being my chief nit-picker; for remaining interested; and for letting me bounce ideas off your brain. Thank you, Son.

To John: For being my friend; for your dialogue ideas; for keeping me honest and on track; and for sticking with me through book two. Thank you, Cowboy.

To Bobbie: Not sure you know how much I appreciate all you have done for me. Thank you.

I Love you all

Rita

Dedication

This series is dedicated to my father, Guy M Ownby. I am eternally grateful to you for not only the bloodline but the legacy of this fascinating family.

The story took roots with Lizzie's granddaughter, Virginia Benson Ashlock. Her initial research and personal stories about Lizzie, Watt, Queen and the others stirred the creative side of my brain.

Virginia, I hope you are enjoying a cup of coffee with Daddy and looking down on me with pride for the story I have told.

A Vow Unbroken

TABLE OF CONTENTS

- WANDERLUST 1
  - Sumner County, Tennessee, October 1826 1
  - Moving 3
  - Lewisburg, Tennessee, April, 1827 4
  - Horse Training 4
  - The Roan Filly 5
  - A Child is born 7
- REST IN PEACE-1866 9
  - On the Road 9
  - Mammy Bess 10
  - Laurie 12
  - Eli Says Goodbye 16
  - Speculation 17
  - Brothers 19
  - Reading of the Will 21
- RECONSTRUCTION, 1866 25
  - Home Again 25
  - Peaches 26
  - Lizzie Visits her Mama 29
  - Queen 30
  - Molasses and Honey 31
  - The Honey Tree 33
  - Bees Light the Way 36
  - Letter from Joe 38
  - Letters from Texas 39
- LOVE IS IN THE AIR 1867 41
  - Yankee Visitor 41
  - Polly 43
  - Molasses 44
  - Watt and Marthey 46
  - Sam and Ruthie 50
  - Luther Peterson 52
  - Venus Rising 55
- Lester and Baxter 58
- WEDDINGS AND BABIES, 1868 59
  - Gathering Stones 59
  - A House becomes a Home 61
  - Lester and Baxter 63
  - Mama Lizzie 65
  - Emmy 67

 Twins for Sam 68
 Amnesty 70
ACQUISITION, 1869 75
 Oh Shit 75
 Spilt Milk 77
 Granma Laurie 79
 Homesteading 80
 Possessed by the Devil 82
 Christmas 85
 Fire 87
Land Grant 92
A TIME TO MOURN, 1870 93
 A Cookie for Ed 93
 Easter 98
 Influenza 100
 Corn Shucking 103
 Bobby Lee 105
QUESTIONS OF LIFE, 1871 107
 Fanny Winstead 107
 Old Ned and Lady Blue 108
 Puppies 110
 Lizzie and Jeff 110
 Henry and Tag 112
 Watt 114
Marriage Bonds 116
JACK AND AGGIE, 1872 117
 The Wrath of Watt 117
 Maggie 118
 Fourth of July Fireworks 120
 Nan Takes a Fall 123
Farm Map 126
A DOUBLE WEDDING, 1873 127
 Joe's Inheritance 127
 Two is Better than One 129
 Wedding Preparations 132
 Fountain Spring 135
 Elopement 139
 Family for Christmas 141
 Christmas Day 143
MOTHERHOOD, 1874 147

    Flooding 147
    Twins for Will 149
    Tomatoes 150
    Maurice and Carol 152
    Craig and Dora 153
    Queen Pines for John 155
CRAIG AND DORA, 1875 157
    Wedding Feast 157
    Babies 159
    Letter from Texas 162
    Dora 164
CENTENNIAL CELEBRATIONS, 1876 167
    Another Double Wedding 167
    A Quilt for Eli 168
    4th of July 169
    Susan B. Anthony 173
    The Election 175
    More Letters from Texas 175
    Naughty Anna Jane 176
TEXAS, 1877 179
    John Murrell 179
    Natchez Trace 181
    Texas 183
    Arbuckle Island 185
    Homeward Bound 192
TENNESSEE, 1877 195
    Queen 195
    The Storm 198
    Aftermath of the Storm 200
    Dora 204
    Eli and Elizabeth 207
    Scarlet Fever 209
GOING TO TEXAS, 1877 211
    Craig and Dora 211
    Shelbyville 212
    Eli and Queen 214
    Crossing the Tennessee River 216
    Tabitha and Queen 219
    Christmas in Mississippi 223
The Natchez Trace 226

A BRAVE NEW WORLD, 1878 227
   Callie Taylor 227
   Crossing the Red..230
   Joseph Franklin Youngblood.......................................232
   Paris at Last...234
   Delays 235
   Home at Last...237
  Mississippi Ferry 240

CHAPTER 1

WANDERLUST

Sumner County, Tennessee, October 1826

"Pack up, woman. We're moving to Bedford County," Neddy Ownby yelled as he stepped over the threshold.

"Where's that, Papa?" eight year-old Eli asked.

"When did you make this decision, husband?" Polly asked as she stirred a pot of stew hanging on the hearth hook.

Two little girls, ages six and four clamped their arms around Neddy's legs while baby Jeremiah screamed from his cradle.

Ten year-old Tabitha tried to soothe the infant.

Neddy lifted the youngest girl, Susan and gave her a tickle then he patted Elvinia on the head and handed the toddler to Tabitha, making certain her hands were securely around the girl's waist.

Born blind, Tabby was always included in family activities and chores. The other children were taught very early to keep things out of her way and to let her know where they were in the room.

"Where's Bellmont County, Papa?" Eli asked again.

"Bedford County, son," Neddy corrected. It's about a hundred miles south of here. Your grandmother Cheek and several of your aunts and uncles are down there and we're gonna join them."

Eleven year-old Cynthia removed a pan of biscuits from the brick oven and started to load them down with fresh butter.

Neddy picked up a hot dripping biscuit. "Edward B Ownby, you'll ruin your dinner," Polly scolded as she smacked his hand with her wooden spoon.

He continued to eat and grinned at her with a buttery mouth. The little girls giggled at their parents' playfulness.

"I got a letter from my brother James this morning. He's all settled in close to your mother and brothers. Mr. Hatcher made me a fair offer, so I sold the acreage but held on to this house in case we don't like it in Bedford. How soon can you get packed?"

With a patient sigh, Polly told her exuberant husband, "I can be ready to go within a few days. Is that soon enough for you?" and she turned back to her cooking.

Polly was born Mary Jane Cheek. Her father, Jeremiah, and Neddy's father, Walter, had been friends and neighbors all their lives. Walter's twelve children and Jeremiah's ten grew up together. Two of Neddy's sisters were married to Polly's brothers. The families were extremely close.

Everyone had moved to Tennessee from North Carolina within a few years and now it seemed that they were all going to congregate in Bedford County south of Nashville.

Walter and Jeremiah had both died in 1823, and Neddy's mother had been dead for years.

Polly's mother, Tabitha Doyle Cheek, was the only one left of her generation, and she regarded all twenty-two of the children as her family.

"I'll be happy to see Mother and the family again, but I hadn't planned on traveling at the present." She sighed with the exhaustion only a mother of six children under twelve years of age could exhibit.

"I suppose it's time I told you, there will be another child in the spring."

Ignoring the spoon in his wife's hand, Neddy picked the little woman up and swung her around the room until they were both dizzy.

Cynthia frowned; the little girls jumped up and down, and Tabby sat quietly and smiled.

Eli was puzzled. He had been hoping for a pony, and the news of another noisy, smelly baby didn't please him as much as it did his sisters.

"Well, well, well, seems like this old man's still sporting strong seed. The new baby will be born in our new home," Neddy boasted as he grabbed another biscuit and headed out the back door.

"Papa! What about your dinner?" Elvie called after his receding back. "Where's he goin', Ma?"

"Most likely, he's going to town to brag. There's no fool like an old fool. Y'all sit down and eat."

Moving

"When I say 'go', slap the reins hard, Eli."

They were stuck in a snow bank, and the cold wet stuff was still falling heavily.

Polly and the children were huddled around a small coal filled brazier in the canvas covered wagon while Neddy and Eli tried to free the wheel from the drift.

Eli had the reins in hand ready to get the mules moving at his father's signal.

"GO!" Neddy called, and Eli slapped the reins on the mules' rumps. Heads down, all four animals pulled together. The wagon rocked forward then sank back into the snow deeper than before.

"Eli, come help me dig this wheel out."

The boy jumped off the wagon seat and started digging around the inside of the wheel. Snow had packed around the spokes, and his small hands were better proportioned to pry out the wet snow. Soon his knitted mittens were soaked and his fingers were numb, but he wouldn't complain or disappoint his father.

"I think that's enough, son. See if you can drive the team out."

Eli climbed up on the seat, freed the reins, and gave a mighty snap as Neddy yelled "Haawwww!"

The wheel rocked and settled back into the rut.

Neddy moved around behind the wagon and yelled, "Try again son."

He pushed as the team pulled and the wheel cleared the packed ice.

Eli stopped the mules so his father could climb aboard and started them moving again when his father was seated.

"Go get dry mittens and warm your hands around the brazier."

"I'll stay and help you, Papa. I'm not cold."

"Do as I say or your Ma will have my hide."

He saw Eli into his mother's care, and then slapped the reins hard. The team moved out slowly and their journey to a new home continued.

Lewisburg, Tennessee, April, 1827

"Eli's coming," Tabby quietly commented from her chair by the fireplace.

"Elvie, go stop him before he wakes Jeremiah," Neddy said as he stroked his young son's hair. He was rocking the baby to get him down for a nap while Polly helped Tabby wind wool yarn into neat balls.

Before the little girl could get to the door and stop her brother, Eli burst into the room with his boots clomping on the plank floor.

"Papa, Mr. Houston's here with the string of horses we bought yesterday."

Jeremiah woke and started to squall.

Polly patiently said to her daughter, "Tabitha, tomorrow you learn to braid this wool into strips. We need to get rugs down on these floors before the baby comes. Cynthia can stitch them together. You girls can be in charge of the rugs."

Neddy instructed Eli, "Go fetch Josiah and tell him to put the horses in the corral, and I'll be there shortly." He continued to rock the baby trying to get him back to sleep.

Polly rose from her chair with care, and Neddy handed his very pregnant wife the now sleeping child and followed his older son out the door.

Horse Training

Neddy had purchased the slave Josiah, a few months ago. The young man had a definite knack for breaking and training horses. Neddy's plan was to buy unbroken stock, train them, and resell as finished horses.

What he hadn't counted on was his son's passion and apparent eye for choosing quality animals. To Neddy, a horse was like any other essential tool. They served various purposes, but above that fact, he didn't give them a second thought.

Eli didn't share his father's material views. At nine years old, he could spot exceptional horseflesh and had proven invaluable at auction every week. Neddy had doubled his investment since January and there were several horses in the pasture in varied states of training.

The Roan Filly

Neddy stood with his foot on the split rail fence and pointed to the horses milling around the corral.

"Cut that black stud, Josiah, and separate him from the others. He needs to be the first saddle broke. I think he will pay for this lot when finished. Turn the three mares out in the south pasture. We'll work them later. Let's take a look at the geldings. That chestnut would look smart pulling a lady's buggy."

As Josiah moved to follow Neddy's commands, Eli spotted a little roan filly off to herself in the far corner. She was a beauty; red face, neck and chest; red and white speckled back and hindquarters; black legs with three white stockings.

The boy couldn't take his eyes off her.

"Eli, you can help Josiah start training those geldings with the ground reins first thing tomorrow. Son, are you listening to me?"

"Yes, Papa. What about that filly? Can I ride her?"

Neddy laughed loudly and said, "If you think you can, go ahead and try."

Josiah looked doubtfully at his master and the boy, but Neddy said, "Josiah, go get a saddle and reins on that filly. Mr. Eli thinks he can ride her."

Dust and hooves flew into the air, and Eli hit the ground hard. He just sat there trying to get his breath, while the filly stood in the corner pawing the ground as an invitation for him to come try again.

Josiah started to climb the fence to help the boy, but Neddy put his hand out to stop him. "He might can pick 'em, but he's gotta learn to ride 'em. Let's see what he does."

The filly had been on the property less than an hour, and the boy was determined to ride her.

Unaware of the men watching, Eli walked up to the roan and put his hand on her nose. She snorted and her ears flicked, but she stood still. He took the reins and put his foot in the stirrup. He waited a moment before swinging his other leg over.

Just as he shifted his weight, the filly went straight up in the air with all four hooves off the ground. Eli's rear end connected hard with the saddle, and then he was air borne over her head.

She stretched her pretty red neck and sniffed at the dusty crumpled boy.

Eli opened his eyes to her face in his. She didn't look mean. Just stubborn.

As Eli got up again, the filly backed away from him into her corner. He walked into the barn and returned in a few moments. He once again took the reins and put his hand to her mouth.

Oats. That might please her.

She sniffed then took the grain from his flat palm and flicked her ears again.

Eli spoke softly in her ear and put his foot in the stirrup one more time. He quickly swung into the saddle and seated himself firmly.

She threw out her back legs then bucked up off all fours.

Eli hung on and the horse seemed to sense that this time he was going to stick. It seemed as if she had known she would do whatever he asked of her. But, she needed to be convinced he was strong enough to command her.

Neddy slapped Josiah on the back and grinned broadly. "I didn't know if he could do it. That boy makes me proud."

Eli was lost in joy as he walked the filly around the corral.

"Ma says to come eat dinner while it's hot." Cynthia startled her father as he stood watching Eli.

"Tell her we'll be there directly, dear."

Neddy called out to his son, "Come eat, Eli, before your Ma takes a broom to the both of us." He turned to Josiah. "Make sure the horses are secured and this one is cooled down then come get your dinner."

Polly met them at the door. "Both of you wash up before you come in my house. And hurry. The food is getting cold. Is Josiah comin' along?"

"Yes, dear. He'll be here when he's finished his chores. Eli, wash your face good. It's all covered in dirt. We don't want to offend your mother's delicate sensibilities."

Neddy gave his big booming laugh as he poured a dipper of water over his son's head.

A Child is born

The family was seated on benches around the big eating table on the porch, and Eli excitedly blurted, "Ma, you should've seen me and Alice this morning. She just does whatever I want her to do, and Papa said I could keep her for my very own."

It had been two weeks since this last group of horses had arrived, and Polly knew Eli had spent every waking moment with Josiah in the corral. She raised her eyebrows with a questioning look directed at her husband.

"Yes, woman! I told the boy he could keep her. She's good breeding stock and will have some fine colts, so consider it an investment in the future." His voice lightened and he ruffled Eli's hair. "Besides a boy needs his own horse before he turns ten."

Polly grimaced and gripped the table edge. Letting out a slow breath, she looked at Neddy and smiled.

"You better hitch the wagon and take Tabitha and the little ones to Mother's. Cynthia can stay and help me. Eli, saddle your filly, and go tell your Aunt Mertie it's time to welcome a new Ownby to the family."

At the stroke of midnight, Polly gave one last push and little Elizabeth Margaret made her voice heard.

Eli watched his father rock the tiny baby girl. He had been hoping for another brother. Girls were such a bother, always giggling and wanting him to play dolls with them.

"Too bad it's a silly girl, Papa," he told Neddy.

Neddy looked at his oldest son and said, "Eli Craig Ownby! Don't ever let me hear you say that again. Girls have many uses. I have two fine sons. You and Jeremiah are all I need. Betsy here is perfect."

CHAPTER 2

REST IN PEACE-1866

On the Road

A loud crack broke Eli out of his reverie. It was dark and the only light was from a low burning campfire.

Where was he and why was he there?

Slowly his confusion lifted, and he recognized his oldest son, Watterson Knox Polk Ownby. He remembered why they were camped on the side of the road.

A letter had arrived from a lawyer in Carroll County. Neddy had died, and Eli was summoned for the reading of his father's will.

Watt had refused to allow his father to make the 165-mile trip alone. They were camped south of Franklin, Tennessee waiting to meet up with Eli's brother Jeremiah and his brother-in-law, Levi Breechan.

A panther screamed. Eli's three-year-old paint whinnied and pawed the ground, while Watt's chestnut mare Belle simply snorted.

Belle was the daughter of Watt's faithful Molly, who was tragically lost in the Battle of Stones River.

"Storm doesn't like that cat following us," Watt observed as his father rose to quiet the young black and white horse.

"That's why I named him Storm Cloud. I knew he was spirited from the moment he hit the ground." Eli smoothed the horse's neck and whispered in his ear. "Just like I knew Scout would have what it took to get Ed through the war. I'm anxious to see what Belle and Scout produce in the fall."

Scout was an Appaloosa stud and grandson to Eli's beloved Alice. The big horse had carried and protected Eli's second born son, Ed through the Civil War.

Meeting Eli's eyes, Watt asked, "I wonder how Ed and Lizzie are making out with us gone?"

Eli chuckled and said, "Don't you fret none about your little sister. She may just be fifteen, but she's raised the young'uns and taken care of the house ever since your mama died. She managed just fine while you boys were gone and even when the Yankees took me captive. As for your brother ... he's grown now and knows what to do."

"Pa, you never talk about your capture or your treatment at the hands of the Yankees...."

"Hallo the camp!" A voice came out of the dark.

Watt was ever alert and reached for his rifle.

Two men stepped into the light, leading their horses.

Eli grabbed the leader who was a mirror image of himself and gave him a bear hug.

"Hello, little brother. We had just about given up on you."

Releasing Jeremiah, Eli held out his hand to the other man and said," It's good to see you Levi. I hope Susan and the girls are all well."

Levi was married to Eli and Jeremiah's sister and was attending the will reading as her representative.

"Susan is fine. I left her and the girls at Jeremiah's place to keep Pricilla company while we're gone," Levi commented as he tied his horse to a tree branch.

Watt took his uncle's horse as Jeremiah laughed. "I don't know why Prissy is so perturbed about this baby that's on the way. She's already had eight."

The horses stamped their feet and pulled on their tethers as the big cat screamed again.

Jeremiah frowned and Eli commented, "He was near us last night. Watt, we may have to take care of him if he keeps following us."

Mammy Bess

The men broke camp at daybreak the next morning and traveled at a long trot, making good time. On the third night, they camped and ate a hot meal of rabbit Watt had shot on the road.

Watt commented, "It's so nice to eat and sleep under the stars without cannons booming in the distance."

Jeremiah took a drink of his coffee and said to his brother, "Tell me something about Ma. I don't remember her."

Eli sighed and replied, "You wouldn't, Jeremiah. You were only two. She was the opposite of Papa, a quiet woman, patient, and strong willed. Where he was loud and boisterous, she was thoughtful and calm. She had definite ideas about how the family should behave and how to live with Tabitha's blindness. She wanted Tabby to be independent within the limits of her affliction. One time Papa took a ball of yarn from Tabitha's hands and started winding it for her. Ma swatted him with a wooden spoon and told him to stop it. The only way Tabitha would learn was to do it herself." Eli chuckled at the memory and thought about his little Lizzie who had her grandmother's practical nature.

"The only mother I knew was Mammy Bess," Jeremiah said softly.

"I remember when Papa bought her and brought her home. She was a young mother, but her former owner had sold the baby to someone else. She really loved us and took to all us children right away. It was as if we could replace what had been taken from her."

Levi had been quiet but commented, "Susan still talks frequently about Bess and how she took care of all you children through the years. Susan was so afraid she would lose her when Mr. Ownby married Nancy Perkins."

Jeremiah said quietly, "I remember. When Papa married Nancy, we thought for sure he would sell Bess, but Nancy liked not being liable for us. She left us alone and under Bess's care. Then when she had K, Harriett, and Will so quickly, she seemed grateful to have help."

"Nancy was never comfortable with Tabitha's blindness, but Bess was like Ma. She protected her but wanted her to be self-sufficient and would go after anyone who didn't feel the same." Eli laughed and continued, "One time Bess scolded Papa about something he had done for Tabitha. He laughed that big laugh of his and said, 'What ya gonna do, little woman? Hit me with a spoon.'"

They all laughed as they pictured the scene. Then a reflective silence settled over the camp.

Watt broke the quiet by saying, "I remember Mammy Bess. She always had cookies for us grandchildren. What happened to her? One day she was gone, and no one would ever tell me where she went."

The silence deepened and finally Eli said, "When Nancy died along with Betsy in the cholera outbreak, Bess took care of Nancy's three babies just like she had your Uncle Jeremiah and your aunts. Then your Granpa Neddy married Laurie and she seemed content to let Bess take care of the children until she had Joe. I think some maternal instinct came to the surface, and she decided to raise Nancy's children by her own rules, 'without that impertinent darkie,' were the words she used. So, Papa sold Bess, her husband Josiah along with their five youngest children. I missed them both."

Conversation died as each man settled into his own thoughts and drifted off to sleep in the peaceful night.

Laurie

After five nights on the road, the four men were glad to reach Neddy's place.

They saw the tall white house from some distance, and as they rode down the lane they noted single story additions on either side of the two story house. Long multi-paned windows filled the front of the house, and a smaller attic dormer was framed by a steep roof.

Neddy had moved to Carroll County before the war, and this was the first time any of them had been to the property.

They slowly approached the house and stopped near the wide front steps. A large black man came out of the barn holding a glowing red horseshoe with a pair of tongs. He was wearing a leather apron, and his rolled up shirt sleeves showed arms the size of hams. A slight touch of silver glinted in his grizzled hair.

Steam rose as he dropped the horseshoe in a bucket of water and with white teeth flashing in the sun, he strode over to Storm Cloud and with huge, callused but deceptively gentle hands, took the reins.

"It's good to see ya, Mister Eli," then, nodding to the others, said jovially, "Mister Jeremiah, Mister Levi, and who's that there? Is that you, Master Watt?"

"Silas, you son-of-a-gun, I had no idea you were still here. We were talking about your mama on the way here. About how much we all loved Mammy Bess." Eli clapped the slightly younger man on the broad back.

"When the war was over, Mister Ned was kind enough to take me to visit Mammy and Pappy down in Lexington. We've visited back and forth a few times. Mammy's real pleased to see her grandchilluns." He turned toward the barn and yelled, "Josiah! You and your brothers mind your manners and git out here to see to these horses."

Three young boys under the age of ten ran out of the barn and each took one of the horses' reins.

"Are these your boys, Silas?" Jeremiah asked.

"Yes sir, Mister Jeremiah. At least it's three of them. Me and Penny, we got us eight sons. Hoping for a girl this time."

The wide double doors to the house opened and Cahal Knox Polk Ownby stood and surveyed the group.

"Hello, Eli, Jeremiah, Levi. Watt good to see ya safe and sound. Welcome to my home." He loudly proclaimed as though someone might disagree with him.

"Boy!" he addressed Silas, "Take those horses to the barn and get 'em fed and brushed down. Give that spotted one extra, he looks plumb poorly. Eli, where did you get that nag? Silas, git a move on, I don't pay you to stand around gossiping." Then, clapping his hands as though scolding a dog, he continued, "I said git, boy."

"K," Jeremiah said to his brother sternly. "You have forgotten your manners. Your elder brothers are here now. You can stop playing Master of the House."

13

Eli grinned at the exchange and turned to Silas and shook his hand. "It's good to see you, Silas. We'll talk some more before we leave." Ignoring K, he stepped up on the porch and entered the front foyer, followed by the others.

K stood a moment and then pushed through the group as they stood gazing around at the spacious but modestly decorated room. A staircase led to the upper floors, and closed doors opened into the foyer.

"Mother Laurie and Tabitha are in the parlor," K pouted as he opened a wide sliding pocket door. The parlor was flooded with sunlight, and two women sat patiently waiting. Fashionably but not extravagantly dressed, the younger of the two rose and floated toward Eli.

Martha Laurie Fisher Ownby had married Neddy when she was barely twenty-years old. He was fifty-eight with seven children older than her. But he had three younger children who needed a mother. They had one son together and for nineteen years had a good life. She was devoted to her older, blind stepdaughter.

Eli moved to meet her. He cupped her tiny soft hands in his huge rough fingers. "Hello, Laurie. I hope you are doing well." His father's widow was eleven years younger than him, and he had never been able to call her mother.

"I'm as well as can be expected, Eli. I'm so glad you came." She moved to greet Jeremiah as Eli stooped to his beloved sister Tabitha and took her hand.

After warm greetings all around the room, Laurie spoke, "K, show the boys to their rooms so they can wash off some of the road dust. Supper will be served at six in the dining room."

After washing and settling into their rooms, Jeremiah excused himself to go check on a loose shoe he had noticed on his horse.

Silas was at the forge and greeted him, "Hello, Mister Jeremiah, your horse had a loose shoe, so I fixed it for you."

"Thank you, Silas. There was no need to do that. I was coming to do it myself." He noticed all of the horses were slick and shiny, contentedly munching on oats. He dug into his pocket and pulled out a three-cent coin and handed it to Silas, or tried to.

"No sir, Mister Jeremiah. I can't take your money. Miz Laurie pays me and gives me and Penny a place to stay. I won't take money for doing my job. 'Sides that, I would do anything for Mister Ned's chillun." And added in a lower voice, "Most of 'em."

When Jeremiah left the barn, he saw young Josiah and called him over. Pressing the coin into his grubby little hand, he smiled and said, "Don't tell your Pappy, but buy you and your brothers some candy." Then adjusting his hat and hooking his thumbs in his waistband he strolled back toward the house.

Supper was served promptly at six in the elegantly appointed dining room. The massive table was set with delicate china in a blue pansy pattern. As Penny and her niece, Opal, passed around platters of roast beef and vegetables, Watt examined the knife laid next to his plate. He had never seen a knife with a china handle. The ones at home had wood or bone handles. He turned the knife over and over and held it close to his face until Eli took it from him and laid it back on the table.

When the meal was finished, Penny brought in a large silver tray with a gleaming coffee service and fresh china cups. Before she set it on the sideboard, Laurie stopped her.

"We'll have our coffee and desert in the parlor, Penny. Please serve us there then clear the table."

Laurie rose, and K gave Tabitha his arm, and the family moved into the parlor.

Tabitha was overjoyed to hear her brother's voices again and was delighted with her nephew, Watt. She plied Levi with questions about Susan and their seven daughters, especially ten-year-old Tabitha.

Watt renewed his relationship with his young uncles, Will and Joe, who were the same ages as his younger brothers.

Laurie told them that Elvinia and Harriett would visit tomorrow. They only lived a short distance away. Cynthia lived in Missouri and couldn't get away to attend but sent her love to everyone.

Eli asked if someone would take him to his father's grave.

"I would like to see it also," Jeremiah agreed.

"K can go first thing in the morning to see if the Reverend will meet us at the churchyard tomorrow. Perhaps he would conduct a simple service at your father's gravesite," Laurie replied.

"Yes, Mother Laurie, I'll go right after breakfast."

Eli Says Goodbye

Chapel Hill Methodist church and cemetery was located just a couple of miles down the road and K was back by mid morning. Not only was the preacher delighted to conduct a service for Neddy's family, but his wife would organize a picnic on the grounds with the church ladies.

Since Eli and Jeremiah had not been to visit their father, the congregation was looking forward to meeting and welcoming Neddy's older sons and grandson.

K had stopped to tell his sisters, and they would meet the rest of the family at the cemetery.

Laurie and Tabitha travelled in Laurie's carriage and the men escorted them on horseback as they made a procession to the church and cemetery. As promised, the church ladies had set up tables that were loaded with food. The tables were flanked by members from the surrounding area.

After the Reverend had greeted the family members he knew and was introduced to Eli, Jeremiah, Levi, and Watt, he looked up and down the road leading to the cemetery.

Watt asked if he expected anyone else and he replied, "I'm uncertain, but knowing your grandfather like I did there could be more of you coming."

Watt laughed and said, "I believe this is everybody for today."

The preacher gathered the family together and led them to Neddy's grave. Laurie had purchased a substantial marker. It was a five-foot grey marble slab with an arched top inscribed with his name, birth, and death dates.

The crowd was solemn as the preacher offered this simple prayer:

"Father, you know our hearts and share our sorrows. We are hurt by our parting from Neddy Ownby, whom we loved; when we are angry at the loss we have sustained, when we long for words of comfort, yet find them hard to hear, turn our grief to truer living, our affliction to firmer hope. In Jesus' name we pray. Amen"

As the others started to drift to the food tables in the church yard; Eli lingered by the gravesite. His father was always bigger than life to him. A vigorous and vibrant man, Neddy had the reputation of being a sharp land buyer and wily trader. He was also known for swaggering through town with a walking stick on one arm and a baby on the other.

Eli knelt by the tombstone, placed his hat on his knee, pulled his hunting knife, and dug into the soft dirt at the base. When he had a small hole, about six inches deep, he removed his silver pocket watch. Opening the watch case, he reached into his vest pocket and removed an old and worn silver dollar. Eli inserted the coin in the back of the watch and dropped it in the hole.

He bowed his head and quietly said, "That's all I have to pay you back for all you've done for me. You taught me to be strong and to stand like a man. You taught me that family comes before everything but God. And I thank you. Rest in Peace, Papa."

Eli was going to miss his father. He was going to miss his frequent and chatty letters, but most of all he was starting to acknowledge his own mortality. As Eli stood by the grave contemplating the future, Watt gently took his father's arm and led him back to the family gathered for dinner.

Speculation

That evening after a light supper prepared and served by Penny, Laurie again excused herself. "I really must attend to today's neglected duties and go over the accounts before the meeting tomorrow with the attorney. Everyone enjoy your coffee and I'll be back shortly."

"I don't know what to expect from Papa's estate," Elvie mused out loud.

"Me neither," Cynthia agreed with her sister.

"Do you know, K?" Harriett asked her brother.

"You know Papa consulted with me on everything but I really can't say until the attorney makes it official," K answered smugly.

Jeremiah leaned over and whispered to Eli, "That means he doesn't know."

Looking around the lovely room, Eli observed, "Papa did quite well here in Carroll County. How did the war affect the farm?"

K thought a moment. "To be honest, big brother, Laurie has handled the accounts since Papa died, but we are still living well, as you can see."

Cynthia said thoughtfully, "Papa was so generous when we married."

"That generosity came from Grandfather Cheeks' Estate," Eli broke in. "Papa held Ma's portion for us in trust. He had to report to the circuit court every year and pay a surety. Our share of that estate is what he gave us when we married. Anything else was just a loan. And the Cheek estate didn't include K, Will, Harriet, or Joe."

Laurie entered the room carrying a tray with a whiskey decanter and a box of Neddy's cigars and sat them on the sideboard.

"I thought you gentlemen might enjoy a smoke and a nightcap before retiring." Then turning to the sisters, "Elvie, Harriett, Cynthia, the groom has your buggies ready when you need them."

Taking the none too subtle hint, the sisters rose and said their goodbyes, giving Eli, Jeremiah, and Watt a hug and a kiss on the cheek. Taking their husband's arms, they thanked Laurie for supper and left. Tabitha rose from her chair and, taking her stepmother's outstretched arm, said her good nights.

K rose to pour the whiskey and Watt waved the glass away and said, "I would prefer a glass of buttermilk if it's not too much trouble."

"Boy, you're still wet behind the ears. At twenty-four, with four years of war under your belt, you're old enough to have a drink with the men."

Watt laughed. His uncle was only three years older.

"Uncle K, I don't like the taste of the nasty stuff. I doubt that my share will go to waste with you in the room." He left to go find the kitchen and see if he could get his buttermilk.

Brothers

When Watt returned from the kitchen with his buttermilk, the men had moved into Neddy's office and taken the whiskey and cigars with them. He noticed Eli and K off to the side and could see his father giving his uncle K a stern "talking to."

He approached and overheard Eli say, "I know that Papa freed Silas when he had to sell Bell and Josiah. Silas stayed out of loyalty so you had best treat him with the respect he deserves."

Seeing Watt approach, Eli changed demeanor and smiled while K slipped away from his brother's wrath.

"I see you found your buttermilk. Let's go have one of Papa's fine cigars, son."

K had taken the chair behind his father's desk and was holding forth in his customary loud and boisterous manner. He had been captured at the Battle of Missionary Ridge and spent the last seventeen months of the war in Rock Island Prison. The experiences there had left him with a permanent facial twitch that got worse when he was talking. Unfortunately, he talked most of the time.

"I tell ya, boy, our general assembly sold out cheap. Ratifying the 13th Amendment so quickly, just so we could rejoin the damned Union was a mistake. All it accomplished was to give the darkies high falutin ideas. Soon they'll think they have the same rights as us white folk. "

Eli cleared his throat and shot his brother a severe look.

K paused and took a long swallow from his glass. He held it up to the light from a lamp on the corner of the desk. Turning the glass so the amber liquid glowed, he spoke softly, "Papa had good taste. This is certainly better than that swill we got in camp."

When no one responded, he shook his head. With the twitch working overtime, he continued his tirade.

"The government still considers us traitors and won't let us vote unless we can sign that God-awful Damnesty Oath. Few men in the south can say they never bore arms or gave support to the Confederacy. I tell you, boys...."

Watt interrupted his uncle by saying, "President Johnson is trying to get Congress to change the oath. He wants it to state that we swear to support the Union in the future and not bear arms against the federal government again."

"You know that doesn't stand a snowball's chance in hell of passing, nephew."

The youngest of the assembled men, eighteen-year-old Joe, spoke for the first time. "I heard yesterday at the Post Office that a group of ex-Confederates down in Pulaski has founded a club. They are calling it the Ku Klux Klan. Nathan Bedford Forrest has been elected their leader. The south just might rise again."

Eli and Jeremiah had been sipping their father's whiskey and both appeared to doze in their chairs. Eli came to life suddenly and declared loudly, "If she does, it will be without my sons." Then he settled back to his whiskey and cigar.

Watt and his Uncle K had fought for the Confederacy, and Will and Levi had fought for the USA.

So far the two Union soldiers had been quiet and pensive. They both knew that Watt and his two brothers, Sam and Ed, had been captured and spent time in Federal Prison camps as well as K. Neither of them wanted to rub salt in the wounds by gloating about the federal victory. But soon the conversation turned to their various experiences during the war. As the level in the whiskey decanter decreased, the dialogue got a bit lively but in true family fashion, stayed good natured.

"Can you imagine my surprise when Will returned home, and we discovered that our units had faced each other at Perryville, Chickamauga, and Missionary Ridge?" K asked the assembled men. "Sure am glad I didn't see this scoundrel. Would have hated having to shoot at him." K laughed a big hearty laugh that was reminiscent of their father and clapped his little brother on the back then drained his glass of Neddy's finest.

"I'd have hated that too, K," Will said with less enthusiasm. "But I'd have hated more to have to tell Pa that I shot and killed you. He was already angry with me for fighting for the Union."

Watt observed, "We each had to follow our conscience, Uncle Will. You and Uncle Levi did what you thought was right, and so did Uncle K, me, and my brothers. I hold no grudge with anyone who fought for the north. But my sister Lizzie is a horse of a different color. She and the other children suffered something horrible at the hands of Yankee troops, and she doesn't have a forgiving nature. So, Uncle Will, Uncle Levi, the next time you see her, be gentle."

Watt and Eli both started laughing at the image of the slight girl taking on her Yankee Uncle's and telling them exactly what she thought.

Eli stretched his long legs and stood. He raised his glass and said, "Edward B. Ownby. May he rest in peace."

All of the men raised their glasses, including Watt with his buttermilk, and Joe summed up the meeting.

"Here's to brothers."

Reading of the Will

The next day, Neddy's children and his widow met with the lawyer at the appointed time.

The reading was brief and to the point.

"Know all men by these presents that I Edward B Ownby of Carroll County Tennessee being of sound mind and disposing memory do make and publish this my last will and testament thereby revoking & making void all wills heretofore made by me.

First: It is my desire that my wife Laurie Ownby act as Executrix to this will and that she pay all my just debts and general expenses as soon after my death as may be convenient.

Second: It is my desire that my wife, Laurie Ownby have all effects both real and personal that I may die seized or possess of after paying debts & to use and exercise the control of it same until my son Joe E Ownby arrives at the age of twenty five years until which time my said wife, Laurie is to provide for my daughter, Tabitha a comfortable and ample support, all of the means bequeathed to said Laurie and after my son Joe E arrives at the age of twenty five years, he is to succeed his mother and become sole proprietor of my estate and after which time he is to provide for his mother and Sister Tabitha a reasonable and comfortable support during their lives.

Third: It is my desire that my son William receive from my Executrix one hundred dollars as his interest in my estate.

Fourth: It is my will and desire that my son Cahal Knox Polk Ownby have the tract of land I purchased of R D Ownby and a sufficiency of the tract purchased of David Jenkins & wife to make him one hundred acres lying in the 10th Civil district of Carroll County provided he survives the war and returns to possess but in case of his death before he receives it to possession it is to follow the disposition made of the balance of my Estate.

Fifth: It is my will and desire that my Executrix as soon as convenient after my death hand over to Cynthia Mitchell & her husband Richard Mitchell, Matilda Perry wife of Ruffin Perry, Susan Breechen wife of Levi Breechen, Harriet L wife of Green Gibson & and to my sons Eli C and Jeremiah J Ownby, the notes I severally hold on them for monies loaned or advanced them by me & said notes are hereby declared canceled as to all persons save & except my self.

In testimony whereof I have hereunto set my hand & seal publish and declare this to be my last will and testament in the presence of the witnesses named below This the 18th day of May 1864.

Edward B Ownby"

Laurie had executed the terms of the will. The lawyer handed over the mentioned notes and the older children were surprised and a bit shocked by the lack of anything else forth coming.

It was a quiet gathering at Laurie's house that evening. Using the excuse of needing to be prepared for spring planting, everyone planned to leave the next morning to travel back to their respective homes.

Eli, Jeremiah, Levi, and Watt went to the stable to make sure the horses were ready to travel at first light.

Silas was busy shutting the forge down for the night. He banked the fire and greeted the men.

"I'm sure glad you all came by. They's sumthin' Mister Ned wanted you to have."

With puzzled expressions, they watched as the big man opened a shed door and pulled out several bags and set them on the work table.

"What is all this, Silas?" Eli asked

"Mister Ned, he had me hide these here sacks just for you all. He knew you would come to visit and thought these might come in handy after the war and all."

Going back to the little room, Silas pulled out some smaller empty bags and handed them to Eli. "Mister Ned, he talked about you all pert near everyday and he said you would know how best to divvy up these here seeds. But he said don't tell the others."

Each of them chose a sack and opened it. Surprised they found seeds. There was cotton, tobacco, oats, and some of the prettiest Indian corn they had ever seen. Some smaller bags held garden vegetables, and sweet corn seed.

"I've never grown Indian Corn," Levi observed. "This just might be the proper time to try it."

Watt commented, "We have grown it and it makes for good inexpensive feed."

While the men divided up the various food and cash crops, they were unaware of Silas leaving the barn. They had finished packing their bags of seeds with their other gear when Silas reappeared and handed Eli three sealed letters.

They were addressed to Eli, Jeremiah, and Susan. The men recognized Neddy's distinctive handwriting and each pocketed his letter to be read in private. Levi would deliver his wife's unopened.

Moved beyond measure, Eli grabbed Silas in a bear hug while Jeremiah stood with tears in his eyes. Watt had never seen his father so emotional and he lifted a silent prayer thanking his grandfather for his generosity and forethought.

Embarrassed by the emotion, Silas took Eli's hands in his and said, "Your father was a good, good man. You boys have a safe trip home and go with God!"

As the sun rose the next morning, the travelers finished packing their gear for the long ride home. Penny had handed each of them a sack of food for the road.

Watt asked his uncle Jeremiah, "Have you seen Pa this morning? Storm's not in his stall and I haven't seen hide nor hair of Pa."

"No, nephew, I haven't. Surely he didn't leave without us."

The stable door opened and Eli entered leading Storm. "Good morning, ya'll. Are you ready to ride?"

"Where you been, Pa? You had us worried."

"No need to worry, son. I went to visit Papa one last time. There was something I needed to return to him."

Puzzled, Watt wondered what his father was talking about. He had seen him leave the watch so he knew there was something else.

"Come on, boys. If we're gonna make time, we better get going. Let's head for home." Eli mounted Storm Cloud and headed out the door, knowing he would be followed.

Eli and Watt parted from Jeremiah and Levi at Franklin.

"Be sure to let us know when the new baby comes. Jeremiah and Levi, give Susan my love."

Watt was very thoughtful on the trip home. He had not known his father had borrowed money from Neddy and had been hoping for cash to help rebuild what the Yankees had destroyed. Relieved to know there were no outstanding debts on the family farm, they were no worse off than they had been before, and Neddy had provided them with a small start toward rebuilding their crops.

Watt recognized how richly blessed he was to have been born into this fine family.

CHAPTER 3

RECONSTRUCTION, 1866

Home Again

Eli and Watt rode toward the house and spotted Ed and Jack plowing in the field.

"Why are they using one mule? Where's the other one?" Eli asked.

"Let's find out," Watt replied, as they rode up to the edge of the field."

"Hello, Pa, Watt," Ed called out. "Welcome home."

"Where's the other mule?" Watt asked.

Ed stopped plowing and walked over to his father and brother. "It's ill. Not sure what's wrong, but he is down in the barn."

"Better go take a look," Eli said as he turned Storm Cloud toward the barn.

The mule was down, lying on his side in the first stall of the barn. He raised his head when Eli entered but couldn't get his feet under him. Examining the mule's hooves and then his mouth, he went looking for answers.

Fourteen-year-old Eli Craig Jr. was crossing the yard from the house to the barn and Eli asked him if the mule had gotten loose lately.

"He got out during last night's storm and I found him this morning down by the creek."

"Was he near that big Black Walnut tree?"

"Yes sir," Craig replied wondering how his father knew where the mule was. "He was standing there fetlock deep in a pile of old hulls."

Eli stood a moment in thought and scratched his chin then said, "Go take my gear off of Cloud but leave him saddled. I need to get to town and see about getting another mule. Then you go over and see if we

25

can borrow one of the Taylor's oxen tomorrow. This here mule will be dead before nightfall, and we'll need to drag him out to the bone yard

Peaches

"When is Sam coming home to help?" Jack asked his brothers one morning in July as they were hoeing weeds in the small patch of cotton from Neddy's seeds.

"As soon as he gets Ruthie's fence repaired," Watt replied. "He owes her a great debt for helping him after the war."

Ed leaned on his hoe, wiped his face with a handkerchief, and smirked. "A debt to repay. You really think that's why he's at the widow Smith's house more than he's here helping us."

Watt looked sternly at his brother and admonished him. "There is no man to help her, and she has four little children to care for. Get back to work, you useless lump of lard."

"Yes, Sir! Sergeant Sack-of-bones," Ed grinned, as he threw his brother a salute.

While his older brothers were playing around, Jack had finished his row and turned up another. Only thirteen when war broke out, he stayed on the farm to help the younger children instead of going to fight. As the oldest male, he had become accustomed to making decisions and working independently. But he was relieved when Watt, Ed, and Sam had returned and Watt had taken control of the farm.

"I'll bet my desert tonight, I can hoe more rows than you two old goats," he yelled in challenge.

The rows of cotton may not have been perfectly cleaned of weeds but the brothers made a game of it and finished in record time.

"I think I'll go see what Lizzie plans for desert tonight, since I get triple helpings," he called, as he threw his hoe down for Watt or Ed to put away, and ran toward the house.

There was smoke coming from the chimney in the detached kitchen.

Jack bounded up the steps and found Lizzie stirring a large kettle hanging from a hook over the fire. The younger girls were peeling peaches into a large bowl on the work table. Both were covered in peach juice and fuzz from forehead to fingertips.

"Be sure to trim off the soft and dark spots and watch for worms," Lizzie told the girls.

They had spent the morning picking up the wind fall and the peaches were bruised, battered, and bug eaten.

"My nose itches," whined six-year-old Maggie, "and when I try to scratch, it gets worse. This fuzzy stuff stings."

Ignoring the girls, Jack asked Lizzie excitedly, "What's for desert tonight, sister? I won a hoeing contest with Watt and Ed and I get their share"

Glancing at her little sisters, Lizzie wiped her sweat covered face with her apron, glared at her brother, and snapped, "I don't know. Until one of you men brings me some game, all we'll have for supper is string beans and cornbread. Pa and Craig have been gone all day hunting, and I sent our little brothers to the garden to see if the tomatoes or radishes are ready yet. Maybe Mack won't eat everything they gather or bury Henry in the dirt. If we get these peaches put up, you can have some with honey for a sweet."

Yankee foragers had slaughtered their sow, Princess, but Ed brought home a young pig after the war. Thanks to a neighbor's boar, Princess Too, or Prinney as she was called, had produced a litter of piglets. In a few months, they would be ready to slaughter for meat. But right now all they had to eat were vegetables out of the garden and what game the men could find.

Grabbing a peach out of the bowl and dodging Lizzie's swat with her spoon, Jack rubbed the only clean spot on his baby sister, the top of her head. He took his rifle out of the corner, grinned, and went out the door.

"I'll go find us some supper."

The younger girls had resorted to eating more peaches than they were peeling and Lizzie was trying to finish the batch over the fire so she could concentrate on supper when there was a blood curdling scream followed by a crash.

Maggie was standing over the bowl of sliced peaches, spitting and shaking her hands as if something were on her, while Queen tried to pick up the spilled fruit.

Lizzie rushed to her baby sister. "What's wrong, baby girl? Did you cut yourself?" She took the little girls hands and examined them for blood. Not finding any cuts, she hugged the girl and tried to quiet her sobs.

"Tell me what happened, Maggie."

But all the child could do was sniff and cry more.

Queen started laughing and held out a half a peach. "I think I know what happened, Lizzie. Look." Wrapped around the pit was a wiggly white worm.

"Kill it! Kill it! Kill it!" Maggie screamed in childish hysteria as Watt and Ed stepped into the kitchen. They both reacted with a soldier's mentality.

Instantly alert, they looked around for the enemy, with their hands on the pistols at their waist.

Queen doubled over laughing as she held out the wormy peach and said, "Kill it, Watt."

Watt pulled out his pistol to shoot the worm, but Lizzie swatted him on the back of the head with her spoon; grabbed the peach from her sister; smashed the worm with the spoon and threw the peach, worm and spoon in the fire.

"Go make me another spoon."

Grinning broadly, Ed reached for a peach in the bowl but Lizzie turned and yelled, "Don't you touch those. Not until you learn how to hoe better'n Jack."

Both men burst out laughing.

"I see we've been told on already." Watt clapped Ed on the shoulder. "I wonder what we can do to get back in Lizzie's good graces?"

Cutting her eyes to her two much-taller brothers, she said with a little smile, "Go check on the boys in the garden... make sure Mack hasn't eaten everything they've picked; and get Henry cleaned up for supper."

As the men left to check on their brothers, she turned to the girls. "Queen, get Maggie and yourself cleaned up. We'll do the rest of the peaches in the morning."

Lizzie Visits her Mama

Eli's beloved wife, Nancy Carol Winstead Ownby died in 1862 at forty years of age. Eleven children in twenty-one years had exhausted her body. Carol's deathbed wish was for a promise from her eleven-year-old daughter.

"Lizzie, make sure the children have clean clothes and that they go to school. You gotta be their mama now."

Today was Lizzie's sixteenth birthday, and she was cleaning her mother's grave. Carol was buried on a hill at the back of the farm, and Lizzie often found solace in the solitude of the hill top. It was mid September and the honey suckle Lizzie had planted was blooming profusely. Lizzie's blue tick hound was rolling around like a puppy in the fragrant vine.

Lizzie laid her hoe down and sat at the head of her mother's grave. Lady Blue ambled over and laid her head in the girls lap. She had a yellow blossom stuck to the top of her nose and another hanging from her long floppy ear.

Laughing, Lizzie pulled the blooms off while the hound looked at her with soulful adoring eyes.

"Did you know, my little lady," Lizzie addressed the dog, "there is a drop of honey at the end of each blossom?" To demonstrate her point, she pulled a bloom and sucked on the narrow shaft to remove the sweet nectar. Looking down she smiled at the dog, asleep on her lap.

"Mama," she said softly. "Nannie Taylor's gonna teach me to knit and crochet. If I knew how to knit socks, we would be so much better this winter. No one in the family has solid socks to wear. I've been cutting off the tops and sticking them down in the children's boots so they aren't embarrassed at church. But Henry is wearing shoes that have been through Jack, Craig, and Mack. Pa repaired the soles but the top's thin, and there's no money to buy new ones.

"He came in from the barn the other day and his toes were bleeding. The cow stepped on him and cut his little toes."

She broke out in tears and her sobs woke Lady who sat up and licked her face. Lizzie stroked the dog's ears until she lay down again. The soft, slick hair felt like velvet between her fingers.

"She's such a good dog, Mama. She's always protective of me and the little ones. I've tried to be a good mama and do what I promised, but I don't know if I have. Maggie and Henry barely eat enough to survive, and Queen and Mack can't stop eating."

A breeze blew a lock of hair across her face and Lizzie looked up to the sky. She knew it was a caress from her mother.

Shaking the sleeping dog gently so as to not startle her, Lizzie rose and gathered her tools and the girl and her dog descended the hill.

Queen

On a bright, crisp October day, the cotton was in and the men were cutting the tobacco to hang in the drying sheds.

The garden was near stripped and food had been preserved, dried or stored for the winter months. A small amount of cash from the cotton sale had prompted Eli to purchase some calico, thread, and new sharp needles.

"Queen, you have to take smaller stitches. They need to be the same length and in a straight line. These will come loose the first time the men raise their arms," Lizzie reprimanded her eleven-year-old sister. "Take them out and do them over right. We don't have enough material to waste any."

"You're so mean, Lizzie." The younger girl pouted. "Why're you so hateful? I'm trying to learn."

"I know you are, sister. I just remember helping Mama sew Watt and Ed's uniforms when I was younger than you. They looked so smart in them when they went off to that awful war."

Lizzie paused a moment and gazed into space, then continued, "The memories made me sad. I'm sorry if I was hateful. Here, let me remove the stitches, and we'll try again tomorrow. You go on in the house and check on the little ones."

As Queen rose, Lizzie reached over and pulled something out of the younger girl's pocket. Bright red hair was glued to a broken china doll face. With only one bright blue eye and half a painted red mouth, the doll had a macabre appearance.

Shocked, Lizzie asked, "Queen Ann Matilda! Why do you carry this in your pocket?"

"Because she's mine. It's all I have to remember when life was happy and we were safe." Queen grabbed the doll head from her sister and ran off toward the woods.

Watt's hound dog, Old Ned, followed and when Queen collapsed on the ground crying, he whined and licked her tears away until she was giggling and rubbing his belly.

"Ned, she wasn't always this cold and mean. That Yankee broke my doll and took her face away. When he came back so badly wounded, he had her in his pocket. Then Lieutenant John showed up and I knew she was a Guardian Angel. If I keep her safe, she will bring him back again."

Lieutenant John Christopher was a dashing young Confederate cavalry officer who had helped the family during the war. He had stolen the little girl's heart when she was six.

Molasses and Honey

November the 11 A.D. 1866
Dear Eli,

Am sending you some of our bestest sorgum seed. With Rufus and William dead in the war and John to weak from the disentary from being a prizoner, there is no one to make molasses this year.

I know how much the little ones like their molasses, but it can't be helped. Maybe your boys can get a good crop from the seed and you can make some next season.

I'm as well as can be expected for 62 years. The rumatize keeps me down on cold days. Lauretha and her husband are staying with me, but Flem's health ain't so good, either.

I mourn my sweet Carol and miss her letters. Tell Lizzie to rite her old grandmother news of the children more often.

I hope you are all good.

Your loving mother-in-law

Fanny Winstead

Grandma Fanny was correct. The customary crocks of sorghum molasses would be sorely missed. Store bought sugar had always been an extravagance but was now extremely rare and expensive.

"Do you think we can clear another acre of that east woodland this winter?" Watt asked Ed that night after Eli read his mother-in-law's letter to the family.

"If we borrow the Taylor's oxen, we should be able to. Why? You thinking about puttin' it under sorghum?" Ed responded.

"I was thinking of plowing an acre of the hay field for the sorghum and clearing the woods for more pasture. We can fence it after we get it burned off."

Jack and Craig groaned at the thought of the extra labor this winter.

Ed grinned and said over his shoulder, "Maybe we'll have molasses this time next year, Lizzie."

After church the next Sunday Lizzie complained to Martha Jane Taylor, "Watt and Ed are excited about making molasses next year. I'm worried about what we'll do for sweets in the meantime."

The Taylors lived on the next farm and had been close friends and neighbors for years. Marthey was engaged to Watt and her youngest brother Jefferson was sweet on Lizzie.

"Ma will share our honey with you. I think she plans to go gather some this week. I'll have Jeff come tell you what day is best to help." The older girl said with a little giggle.

A few days later Jeff stepped into the kitchen as Lizzie took a pan of corn fritters out of the brick oven. She turned them onto a platter and Jeff grabbed one and popped it into his mouth.

"Jefferson Lafayette Taylor, stop that," Lizzie scolded, and Jeff grinned and grabbed another, retreating across the room out of reach of the wooden spoon she held in her hand.

"What do you want?"

"I was down fishin' by the creek and smelled your fritters cooking. Ma is going to go rob the bee tree before dawn tomorrow. She says to come over after the little ones leave for school. She thinks there will be a good haul. Do ya want me to come walk you over?"

"Now, why would I want you to do that? I know the way. Tell Nannie Taylor that I'll be there as quick as I can. Now shoo. I have supper to fix."

Jeff smiled and pulled her apron strings. She scowled and as she used both hands to retie the too-big apron, he swiped another fritter and ran out the door.

Adjusting the apron, Lizzie smiled, started to hum softly, and turned back to her task.

The Honey Tree

Nancy Jane Canaday had been married to Anderson Lafayette Taylor for close to thirty-five years.

Both were from established Old Virginia families but had journeyed across the Cumberland Gap in 1841 while Tennessee was still a frontier.

Nannie made the eight month sojourn on horseback with four children, a baby in her arms, and another in her womb. They lost six-year-old William when he fell from an incline and broke his neck. Eighteen-month-old Mariah Jane died of cholera shortly after they arrived in Tennessee. Nannie delivered six more children after their move.

Four of their sons had gone to the war. Virgil Stewart and Anderson Lafayette Jr. both died. Virgil died from illness early in 1861, and Fate was wounded and died in Chattanooga. Their oldest son, Creed, and middle son, James David, had both returned and were helping on the farm.

"Thank You, Lord, for my family and all the blessings you bestow. And thank you for the bees in this hive. They will sweeten our lives with their nectar and brighten our home with their honey comb." Nannie prayed reverently as she made the first slice in the massive honeycomb being careful to leave enough of the top for the bees to rebuild.

She worked diligently and peacefully; seemingly at one with the bees. Finally, the sun was peaking through the trees and two of her pails were full. Stepping back, she placed her hand over her heart and addressed the ancient tree containing the massive hive.

"Go raibh maith agat as do fhlaihuilacht, do SOILSE." ('Thank you for your generosity, your majesty,' in Gaelic.)

On her way home, she stopped at her eldest son's home. Creed, his wife Sarah, and their three children lived on the edge of the Taylor property.

Since the war, Creed's profession as a stone mason wasn't in demand so he had been helping his father with the farm.

"Good morning, Ma," Creed greeted his mother as he headed out the door. "I see you robbed the bees this morning. Sarah is ready to go with you and I'll carry the pails."

"Thank you, son. Do the girls know to come to our place after school?"

"Good morning, Ma Taylor," Sarah said pleasantly as she exited the house with her four-year-old son on her heels. "The girls will come to your house after school. Let's go render that honey and wax so they can have a treat when they get there."

"Ellen's here, I see. She'll have everything set out and ready to go," Sarah commented as they approached the house.

Ellen was the oldest Taylor daughter and lived a few miles down the road with her husband Joseph Lance.

"Set the pails on the back porch, son. Your papa and brothers are waiting for you down in the horse pasture." Nannie told Creed, and then greeted the women gathered there.

There were pans and bowls and mashers of all types set on a large worktable on the end of the porch.

The side yard held a permanent fire pit and tripod with a large kettle. It was used for laundry and various chores throughout the year. A hook hung from the apex of the tripod. A large tin bucket was almost obscured by steam rising from the boiling kettle of water.

Nannie went to wash the dust from her face and hands at the kitchen washbowl as the other women went to work extracting the precious honey.

Ellen removed the warm bucket from the hook and brought it to the table and suspended a large copper colander by the handles over the bucket. She placed a few pieces of the dripping honeycomb in the colander.

With a large wooden masher, Marthey crushed the comb to release the sweet honey from its cells. As the comb was crushed, Lizzie added more pieces until the colander could hold no more.

Nannie returned and smiled to see Lizzie licking her fingers. "Oh what a glorious day it is. The sun is shining and the Queen graced us with an ample supply of her sweet nectar. Lizzie, when you get done licking your fingers, help Betsy and Callie cut straining cloths for the crocks."

The bucket was beginning to get full, but there was still honey in the combs so a second bucket was slipped under the dripping colander.

The last pieces of comb were added and crushed and the bucket was set over the hot water.

Linen straining cloths were stretched over the crocks and the warm, golden liquid was poured into the waiting containers. When the bucket was drained, Ellen appeared with a platter of hot, buttered biscuits and set them on the table.

Nannie said, "Shall we test the Queen's gift?"

Her question was met with an enthusiastic chorus of "Yes!"

"What about Mr. Taylor and the men?" Lizzie asked with butter and honey dripping off her chin.

"They can eat their fill at supper. This first taste is ours by right of effort."

When they finished their snack, the women all rose and brushed the crumbs from their skirts and washed up at the well. By now, the second bucket was full and all the honey had drained from the crushed comb.

They got busy pouring and straining the honey into the crocks while Nannie carefully and with reverence wrapped the honeycomb from the colander in a large square of doubled cheesecloth. She tied the top off with some twine. Calling out to the two youngest girls, "Betsy, stoke the fire under the kettle and, Lizzie, add some water from the well."

Once the fire was going again, Nannie took the bundle of honeycomb and placed it in the steeping water. "We'll let the wax melt and cool overnight and tomorrow we will make candles to light our way."

She turned to survey the day's work. There were several crocks of varying size. Enough to sweeten their tables for a few months.

All in all it had been a glorious day.

Bees Light the Way

Lizzie was late arriving at the Taylor place the next morning. "I'm so sorry I'm late, Nannie Taylor. Queen and Mack made themselves sick eating too much honey last night."

Both of the children remembered the time of plenty before the war and were affected by the deprivation of the war years. It seemed that neither of them ever got enough to eat.

Showing concern Nannie asked, "Are they better this morning? Do I need to take a look at them?"

"They are fine. Watt reminded them both that they needed to take Maggie and Henry to school and made them go even though they whined about it. What can I do to help?"

Nannie laughed but Marthey frowned and pursed her lips at the thought of her future husband being so stern with the children.

"You and Betsy take the honey pans and the colander into the woods. Bets, you know where I leave them. By the time you get back the wax should be ready to work with. Ellen and Sarah aren't coming today, so we have plenty to do."

Nannie knew the best way to clean the sticky honey from the utensils used was to set them out in the open for the bees to reclaim their honey. In a couple of days the pans and colander would be clean and ready to scour for their next purpose. This also served as her tribute to the Queen for her generosity.

As the wax had melted in the hot water, the cheesecloth had captured the comb cells and any dead bees or other debris. Left in the water overnight, the beeswax had solidified into a thick bright yellow ring.

Once again the big wash kettle was filled with water and brought to a boil.

A deep and narrow tin bucket was hung from the tripod hook so it was resting but not submerged in the hot water. The wax was broken into pieces and placed in the bucket to melt.

A pile of candle wicks was waiting. Cotton twine cut into two foot lengths had a small stone tied to each end.

When the wax was completely melted, it was a simple but tedious task.

Marthey picked up a piece of twine and held it in the middle. Suspended over three fingers so the ends were separate and of equal lengths, she slowly dipped the weighted ends into the hot wax and slowly withdrew them. The wax coated twine was then hung over the bottom rung of a quilt rack.

Callie, Betsy and Lizzie then repeated the process one at a time. By the time they had dipped all of the prepared wicks, the first ones were ready to dip again.

It required several dips before the candles were thick and straight. Nannie cut the stones off the bottoms and the tapers were dipped a few more times.

At mid-afternoon, she declared the candles sufficient and ready to dry completely.

Three hundred fat, yellow candles hung from the quilt rack and a handy tree limb.

Enough bees wax to light their way for several dark months.

Letter from Joe

Carroll County, *Dec 1st, 1866*

Dear Brother Eli

After so long a time I thought to write. Summer was brutal but we managed to get a good crop of corn and the apple orchard gave us surplus.

Mother got married the first of November. Her mourning period was over so she married Hezekiah Coble who lives down the road. He is a widower with several grown children and some still at home. Since Papa's will made no provision for her remarriage, her new husband will manage the estate until I turn twenty-five in seven years. They are living in Mr. Cobles place.

K married Orpha Jane Malear and they are staying here with me until K can build his property to support them. Uncle R D's place doesn't have a house on it. Jane is a very nice lady and is good company for Tabby, since Mother moved out.

Will is still here and saving his money from Papa until he can find a place he wants to buy. I'm glad for the company and so is Tabitha.....

Joe was laboring over the letter to his oldest brother when K burst into Neddy's office.

"I just came from Papa's grave. Have you been there lately?" K excitedly asked his little brother. His twitch out of control. One eye kept closing rapidly and his mouth curling toward his nose in a snarl.

Joe put his pen down and looked at K. "No, not since the service in January. Why?"

"There's a big stalk of tobacco growing next to the headstone. Now, boy, we both know that tobacco doesn't come up on its own. And if it did, there isn't a tobacco field within a mile of that cemetery."

"Well, I'm sure I don't know why. Probably just some strange coincidence. Did you pull it up?"

K calmed a bit then shivered and slowly said, "No. When I reached for it, I got a chill and it felt like a rabbit ran across my grave." K shivered again and turned and left the room.

Eli, K just came from the cemetery, upset due to a stalk of tobacco growing on Papa's grave. Sometimes I don't understand our brother.

Had better close for now.

Please write soon and let us know how you all are.

Tabby sends her love.

Your baby brother

Joseph E

Watt read the letter to Eli as they rocked in front of the parlor fire. When he got to the passage about Neddy's grave, he stopped and looked at his father questioningly.

Eli just smiled and continued to rock, holding little Henry closer.

Letters from Texas

Just before Christmas, Watt received a letter from, John Christopher. He had left Tennessee and moved to Arkansas with his father. They had heard from relatives who had moved to Fannin County, Texas. John wanted to know if Watt or Ed remembered, Ezekiel Skaggs who served in Terry's Texas Rangers and fought alongside the 4th TN Cavalry. It seems the relatives were living close to Skaggs.

John added a postscript in his letter to "Queen of my Heart" saying he would see her again someday and hoped she was well.

The next day a letter came to Eli from W. C. Reeves, the neighbor who had swapped for the roan stud. He was settled in Texas, and also mentioned Skaggs. Reeves loved the roan and already had the start of a horse ranch. The land was similar to the land in Tennessee. Water was plentiful and the soil was perfect for wheat, corn, and cotton. The area in Grayson County he settled in was full of Confederates and was known to show hospitality to Jessie James and William Quantrill. He also added a postscript to his letter. If ever Eli or his family wanted to relocate, he would be happy to be their neighbor again.

CHAPTER 4

LOVE IS IN THE AIR 1867

Yankee Visitor

In August of 1867, Will married Deliah Huffman and the couple came to visit Eli after stopping in Marshall County to visit with Susan and Jeremiah. On their arrival at the farm, as they rode in the buggy up the long drive toward the front porch, Deliah took Will's arm and whispered, "Why are all those boots lined up on the porch?"

Will frowned and pondered how he should respond. Watt had told him about some of Lizzie's quirks regarding housekeeping. Will informed his bride, "The war was very difficult for Lizzie and the children, and she has developed some quirks about the household and cleaning. One of the things she insists on is work boots must be removed before anyone enters the house; especially if they have been in any of the animal pens."

"Does that include the little children?" she asked. The boots were lined up by size all along the front wall of the house. All ten pair in various sizes and wear patterns including the tiny pair belonging to Henry.

Laughing, Will squeezed her hand and said, "Yes, I believe it does, but don't worry, my dear. Your shoes are clean so she shouldn't make you remove them."

The front door opened and Eli stepped out on the porch to welcome his young brother and his new wife. Soon the couple was surrounded by family members, and all thoughts of stray boots had left Deliah's mind.

Ed was three months older than his Uncle Will and they had spent a lot of time together as children. They renewed their former friendship instantly and their opposite stance on the war was easily forgotten.

Sam and his younger brother Jack shared their brother's sentiments and Watt had already made his opinion clear. For all of the men, family unity was more important than politics.

Unfortunately, Lizzie didn't share her brothers' tolerant attitude. She liked Deliah immediately but she could barely look at or speak to her Uncle.

That evening the family was gathered around the big table on the back porch enjoying supper. Deliah had helped Lizzie and the girls with the garden and in preparing the meal.

Lizzie went to get a fresh batch of her fluffy biscuits out of the brick oven and as she returned Will complimented her cooking.

"Lizzie, that is the best meal I've had in ages. You should come teach Penny how to make biscuits like those. May I have another one, please?"

She was standing at the opposite end of the table. Starting with her father, she placed a fresh hot biscuit on each plate. There was only one left when she reached her uncle. Just as she got to his place, she stumbled and the biscuit tumbled to the porch floor.

As she stooped to pick it up, Old Ned ran out from under the table and grabbed the hot delicacy and took off across the yard. Lizzie looked up, hidden from sight of everyone but Will, met his eyes and smiled a tiny little smile.

Ever gracious, Will understood and reached out to help his niece to her feet. He understood her anger.

Later that evening, Eli found her alone in the kitchen. "What is wrong with you, girl? I've never known you to be rude to a guest in this house, especially to one of your uncles."

She looked at him incredulously. "But, Pa. He's a Yankee. How can you still call him brother, after what the Yankees put us through?"

Uncharacteristically stern, Eli responded, "You listen to me, young lady. I am still head of this house and I will not put up with inhospitable behavior from you or any of my children. William is blood-of-my-blood, and you will be pleasant and courteous and give him the respect he deserves, while you are under this roof. Is that clear?"

Thoroughly chastised and not convinced she was capable of what her father demanded, the girl obediently said, "Yes, Sir."

Remembering his daughter was just sixteen and still not a woman grown, he put his arms around her and gently said, "We must let bygones be bygones, Lizzie. If we don't, the hatred will eat us up inside. What are you planning for tomorrow's supper?"

Polly

"Polly's here!" Queen yelled from the yard into the house. "Her buggy's coming up the road."

Eli stuck his head out of the tool shed, knocked the dottle out of his pipe, and walked toward the house.

Watt, Ed, and Jack were in the field but the rest of the family gathered on the porch as Eli stood in the yard waiting for his first born to stop the buggy near the steps.

Mary Smith "Polly" Ownby Brown let her father help her descend from the buggy as Queen lifted three-year-old Nancy Ann into her arms.

Henry ran up and grabbed his nephew John's hand, "Ya gotta come see Lady's pups. They just opened their eyes this week." The boys were only a few months apart in age and enjoyed playing together like all six-year-olds.

"Mack, take your sister's bag into the house," Eli directed, "and Craig, get this buggy unhitched and rub down the horse."

Polly hugged her father tight and kissed him on the cheek. "How are you feeling, Pa?" she asked as though she were the parent instead of the child.

"I'm fit as a fiddle, daughter, but sad that Roy couldn't come with you." Polly's husband, Leroy Spencer Brown owned a farm near Shelbyville and couldn't get away. She spotted her uncle Will standing near the corner of the porch and moved toward him.

He took her hands and said, "It's so good to see you, Polly. Lovely as always."

"I'm pleased to see you, Uncle Will," and she turned to the young woman standing next to him. "You must be Deliah; you're even prettier than Grandmother Laurie said you were."

She put her arm around Deliah's slim waist and said, "Let's go find Lizzie and see where we're all to sleep."

The house was crowded that night. The children and young people slept on pallets on the porch, the men slept in the barn, and the women doubled up wherever they could in the loft. Eli had already given his room to the newlyweds and slept in the barn with the other men.

Molasses

After much discussion with his father, brothers and neighbors, Watt decided to try a half acre of the Winstead sorghum.

Early in October, he started watching the seed heads every day and when they turned dark brown and started to shed he told Ed, "Tomorrow we cut the sorghum."

At first light the next morning the brothers descended on the small field. As Watt and Ed stripped the blades from the stalks, Sam and Jack tied the long thin leaves into bundles to be dried for cattle feed during the winter. Craig and Eli followed with a sled to carry the bundles to a crib.

Once the stalks were cleaned, Watt started cutting the canes. Using a long, thin blade, Ed had forged just for the task. Watt cut the stalk six inches above the ground and let it lie.

Ed came along behind Watt and cut the seed head with a smaller knife and collected the seeds in a cotton sack.

Eli drove a team with the sled along the edge of the field while Sam, Jack, and Craig stacked the cut stalks on the sled.

The sun was getting low as the men stood the final stalks up, teepee fashion, next to the newly constructed cane mill.

Eli surveyed the now-stubbled field and the stacks of cane. He lit his pipe and passed around a twist for his sons. "This was a good days work, boys. My tongue can taste the sweet already. Let's go see what Lizzie has for supper."

Watt had been advised to let the stalks stand for a week to let the sugar deepen. So at supper a week later, he announced, "Tomorrow is Molasses Making Day. Is everybody ready?"

In unison they all said, "YES!"

Everyone was ready for the bittersweet change from the honey they had been eating for the past year.

Lizzie had collected and washed all of the crocks she could find, and they stood ready to be filled.

Queen, Mack, Maggie and Henry were allowed to stay home from school to help on this special day.

Shortly after dawn, Eli led a mule to the mill where the entire family was gathered.

Creed Taylor had fashioned two stone rollers and Jack had built the mill frame.

The mule was hitched to a long pole and as he was led in a wide circle, the rollers crushed the canes squeezing the sweet liquid into a waiting bucket. A piece of woven hemp covered the bucket to catch dirt and debris.

Queen and Mack were in charge of feeding the sorghum cane through the mill while Eli led the mule in circles. When the bucket was full, Eli would stop the mule and carry the bucket to a huge kettle set over a fire pit.

Lizzie would remove the straining cloth and pour the unappetizing green liquid into the kettle while Jack and Craig held a clean straining cloth. The juice smelled like the insides of a gutted pumpkin.

Once the fire was lit and the kettle full it would need to boil for five or six hours.

Everyone in the family including Maggie and six-year-old Henry took turns skimming the green slime that appeared on the surface. A long wooden paddle with holes in the end was used to constantly catch and discard the scum.

By mid afternoon, the scum had turned yellow. Thick bubbles appeared on the surface and popped, leaving fish eyes.

Lizzie stirred the dark mixture with a clean spoon. Holding the dripping spoon above the kettle, she watched the thick syrup slowly gravitate back into the pot in threads.

"Grandma Fanny said when it's thready it's ready. Jack, Craig, put the fire out."

A wooden table had been set up close by and the crocks were waiting. Each was covered with a fresh piece of hemp to act as a final filter. It was important to pour the finished molasses up while it was still hot to keep it from hardening and turning to sugar.

The first crock was delivered to the kitchen and the others were sealed and stored in the spring house.

Supper was simple that night. Everyone was exhausted. There was bacon, cornbread and enough molasses to satisfy every sweet tooth.

As she was clearing the table, Lizzie spoke to Watt. "Why don't you take the Taylors a couple of crocks of molasses tomorrow? I'm sure Nannie Taylor would be pleased."

Watt grinned at his sister and said, "I believe I will."

Watt and Marthey

On October 31, the harvest was in. Everyone was waiting for first frost to slaughter the hogs. The Taylors decided to revive the ritual of Snap-Apple Night and invited Eli and his family to join in the celebration.

Nannie Taylor's Celtic roots provided many customs for this All Hallows Eve party. A fire to keep the ghosts, goblins, and witches away was built in the yard, and candle lit Jack-O-Lanterns lined the wrap around porch.

A large tub of water and apples stood ready for the children and young people to bob for apples later in the evening.

The dining table was set up on the front porch, decorated with autumn leaves and bright chrysanthemums from Nannie's garden. Platters of ham and biscuits; large bowls of squash, sweet potatoes, sauerkraut and turnip greens; apple pie and baked pumpkins with cream filling were waiting to be devoured.

After everyone had eaten their fill, Watt and Marthey took a walk around the farm. When they reached the edge of the woods, Watt reached for her and took her in his arms. "I thought we'd never be alone. It's been so hard since the war ended, and there is still so much work to do. I don't know if it's possible to rebuild, but I have to try. Will you be patient a little longer?"

Marthey sighed and raised her head from his chest to look into his eyes. She quietly replied, "I'll wait forever if that's what it takes, Watt. I know you have to take care of the children and your Pa."

They stood holding each other for several minutes until the sounds of the children laughing and Jim tuning up his fiddle intruded on their quiet time.

"We had best get back, Marthey, before your Pa comes looking for us with that shotgun of his." Watt laughed as he took her hand and reluctantly walked her back to the house.

As they walked, Watt started humming a tune.

"Why do you hum that tune, Watt? The war is over. It should be put to rest."

"Oh, Marthey, I didn't realized I was humming. The words running through my mind aren't of war and rebellion but of peace and tranquility."

Marthey stopped and looked at him. "I know that song and I hate it. That song caused nothing but heartache and death. I want to have nothing to do with it ever again."

Watt realized she was extremely upset and a little angry, so he sat on the edge of the porch and pulled her down beside him. He put his arm around her shoulders, pressed her head to his chest, and held her tight.

"Let me explain, sweetheart. I'm not humming the Bonnie Blue Flag. When I was imprisoned at Camp Chase, a song circulated the various prisons. It became a symbol of hope for all of us; a hope for a brighter future. The tune and cadence was the same as the Bonnie Blue, but the words were different and it was entitled The Bonnie White Flag."

As Marthey raised her head and gazed at him in wonder, Watt began to softly sing.

Though we're a band of prisoners,
Let each be firm and true,
For noble souls and hearts of oak,
The foe can ne'er subdue.
We then will turn us homeward,
To those we love so dear;
For peace and happiness, my boys,
Oh, give a hearty cheer!

Hurrah! Hurrah! for peace
And home, hurrah!
Hurrah for the Bonnie White Flag,
That ends this cruel war!

Comprehension showed in Marthey's eyes as Watt sang the chorus, and she began to hum the tune in accompaniment.

The sword into the scabbard,
The musket on the wall,
The cannon from its blazing throat,
No more shall hurl the ball;
From wives and babes and sweethearts,
No longer will we roam, For ev'ry gallant soldier boy,
Shall seek his cherished home.

Hurrah! Hurrah! for peace
And home, hurrah!
Hurrah for the Bonnie White Flag,
That ends this cruel war!

Our battle banners furled away

No more shall greet the eye,
Nor beat of angry drums be heard,
Nor bugle's hostile cry.
The blade no more be raised aloft,
In conflict fierce and wild,
The bomb shall roll across the sward,
The plaything of a child.

Hurrah! Hurrah! for peace
And home, hurrah!
Hurrah for the Bonnie White Flag,
That ends this cruel war!

No pale-faced captive then shall stand,
Behind his rusted bars,
Nor from the prison window bleak,
Look sadly to the stars ;
But out amid the woodland's green,
On bounding steed he'll be,
And proudly from his heart shall rise,
The anthem of the free.

Hurrah! Hurrah! for peace
And home, hurrah!
Hurrah for the Bonnie White Flag,
That ends this cruel war!

The plow into the furrow then,
The fields shall wave with grain,
And smiling children to their schools,
All gladly go again.
The church invites its grateful throng,
And man's rude striving cease,
While all across our noble land,
Shall glow the light of Peace.

Hurrah! Hurrah! For peace
and Home, Hurrah!
Hurrah for the Bonnie White Flag
That ends this cruel war.

Sam and Ruthie

Three weeks before Christmas, twenty-one-year old Samuel Mortimer Ownby married thirty-five-year old, twice widowed Ruthie Springer Wilburn Smith.

Ruthie inherited a small plantation and a mercantile Store in Bradyville when her second husband died of cholera in 1863. She had closed the Mercantile and moved her four children to the country.

Sam had stopped there on his way home from the war and had gone back as often as possible to help the lovely widow.

The wedding was held in the spacious but modest plantation house, and Ruthie's former slave, nineteen-year-old Tennessee Smith had been busy cleaning and polishing until the house and everything in it was sparkling. All of the neighbors had prepared dishes and special treats for the upcoming nuptials. Ruthie's children loved Sam and were excited to welcome him to their little family.

Weddings were an especially joyous occasion and everyone for miles around was expected to attend. Only extreme and serious illness would keep family and friends away. After the solemn ceremony, the festivities began with much food, drink, music, dancing, gossip, and flirting among the single folks.

Nannie Taylor made the bridal cake. Flavored with rose water, lemon, nutmeg, and cinnamon, it was frosted with a rich icing of sugar and egg whites. It looked simple on the outside, but it was the inside that was an art. Placed in the batter and baked into the cake were various prizes, each signifying something special for the guest who received the token.

As the bride cut the first piece, and carefully bit into the slice, Ruthie was delighted to find a small coin, which symbolized a prosperous fortune. Sam hugged her tightly and they both beamed with happiness.

As the rest of the cake was sliced and passed around to the guests, Lizzie received the thimble, which signified many to feed or sew for.

Watt bit into the darning needle, which foretold much blessedness.

Queen was appalled when she found a button representing fickleness or disappointment.

But the largest laugh came from the gathering when Ed discovered a ring in his piece of cake. The ring predicted the very next bride or groom. Laughing his deep booming laugh, he told the assembled crowd, "Not anytime soon, y'all," and he nodded toward Nannie, "so don't go makin' the cake just yet."

Since a man got the ring in the cake, the single women all wanted a chance at good luck, so Tennessee brought a quilt into the parlor. Ruthie's big gray house cat, Mouse, was dragged out from under a chair, and all the single girls over sixteen years old held an edge of the quilt. Mouse was placed in the center of the quilt. The object of the exercise was to see who he came closest to on leaving the quilt. That lucky girl would be the very next bride.

The quilt was given a light toss to encourage Mouse to run off. Martha Jane Taylor was surprised when the cat came right to her and brushed her arm as he jumped to the floor. Meeting Watt's eyes across the room, she gave him a radiant smile and blushed.

The music began and Jim Taylor joined in with his fiddle. Sam escorted his bride onto the floor for a first waltz as man and wife. Soon the music turned livelier with Virginia Reels and the young people monopolized the dance floor. The older men drifted toward the porch and their pipes. The women went in search of their children or tended to their babies.

Eli took Sam's arm and said, "Follow me outside, Son." As they headed out the back door, Sam saw a beautiful chestnut colt hitched to the back porch railing. "I know how you have missed Fitzwilliam since the Yanks took him from you. Maybe this fella will get you and Ruthie started with your own strong horse stock."

51

Luther Peterson

Standing in the doorway, Watt was watching the couples dancing in Ruthie's parlor through silted eyes. Anyone observing would assume it was from the smoke of the pipe his teeth were clenched around.

But Ed knew his older brother better than anyone. Two years younger, Ed had followed Watt through the war and had seen his brother act with the authority and responsibility of a cavalry sergeant.

"What's stuck in your craw, you old sack of bones?" Ed asked as he surveyed the room. Then he saw why his brother was angry.

A dashing and handsome man was twirling Marthey around the room. His black hair and dark eyes shone in the lamp light. His white teeth sparkled in a tanned clean-shaven face. With graceful movements, he floated Watt's prospective bride across the floor as if she were a feather.

The floor had cleared of all but the one couple. The crowd had encircled the dancers and was watching. Marthey's face was flushed, and Watt had never seen her look lovelier.

"I see what's got your dander up." Ed commented wryly.

"Do you know who that man is?" Watt asked.

"He's from Chicago. He showed up in Bradyville a few weeks ago and bought Ruthie's Mercantile. Says he plans to reopen with new stock from up north. Sam said his name is Luther Peterson. Surely you aren't jealous of a good looking, smooth talking carpetbagger?"

Watt shot his brother a scathing look and said, "Don't be ridiculous," as he squinted his eyes again.

"Open your eyes and look at the man closely, you useless lump of lard. Put him in a Yankee uniform and prop him up against a tree. Does he look familiar?"

The music stopped and Peterson escorted Marthey toward the drink table. She was furiously fanning her face and accepted the cup of punch he poured for her. Bowing politely, he excused himself and walked toward the doorway.

Stepping outside, he met the two brothers. "Evening, gentlemen. Lovely wedding and fabulous party don't you think?" he said pleasantly.

"Yes it is," Ed said with a crooked smile as he hooked his arm through Peterson's.

"Lovely evening for a stroll," Watt said as he felt a weapon in the man's waist band and removed it. He took the other arm and the brothers walked Peterson across the porch and down the steps toward the dark barn.

Sensing the hostility, Peterson tried to resist, but the brothers' death grip on his arms kept him moving forward.

When they reached the barn, Watt released the arm and stood in front with the gun pointed at Peterson's chest.

Ed lit a lamp hanging from a post.

As the lamp brightened so did Peterson's eyes. Recognition had set in and he smirked and said, "Well, well, well. If it isn't the rebel Ownby brothers. What is white trash like you two doing at a fine lady like Mrs. Smith's wedding party?"

Ed drawled in a deceptively lazy manner. "We were wondering the same thing about you, Yankee. How did you get an invite to our brother's wedding?"

"Your brother? You mean there's more than two of you spawn of Satan?"

Ed started toward Peterson with clinched fists, but Watt put his hand out to stop his brother.

Peterson went on, ignoring the threat of Ed's anger. "Do you know what hell I went through after you boys escaped from Butler Prison? You two made me the laughing stock of the Union Army. Not only did you escape but took thirty others with you. I was on shit detail for two months. And you took my horse. The quartermaster wouldn't give me another one so I had to walk. I barely escaped going to prison myself. You boys owe me a lot."

"We owe you nothing, you Yankee scum. That'll teach you not to nap on duty." Watt growled low in his throat.

Peterson laughed. "I'm a respectable business man now. Your brother's new wife guaranteed that for me. All I need now is to find me a wife, and I'm set for good in this community. Perhaps that sweet little Marthey I was dancing with would be willing. A man could get lost in her charms for days at a time. Or...that little skinny gal I met earlier tonight. Name was Lizzie. She's small but seemed like she could be a wild cat if she let her hair down."

Watt and Ed both lost their angry expressions and broke into wide smiles, just as Peterson jumped, turned and said, "What the hell!"

Standing behind him holding a pitchfork was the skinny little wild cat.

"I'll show you what a wildcat can do, you Yankee bastard." Lizzie had seen Watt and Ed take the Yankee off the porch and had quietly followed.

"LIZZIE!!! That's no language for a young lady," Eli said from a dark corner. He had seen Lizzie leaving the party and had followed her.

Both had heard the exchange with Peterson.

Sam and Jack stepped through the barn door, having seen the light in what was supposed to be a dark building. The two younger brothers moved to flank Watt and Ed.

Peterson felt like he was seeing double or quadruple. The four brothers resembled so closely it was hard to tell them apart and all four were younger versions of the old man standing in front. Turning to look over his shoulder, he realized the girl was a tiny, feminine replica of the men.

The six similar faces were more frightening than the gun or the pitchfork, and Luther Peterson began to sweat.

"Well, son," Eli looked at his eldest. "What should we do with this Yankee scoundrel?"

Watt handed Peterson his gun and smiled a smile that didn't reach his eyes. "I think Mr. Peterson has worn out his welcome in these parts. We have extended all the hospitality he is entitled to. He'll be moving along on the morrow. Right, Peterson?"

Sputtering and still sweating, Peterson said, "But I can't leave. What about my property?"

"The land agent in town can handle a sale for you. Leave him a forwarding address and he can send you the money if it sells. But don't come back to collect it. Understand?"

"Yes. I think your plan is wise. I need to visit my mother in Chicago. Good evening gentleman, ma'am."

With his head held high, Luther Peterson walked to the barn door then ran like the devil was after him.

Ed watched him run and turned to his family, "Looks like Peterson is afoot again. He left his horse tied to the porch railing."

"What in thunder was that all about?" Sam asked.

Clapping his brother on the back, Watt said, "Old war debt now paid in full." Go enjoy your wedding night, and I'll explain later. At least Ruthie got paid before the carpetbagger was found out."

Venus Rising

Ed reined Scout in and dismounted at a creek bank so they could both get a drink. Watt and Jack could handle the farm chores at home so he had taken a few days to go visit Sam and take a look at Ruthie's horse stock. Breaking the thin ice on the creek with his front hoof, Scout drank his fill, as Ed noticed the big stud favoring his left back foot. Lifting the Appaloosa's leg, he realized that Scout had a loose shoe and two of the nails were missing.

He removed the shoe and wondered where he could find some nails when he saw chimney smoke drifting from a stand of trees. He headed toward the smoke, hoping to find a farmhouse where he could borrow what he needed. A small but neat farmhouse was set back in the trees with a hog pen, several outbuildings, and a fenced in garden. He approached the back kitchen door and tied Scout to the porch railing, stepped up on the porch, and knocked on the door.

He could hear a woman singing as she went about her housework, and when the singing didn't stop at his knock, he opened the door and entered the warm kitchen.

Surprised, he saw a young woman sitting in a large copper bathtub in front of the kitchen hearth. Her back was to him. Her long chestnut hair was wet and plastered to her neck and shoulders. She stood and the hair fell below her buttocks. As she raised her arms to squeeze the water from her hair, Ed was mesmerized by the sight of her charms.

Scout decided he was bored and snorted loudly. Startled, the woman turned, saw Ed and his horse, and screamed. She reached for a large cotton sheet to cover herself and slipped and fell back into the tub.

Alarmed, Ed rushed to help her up but couldn't seem to find a place to put his hands that didn't invade her privacy. She squirmed and fought, but he kept fumbling to help her. She was too slippery and fell back under the water. His boots slid out from under him on the now wet kitchen floor, and he tumbled head first into the tub of water landing on top of her.

He came up sputtering. Scout whinnied. Ed raised his head to look at the woman. As blue eyes met brown, they both burst out laughing.

"Eduss Dallard Oby, I mean Edward Dallas Ownby at your service, ma'am," Ed said as he regained his feet, if not his dignity. He then simply bent over and scooped her up and carried her to a chair by the fire where her clothes were folded neatly in a pile. He handed her the wet sheet and put her on her feet.

She covered herself with as much modesty as she could muster under the circumstances and said, "Cynthia Emeline Knox. Thank you. Now would you please turn around and let me get dressed?"

Ed, red-faced, cold, wet, and uncomfortably distracted, reluctantly turned away and stepped out on the porch. He rubbed Scouts nose and heard the woman behind him humming a tune.

Lost in thought and thinking of a drawing he once saw called *Venus Rising from the Sea,* he jumped when he felt a tap on his shoulder, turned and faced a vision even more troubling. A beautiful young woman in yellow calico offered him a steaming cup of coffee she held in her pretty little hand.

She smiled a radiant smile and playfully said, "Would you like some coffee? I guess you'll have to marry me now, Edward Dallas Ownby, since you've seen all of me there is to see."

Before Ed could respond, the sound of a wagon approaching drew their attention. "Well, ma'am, if that's your Pa, I guess we'll have to see what he says about that."

Lester and Baxter

CHAPTER 5

WEDDINGS AND BABIES, 1868

Gathering Stones

After a brief one-month courtship, Ed married Emmy Knox.

The wedding took place in the Knox home. Emmy's father, Joseph Knox beamed proudly while her five older brothers scowled. Her mother, Cynthia, cried to see her baby and only daughter leaving home.

It was a simple but festive wedding with all the family there. Polly came with her children to stay a few days. Sam and Ruthie brought her family and of course the entire Taylor clan attended.

As the party started to wind down, Ed was trying to get Emmy away from her friends. "Come on, woman. Let's get out of here before my brothers decide to honor us with a Chivaree. Anderson and Nannie are letting us use a cabin on their land, and I don't like the way Watt and Jack keep looking at me."

Before he could pull her away and out the door, seven-year-old Henry stopped him. "Here's your rock, Ed," he said as he struggled to hand his brother a large flat rock.

Too impatient to be curious, Ed patted his baby brother on the head and said, "Not now, Henry. Give it to me later," and he pulled Emmy toward the door.

The couple didn't get very far. This time they were stopped by Creed and Sarah Ann Taylor's seven-year-old son, James. "Where do you want your rock, Mr. Ownby?" he inquired politely.

Before Ed could comprehend and respond, eight-year-old Maggie handed Ed a small, smooth, oval rock and sweetly said, "I think this will be pretty on the hearth. Don't you, Emmy?"

Ed looked around and realized that the room was quiet and everyone was watching him and they were all smiling. Ed looked for his brothers and spotted Watt, Sam, and Jack in the corner. As the brothers took long strides toward him, he wanted to run but couldn't. They had him in their sights. All he could do was stand there and wait. To Ed it looked like they were walking through molasses.

Fuming and muttering under his breath, "it's not their wedding night, why do they have to stop and talk to everyone? Come on, let's get this over with. Damn Chivaree!"

When Watt reached the newlyweds, he reached for his brother's hand and saw Maggie's rock and Ed's puzzled face. He grinned and said, "What ya got there, little brother? Looks like a rock."

"You know damn well it's a rock, Watt. The children have been bringing me rocks all night and I still don't know why, but I think you are about to tell me why. RIGHT, BIG BROTHER?"

Eli and Anderson walked up behind Ed. Eli put his hand on Ed's shoulder and said to his oldest son, "Let the boy in on the secret, Watt."

"Where do you plan to live, Ed? You and your new bride? The house is pretty full now but you could keep your old bed and Emmy could sleep in the loft with Lizzie and the girls."

"WATT!!!! That's enough," Eli interrupted. "Ed, for a wedding present, I would like to give you five acres of woodland and a single pen house for you and Emmy to live in."

"But Pa," Ed sputtered, "there's no cash to buy supplies or to pay anyone for helping."

Anderson Taylor spoke up, "That's what friends and neighbors are for, son."

"I'll take those rocks the little ones have been bringing you, Ed. I'll set Maggie's stone in the middle of the hearth just for her," Creed said proudly.

Soon a competition began. Who could come up with the most unique gift to contribute to the new house? "Me and Craig can cut the trees," offered Jack.

Not to be outdone, Jeff said, "And me and Jim can get more rocks. Those three won't build much."

The crowd laughed and everyone started talking at once. Emmy was still in shock. They had figured it would be a couple of years before they could have a home of their own. Eli quietly asked Ed if this is what he wanted and Ed finally came back to reality long enough to accept the gracious offer.

A House becomes a Home

Cynthia Emmeline Knox Ownby chose her home site the very next morning. It was about two-hundred feet behind and to the east of the main farmhouse.

Watt, Jack, Ed, and Craig started felling trees that week. Jim and Jeff helped Creed find the perfect cornerstones for the foundation. The Taylor's oxen, Ole Hickory and Stonewall, came in handy.

Jack had a distinct talent for working with wood, which he inherited from his great-grandfather, Thomas Ownby, who was a wheelwright. Before the foundation was complete and the fireplace was set, Jack started shaping logs for the floor and walls.

Sam came home a couple of times a week and helped where he could.

Once the walls were placed, the girls and children spent all their spare time collecting twigs and moss to chink the logs.

Ed and Emmy were staying with Eli, and he had given them his bedroom and was sleeping with the boys in the loft. Emmy had spent the time getting to know Lizzie and Queen and helping with Maggie and Henry. Eleven-year-old Mack adored her and followed her around like a lovesick puppy.

When the last of the lime was daubed on the interior walls, Emmy went with Ed to get her bed and rocker, from her father's house.

The wagon was loaded with other household goods that Emmy's mother insisted she take with her, including her spinning wheel and loom. As they drove away, Emmy's father came running out of the house calling for Ed to stop.

"Your Ma says for you to take this. She says she won't need it no more." He carefully placed a sturdy quilting frame in the back of the wagon and with a mournful look at his daughter turned to go back and comfort his sobbing wife.

Emmy was crying quietly and Ed patted her leg, "We'll visit often. It's only three miles, honey."

Wiping her eyes with the back of her hand, Emmy pushed a loose strand of hair back and smiled at her husband. "I'm not crying for me. I'm sad because Ma is so sad. She's so lonesome since I left. But she knows how happy I am."

As they drove up to their new house, Mack ran out to help, along with Henry and Maggie. Lizzie waved from the back porch. Eli, Watt, and Jack soon followed and they had the wagon unloaded quickly with Emmy directing where each piece should go in her new home.

"Mack, take the wagon to the shed and put the team away." Eli told his son.

"I'll put it away, Pa." Ed said. "I'm sure you all have other things to do." Then he looked at his wife with a look, Eli understood all too well.

"Yes, you boys get back to work and, Maggie, I think I hear Queen calling for you."

"I don't hear her, Pa," the little girl said hanging onto Emmy's skirt. "I wanna stay here with Emmy."

"Don't sass me, young lady. I'm sure your sisters have something for you to do. Now go on. Git."

When everyone left, Emmy started making their bed with a stack of quilts her mother had sent, but Ed said, "Come out to the porch, wife."

She stepped out and he swooped her up in his arms.

"But Ed, what about your hip?"

Ed had been shot in the left hip by a bushwhacker during the war. Scout had stood over him until he could be rescued. The mini ball had struck the fleshy part of his buttocks and done no serious or permanent damage although it still pained him when the scar tissue contracted.

"My hip is fine. Let me worry about that. Come here, woman."

"Ohhhh," she squealed as he spun her around in a circle.

"I need to carry you over the threshold, my darlin, so we are blessed with luck in our new home."

"Ummm," Emmy murmured as she buried her face in his neck.

As was always the case when he was near his chestnut beauty, Ed's reaction was instantaneous

Kicking the door closed with his right leg, he gently placed Emmy on the pile of quilts on the bed.

Two hours later, Watt approached Eli, who was standing on the back porch smoking his pipe.

"Looks like Ed forgot to put the team and wagon away. I guess I better go see if something is wrong over there."

"Just stay put, Watt. Give your brother some time. He'll remember eventually. The mules won't die standing there a while longer." Grinning as Watt seemed to understand, he walked into the house.

Lester and Baxter

"I'm against it, Watt," Ed stated. "It's a waste when we can borrow the Taylor's yoke anytime we need them."

The brothers were returning from Woodbury where they had gone to look at some livestock. Watt had been impressed with the Taylor's oxen. Ole Hickory and Stonewall had made a major difference while clearing the land and building Ed's house. Watt wanted to own a pair of the big animals.

"There's money in horse flesh, Ed. We can sell that two-year-old stud and the little chestnut filly and buy that yoke Johnson has for sale." Watt reasoned with his brother. "There's two hundred acres of woodland that can be cleared. If we cut and sell the wood, we can turn the land into fields and pasture much quicker, and it will give us some money for other improvements."

Ed grunted and said, "Let's train a yoke. We can pull two of the steers and work with them until they are ready in three years."

They were still arguing as they made a sharp turn and saw a wagon crammed full of household goods stopped in the middle of the narrow road. A man's feet protruded from beneath the wagon and he wasn't moving. Two oxen were hitched to the wagon and were standing there patiently waiting.

The brothers stopped, and Ed crawled under the wagon and called to Watt, "He's dead. Looks like his neck is broke. Must have fallen off. I'm surprised the oxen didn't bolt."

"Oxen don't bolt like mules or horses, you useless lump of lard. Don't you know anything?"

"I know as much as you do, you old sack of bones," Ed retorted back. "I guess we should take him and the rig back to town. Do you recognize him?"

Watt looked the man over and said, "No, I've never seen him before."

They tied the man over Belle's saddle and turned the yoke and wagon around and, with Watt driving the wagon and Ed leading Belle, they went back to Woodbury. Stopping at the Sheriff's office, they told him how they had found the man. The sheriff didn't recognize him either.

"I'll arrange for a proper burial and send word to the surrounding counties. Why don't you boys take the rig on home. If no one claims it in a month or two, it's yours."

No one came to claim the rig so the sheriff told Watt to dispose of the goods however he wanted to.

The wagon was full of household items and Emmy made good use of the table and chairs. Lizzie appreciated the kettles and crocks. There was no identification or names in any of the things. A bible had birth and death entries, but they were first names only.

Watt acquired his yoke of oxen and Ed didn't have to give up his horses. They named the big animals Lester and Baxter.

Mama Lizzie

"For seven years I've been a mother to these children. All I've done is cook and clean and wash clothes and wipe runny noses. When is it my turn to have my own life?" Lizzie sobbed to Nannie Taylor.

Not quite eighteen, Elizabeth Nancy Ownby was a young woman with little time for frivolous things.

At eleven years of age, she had promised her dying mother to look after her younger brothers and sisters. She had done just that. During the war years she was often alone and frightened and hungry and didn't know what to do. Somehow, she found the strength to persevere and they had all managed to survive.

The war had been over for two years, but the deprivation was still prevalent and Lizzie worried constantly about the family's welfare.

Crying on Nannie's shoulder was Lizzie's only emotional outlet. It wasn't a frequent occurrence, but occasionally Lizzie needed the older woman's comforting wisdom and experience.

"This is your life, sweetling. It's not one you would have chosen, but it's the one the good Lord gave you. Your family is like a twist of tobacco, layered and entwined until you are all inseparable." She patted Lizzie's back, feeling the shoulder blades poking through her dress. Never plump, the tiny girl was downright scrawny.

"Your time will come to sing in the sun. Read Ecclesiastes chapter three.

Before Lizzie was forced to stop school when her mother died, she loved to read and exhausted the meager offerings in the schoolhouse. Her brothers and sisters would bring her books from school. But with the scarcity of reading material and limited time, she didn't indulge often, except for her daily bible readings.

When Nannie left, Lizzie opened her bible to study Nannie's suggested passage:

Ecclesiastes Chapter 3:

1. To everything there is a season, and a time to every purpose under heaven:

2. A time to be born, and a time to die; a time to plant, and a time to pluck up that which is planted;

3. A time to kill, and a time to heal; a time to break down, and a time to build up;

4. A time to weep, and a time to laugh; a time to mourn, and a time to dance;

5. A time to cast away stones, and a time to gather stones together; a time to embrace, and a time to refrain from embracing;

6. A time to get, and a time to lose; a time to keep, and a time to cast away;

7. A time to rend, and a time to sew; a time to keep silence, and a time to speak;

8. A time to love, and a time to hate; a time of war, and a time of peace.

Lizzie found the words comforting and strangely enough, they gave her strength.

Lizzie sent her excess butter into town with her father and this gave her a few pennies to spend on herself or the children now and then.

Lady Blue and Old Ned produced excellent hunting dogs, which Eli traded in town.

Jeff Taylor visited her frequently, under the pretext of seeing how Lady and her pups were getting along.

Craig would soon be fifteen and had decided his time was better spent with the cows and pigs than in school

Queen, now twelve, was in charge of Maggie and Henry who were growing up healthy and were being schooled like Lizzie had promised.

Mack, at ten, would rather stay home with his chickens than go to school. Some mornings Watt had to severely remind the boy that the chickens would survive a few hours a day without Mack's care.

The war had been hell here on earth. But they had come through it and were in the process of rebuilding what had been broke down.

She struggled to concentrate on the positive things happening for the family; all the while understanding that she would never forget the bad.

Eli spent his time hunting and going into Woodbury to barter, trade, or visit, when he wasn't sitting in his rocker lost in some kind of fog. He completely turned over the management of the farm to Watt who, with Ed, spent many late night hours at the desk in his father's bedroom going over the farm accounts trying to increase yield and profits.

Emmy

"Tarnation, the heat was brutal today," Eli commented to his sons as he sat rocking on the porch after supper. It was a hot July night with no breeze blowing. He could hear plates and pots rattling in the kitchen.

Ed and Emmy had settled into their home, but since it didn't have a real kitchen yet, they took most of their meals with the family.

Lizzie appreciated Emmy's help with the cooking and gardening and the two women grew closer every day. Emmy tried to understand Lizzie's little quirks and acknowledged that the younger girl was in charge of the house and the younger children.

"Emmy sure is the picture of health these days," Watt observed.

As if on cue, Eli replied, "She is absolutely radiant. Don't you think, Ed?"

"She resembles a fattening hog," Ed grunted. "All she does is eat. I found an apron wrapped around a dozen buttered biscuits in the foot of the bed the other morning.... and all she does is want to sleep. I think she'd go to bed with Mack's chickens."

Eli stopped rocking and looked at Ed with sympathy in his eyes. "Son, she hasn't told you yet?"

"Told me what, Pa? Is there something wrong with her? Is she ill?"

Watt stood and walked away to keep from laughing in his brother's face, while Jack and Craig merely looked confused.

Eli doubled over with tears in his eyes from laughing, "No, son, she's not ill. It will come clear to you soon. Just as soon as you see that little baby at her breast."

"Little baby? What little baby? You mean I'm gonna be a Pa?" Ed stood so fast, he knocked his chair over on the wooden porch with a loud crash. "Emmy! Cynthia Emmeline Ownby, you get out here right now!" he yelled toward the kitchen.

Everyone in the house came running. But leading the crowd was Emmy. Her apron was pulled tight over her growing belly. Wiping her hands on a dishtowel, she noted the overturned chair and rushed to her wild-eyed husband. "What's wrong, Ed?"

"Are you expecting a baby?"

She had confided in her mother, Lizzie, and Nannie Taylor months ago and by now everyone in the area knew. Everyone except Ed. Never finding the right moment to tell him, she hoped he would notice. Eli and Watt had decided to help her out a bit.

The family encircled the couple, Watt and Eli laughing, Jack and Craig clapping their big brother on the back and everyone talking at once. Ed and Emmy stood lost in each other's gaze.

Lizzie broke the spell. "Queen, take Maggie and Henry to bed." Reaching for her broom, she swatted Watt on the backside. "You quit laughing and leave them alone." Taking the dishtowel from her sister-in-law, she pointed the couple toward their own house.

Watching them stroll to their home in the hot summer moonlight, she sternly said to Eli, "You oughta be ashamed of yourself, Pa. Upsetting poor Ed like that." Then, snickering behind her hand, she whispered to her father, "But it sure was funny."

Twins for Sam

Harvest went smoothly. The corn cribs were full once again, and the root cellar was stuffed. Bundles of herbs hung from the kitchen rafters, and three fine pigs were fattening for slaughter.

On a crisp, sunny Saturday morning just before All-Hallows-Eve, Eli was rocking on the porch while his sons tended to various chores in the sheds and animal pens.

Lizzie was sweeping the parlor while Queen instructed Maggie in how to clean a lamp chimney.

"Someone's coming down the road," Eli yelled to his daughter. "But I can't tell who it is, yet?"

Lizzie stepped out onto the porch and squinted into the sun. "It looks like Sam's chestnut. Maybe Ruthie had her baby. I wonder what it was."

Sam reined in at the porch railing and before he could dismount Eli said, "Well son, tell us about your first born. Was it a boy or a girl."

"Girls, Pa. Two of 'em. Mary Ida and Nancy Alice."

"Congratulations, Sam. Lizzie, go get your brother a drink of water and see if we got some biscuits left from breakfast."

"Mack ate the last of the biscuits, but I'll see if I can find something else if you're hungry, Sam."

"Just a drink will be fine, Lizzie. I'm not hungry."

Queen ran out on the porch followed by Maggie. "Twins? Did I hear you say twin girls?" she threw herself at her brother and nearly knocked him down as she wrapped her arms around his waist. "When can I see 'em? I've never seen twins before."

Sam chuckled and hugged his little sister tight. "I don't know, but I promise this will be their first trip as soon as Ruthie and Tennessee say so."

Lizzie handed Sam a tin cup of water and asked, "How is Ruthie? Did the birth go easy?"

"Ruthie is good and back on her feet. She had no problems with the other four and she said these two were so small they just slid right out."

He took a drink of his water and stared into the cup, as though it were a crystal ball. Finally, he looked up at his father.

"Wow, Pa! I've got myself quite a family now. The other four were a handful, but there is no rest to be had in my house. Those three baby girls have everyone in the house tending to 'em around the clock."

"Three babies?" Lizzie questioned.

Yes three. Two days after she helped the twins into the world, Tennessee delivered a beautiful baby girl she named Gracious."

Queen pouted. "Tennessee got married and we weren't invited to the party?"

Sam looked to his father for help.

Eli rose and said, "You know, sweetheart, the darkies don't always have a big wedding." He swatted her on the backside and said, "Take your little sister and y'all go find your brothers and tell them Sam is here. Lizzie you better go start dinner since we have a guest."

When the girls had left Eli turned to Sam and asked, "Is there a buck hangin' round?"

"No, Pa. Not so's you'd notice." And both men sat down and lit their pipes and smoked in silence.

Amnesty

The week after Christmas, the men were in the tool barn repairing tools and harness, and the children were in school.

Lizzie and Emmy were in the kitchen when Emmy doubled over in pain. Looking horrified, she groaned as her water broke and spread over the oiled kitchen rug.

Lizzie dropped the wad of dough in her hands and rushed to help Emmy. Her feet slipped out from under her and she went flat on her back.

Emmy doubled over with laughter mixed with agony as another cramp hit her midsection.

Rolling over to all fours, Lizzie got up and said, "If you'll stop laughing long enough we need to get you to bed."

"Are you alright, Lizzie? You fell pretty hard, and I'm fine now. You looked so funny sprawled on the floor............ohhhhhhhhhhhhh...I think you're right," as a second pain hit her.

Lizzie got her sister-in-law settled in Eli's soft bed. The same bed she and her siblings had been born in. She calmly and smoothly got Emmy undressed and as comfortable as possible when another contraction swept over the taut belly. Smiling she patted Emmy's hand and said, "I'll go put some water on to boil. I'll be back shortly."

Then she ran. She ran like the devil was after her to find Ed.

He wasn't in the barn with the others. "Where's Ed? Emmy's having her baby."

"I sent him to town to pick up some supplies," Watt told his panicked sister.

"Well, go find him. And someone needs to fetch Nannie Taylor and Mrs. Knox. I've never birthed a baby. You boys saddle up and get me some help."

Not accustomed to seeing the tiny woman in an uncontrolled terror, the men simply stared.

"GET MOVING!" she screamed and ran back to the house.

She was getting another bucket of water from the well when she saw the barn door open. Three horses with tall riders exited. Jack went east, toward the Taylor's; Craig went west, toward the Knox's, and Watt tipped his hat as he saw his sister and headed north toward town.

Eli followed without a horse and closed the barn door securely. He walked up to Lizzie and gently spoke. "Go tend to Emmy. Help will be here soon. I'll get the kettle hot for you."

Mrs. Knox arrived first. Her husband was following with the buggy. Clutching her bonnet to her head and hanging on for dear life, she had insisted on riding behind Craig. As fast as possible.

Anderson brought his wife and daughters in their buggy. Lizzie had never been so glad to see anyone as she was Nannie Taylor.

Mrs. Knox sat by Emmy's head. She washed her daughters face with a cool rag and held her hand and sobbed softly.

"Mother, let me breathe. You are smothering me. I'm having a baby, not dying..........ohhhhhhhhhhhhhh."

"Almost ready," Nannie said cheerfully. "With the next pain push hard, Emmy."

With a final big push, William Anderson Ownby entered this world, amid his grandmother's wails.

"Mother would you please be quiet. I want to hear my baby cry, not you." Emmy told her mother irritably.

Once little Billy was cleaned and nursing loudly at Emmy's breast, all of the women in the house were thinking "Now that's the way it should be done."

Ed galloped up the road whooping and hollering and shooting his pistol. Scout was lathered and his ears were laid back. He hadn't seemed to enjoy a run like this since the war.

In the house everyone heard the racket and shots and assumed Watt had found Ed and told him the news.

Not noticing the buggies and saddled horses at the porch rail, Ed slid Scout to a stop and bounded up the steps and into the parlor. Seeing his father in his customary rocker in front of the fire, he whooped, "Wooooo, Pa, look what I brought from town."

"Shhhhh," Eli smiled. "You'll wake your son."

Ed's eyes got wide as he saw the baby in Eli's arms. He dropped the newspaper he was holding and reached for the bundle just as Watt stepped through the door.

"There you are, you useless lump of lard. I've been looking everywhere for you. What ya got there?"

"My son," Ed said in awe. For once not responding to his brother's jests. His voice was low as if in a trance. He looked up from his son's face and said one word. "Emmy?"

"She's fine, son. She's in the bedroom with all the other hens. Go to her."

Watt had picked up the paper and was reading intently.

"Listen to this, Pa."

By the President of the United States of America
A Proclamation
Whereas the President of the United States has heretofore set forth several proclamations offering amnesty and pardon to persons who had been or were concerned in the late rebellion against the lawful authority of the Government of the United

States, which proclamations were severally issued on the 8th day of December, 1863, on the 26th day of March, 1864, on the 29th day of May, 1865, on the 7th day of September, 1867, and on the 4th day of July, in the present year; and

Whereas the authority of the Federal Government having been reestablished in all the States and Territories within the jurisdiction of the United States, it is believed that such prudential reservations and exceptions as at the dates of said several proclamations were deemed necessary and proper may now be wisely and justly relinquished, and that an universal amnesty and pardon for participation in said rebellion extended to all who have borne any part therein will tend to secure permanent peace, order, and prosperity throughout the land, and to renew and fully restore confidence and fraternal feeling among the whole people, and their respect for and attachment to the National Government, designed by its patriotic founders for the general good:

Now, therefore, be it known that I, Andrew Johnson President of the United States, by virtue of the power and authority in me vested by the Constitution and in the name of the sovereign people of the United States, do hereby proclaim and declare unconditionally and without reservation, to all and to every person who, directly or indirectly, participated in the late insurrection or rebellion a full pardon and amnesty for the offense of treason against the United States or of adhering to their enemies during the late civil war, with restoration of all rights, privileges, and immunities under the Constitution and the laws which have been made in pursuance thereof.

In testimony whereof I have signed these presents with my hand and have caused the seal of the United States to be hereunto affixed.

Done at the city of Washington, the 25th day of December, A. D. 1868, and of the Independence of the United States of America the ninety-third.

ANDREW JOHNSON.
By the President:
F. W. SEWARD,
Acting Secretary of State.

"This means all you boys are pardoned and are no longer considered traitors," Eli said with tears in his eyes.

"It also means that Jeff Davis can come home from exile in Canada." Anderson smiled broadly.

Ed entered the bedroom, holding his infant and watched his sleeping wife. Lizzie and the other women quietly left their cleaning chores to give the couple privacy.

As the door closed, Emmy woke and her eyes met Eds. She put out her hands and took the baby and started to nurse him.

Tears rolled over Ed's high cheekbones. With a catch in his voice, he softly told her, "Did ya hear the news? Our boy is no longer a traitor's son."

There was a soft knock on the door, and Ed took a moment then opened it. There was no one there. He started to step out but tripped and banged his ankle on something hard. Crying out in pain, he looked down and saw a shiny new cradle with hand carved cherubs on the head and footboards.

Recognizing Jack's craftsmanship, he was overcome with love for his thoughtful brother.

CHAPTER 6

ACQUISITION, 1869

Oh Shit

Every day after school, Queen ran to Emmy's house to help with little Billy.

Emmy was grateful for the time alone to rest or have a few quiet moments to do things without interruption.

One warm spring afternoon as Queen carried the baby to her house, he started to fret and she realized that he needed to be changed. After she had cleaned him and was fastening his diaper, Lady and Ned set up a tremendous howl in the front yard.

Picking up the baby, she went to the front porch to see what had the hounds in such an uproar.

Both dogs were jumping and howling and trying to climb the peach tree.

Lizzie was poking into the branches with her broom handle and tripping over the moving dogs. Peach blossoms covered the ground, the girl, and the dogs.

Through the limbs, leaves, and blossoms, Queen could see a boot clad foot beneath a work pant-covered leg.

"Git down from there, you mangy varmint," Lizzie screamed as she poked again with her broom handle. "I said get out of there. I mean it."

A male voice cried out, "Be careful, Lizzie, stop poking me."

Confused, Queen yelled out, "Lizzie it's just Jeff Taylor. Why are you poking him with a broom?"

"I'm not poking him. We're trying to get this coon out of the tree." She poked again; Jeff hollered, again; the dogs barked louder and Queen laughed.

"Give me that damn broom and I'll get him from up here," Jeff said as he yanked the broom handle out of Lizzie's hands.

The raccoon fell, right on Lizzie's head. It didn't stay long but took off toward the house; ran up the porch steps and as Queen squealed and moved out of the way, the raccoon ran through the foyer and out to the back porch. Ned and Lady gave chase at full speed.

Knocked down by the falling raccoon, Lizzie was sprawled under the tree trying to get her senses back when a ruckus in the tree made her look up. That's when Jeff fell, on her lap.

She screamed and scrambled away. "Jeff Taylor, you should be more careful. You could've hurt me bad."

Jeff lay there still as death. Lizzie became alarmed and crawled toward him. "Jeff, are you alright?" He still didn't move.

Queen ran down off the porch holding Billy close.

Lizzie pulled Jeff's head into her lap and pushed the hair out of his eyes. "Jeff, talk to me. Say something, Jeff."

Slowly one eye cracked open and a wide grin split his face.

Lizzie dropped his head in the dirt. "You rascal. You were playing possum. How dare you scare me like that?"

Queen doubled over, nearly dropping the baby from laughing, as Lizzie stomped up the steps and into the house.

She headed straight for the wash basin to clean the dust and sweat from her face. With water in her eyes, she grabbed the rag lying on the rim of the basin.

A blood-curdling scream, worse than a panther, halted Jeff and Queen's laughter.

Running into the house, they saw Lizzie standing by the basin. One glance at the rag in her hand told Queen what had happened.

In her haste to see what the commotion was, Queen had not rinsed or disposed of the rag she used to clean Billy's bottom, but had laid it on the basin rim.

Clutching the baby tight, Queen collapsed on a chair while tears of laughter ran down her face. Jeff reached out for Lizzie and seeing the anger on her face, changed his mind and ran.

Lizzie never did see the humor.

Spilt Milk

Lizzie cut into a tomato and the aroma made her head swim. The ripe red flesh was firm but juicy. Inhaling the scent, she put a slice in her mouth and groaned. It was sheer pleasure.

"Ruthie, what do you do to these tomatoes? They are the tastiest in the county. I grow your seedlings, but they don't taste like this."

"I just grow 'em. I don't do anything special. Here, try some of Tennessee's plum jam. We had a surplus of plums this year."

It was a beautiful Sunday in May, and Sam and Ruthie had brought their family for church and dinner.

Two tables had been set up on the back porch with benches and wood crates brought in from the barns for seating. There were eighteen people from five to fifty years old. The four babies were sleeping on a pallet up against the wall, under the watchful eyes of their mothers.

When everyone had eaten their fill of fried chicken, fresh vegetables out of the garden, and lots of biscuits with plum jam, Eli and his older sons pushed back their chairs and lit their pipes. Lizzie and Emmy rose to clear the table.

"Keep your seat, Miz Lizzie, Miz Emmy. I'll get them dishes," Tennessee said. She was wiping Will Smith's face. Ruthie's five-year-old son by her second husband had smeared plum jam all over his chin and cheeks.

Queen, seeing a reprieve from cleaning the dishes, jumped at the opportunity and grabbed Mary Smith's hand. "Come on Maggie, let's go show Molly Sassy's new litter of kittens. Three of them are calico like her," Queen said as she pulled the little girls up and off the porch before Lizzie could stop them.

James Wilbourn, Ruthie's sixteen-year-old son by her first husband, was in deep conversation with Craig and Sam about the merits of changing from Yorkshire to Duroc hogs.

One of the babies started to whimper. "That will be Nan," Ruthie said as a dark stain blossomed on her bodice. "She always wants to be fed first. Of the three of them, she is the liveliest. She'll be crawling by next week." She reached for the fussy baby and placed her at her breast where little Nancy settled in for her dinner.

The men all rose to go have a look at the hogs, but Mack asked Tom Wilbourn, "Wanna go fishing?"

"Sure" the boy said looking to his mother for permission.

Ruthie nodded and the adolescent boys went to gather poles and head for the creek.

Mary Ida woke and entertained herself by playing with her feet while she waited for her twin to be fed. Getting bored with that game, she rolled over, sat up, and starting playing with Billy's ears and nose and mouth. When she stuck her tiny finger in his eye, he started to scream. Emmy sighed and picked him up to feed him his own dinner.

With her newest plaything removed, Ida rolled over to a familiar toy. Gracious lay quietly and contentedly cooing softly. She kicked her foot and Ida grabbed at it. It was obvious that this was a game the girls played often.

"Did you finish your milk, Will?" Ruthie asked as he and Henry started down the steps.

"No ma'am. But I will." He reached for the cup of milk on the table.

Queen and the girls were coming back from the barn, and Queen stepped up on the porch and was watching the babies play.

"Gracious is such a beautiful child, with that mulatto skin and those big grey eyes. The twins create perfect bookends with their blond curls and dark blue eyes."

Will was gulping his milk and walking across the porch when he tripped on the blanket and spilled his milk in Gracious' face.

As the creamy, thick white liquid spread over the baby's face, Queen gasped. "Oh my, Gracious looks like Granma Fanny."

Lizzie jumped up and pulled her sister away and declared loudly. "Don't be silly, Queen. All six month old babies look alike."

Granma Laurie

"We have a letter from Uncle Joe," Watt called out to his father as he dismounted Belle in front of the house.

Eli was rocking Billy and dozing on the porch. He opened one eye and said, "Well, read it to me, son. What does the young'un have to say?"

Since Neddy's death, Joe had taken over the role of family scribe and wrote chatty letters to his brothers and sisters.

Carroll County *Aug 29, 1869*
Dear Eli and family
K moved Jane and their baby boy to that property Papa bought from R.D. and left to K in his will. He got the house fixed up and plans to farm the land.

This time Eli opened both eyes and lit his pipe. "That's good news for Joe and Tabitha. I figured K would stay there in Papa's house forever."

He started blowing smoke rings for Billy to try to catch.

Watt smiled at the baby's antics and continued.

Will and Deliah have a baby boy also. Born last month. They are staying here with me. He helps in the field and Deliah takes care of the house and is good company for Tabby.

The Indian Corn is high and the heads should be full to bursting soon. We only have eight acres planted. Mr. Coble keeps the accounts for the estate since he married Mother. I'm not sure what is happening, since he won't let me see the books. I have heard rumors in town that he has sold some of Papa's holding but I don't know which pieces have been sold.

  Silas and Penny left when Mr. Coble refused to pay them. They moved to Lexington to be near Mammy Bess and Josiah. Silas said there was work there for him.
  Mother doesn't visit often. Not since....

  Watt stopped reading and dropped the letter in his lap with an incredulous look on his face.
  Eli sat up straight, with a tight grip on the baby and asked, "What is it, son?"
  Watt threw back his head and laughed. "You have a baby sister. Granma Laurie had a little girl with her new husband."

Homesteading

  THE STATE OF TENNESSEE,
 To all to Whom these Presents Shall come, Greeting;
 Know Ye, that in consideration of an Entry made in the Entry Taker's Office of
  Cannon County, dated 10th day of September, 1869

  There is Granted by the STATE OF TENNESSEE, unto W. K. P. Ownby
  a certain Tract or Parcel of Land, Containing Six Hundred Acres
  by Survey lying in 5th District of same County.

  Beginning on a blackjack oak the N.E. corner of E. C. Ownby's tract of land he bought of John Teal supposed to be 5 poles. South of the old Perk womans Home. South with said line facing a postoak at 163 poles supposed to be the Perk womans in all 260 poles to a stake in the Coffee County line, bear East with said line to the N. E. corner of said Coffee County on the Warren bounty line, Bear North with said Warren Co Line 442 poles to a stake in a 8000 acre survey known as the Barrell land. M. Hill acting as agent, Bear West with said line 550 poles to the Beginning.

With the Hereditaments and Appurtenances. To HAVE *and to* HOLD *the said* TRACT OR PARCEL OF LAND, *with it Appurtenances to the said* W. K. P. *Ownby and his heirs forever.*

"TIM...BERRRRR!" Watt yelled as the massive oak tree fell. It was three foot in diameter and seventy-five feet tall. Watt and Ed had chopped all morning to bring it down.

The branches softened the fall and the tree settled on the ground with a soft "swoosh."

Watt leaned on his axe handle and wiped his face with a handkerchief as Ed collapsed up against the trunk for Mack and Henry to drag toward the burn pile. The larger limbs would be saved to cut for firewood but the smaller branches would be disposed of in one big bonfire.

"Here comes Pa. I wonder if he brought dinner?" Ed said.

"Always thinking with your belly, you useless lump of lard." Watt grinned.

"Not always, you sack of bones," Ed retorted, then asked his father, "Why are you bringing dinner? How's Emmy?"

Emmy was very pregnant and expecting her second child any day now and Ed barely left her out of his sight.

"Emmy's good, son. Her and Lizzie were busy with women's work, and they asked me to bring you boys your food. 'Sides me and little Billy here, been to town and have some news for ya'll"

Billy reached his arms out for his father and as Ed took him, the other three brothers started to dig through the dinner pail. There was chicken, buttered biscuits and a small crock of peach preserves.

"What's the news, Pa?" Watt asked with a mouthful of chicken.

"I know you boys want to clear as many acres as you can this winter, but we need to move the fallen timber out-a-here so you can. So I went to see Joe Clark at the sawmill. He said he'll take all the trees you can get to him and will be happy to finish some into plank lumber on a half and half basis.

Jack spoke up, "But we don't need that much lumber Pa. A few repairs to the barns but there's more than enough right here on the ground."

"I been promising Emmy I'd try to add her a kitchen this winter. With two babies it'll be easier for her to at least fix breakfast in our own home."

Eli smiled and took Billy from Ed and bounced him on his hip and said," A kitchen is a good addition and when we have all the lumber we need, Clark said he'd pay us the going rate for timber. He says he's got a man in Nashville buying furniture grade oak and maybe some of that maple over yonder too."

The men finished their dinner and Watt handed the bucket back to his father. "We better get back to work if we are going to clear five acres by the new year."

"I'll take Billy home and come back with the wagon when Mack and Henry get home from school. We'll load some of these branches and stack 'em out by the woodshed. Y'all might think about girdling some of those smaller oaks to kill off for firewood next winter."

Greenwood was best for furniture and building, but firewood needed to be dried. Cutting a ring around a tree trunk a few inches wide would choke off the nutrients and kill a tree. The smaller diameter trees would be easier to clear and to burn.

By the end of November, Jack had taken several wagons of full size logs to the sawmill and had returned with a nice supply of planked lumber for repairs to outbuildings and a kitchen for Emmy.

Lester and Baxter had earned their keep dragging the huge trees and helping load them.

Possessed by the Devil

One afternoon a few days before Christmas the men were working hard to get another load to the sawmill when Eli came galloping Storm Cloud across the clearing.

"Get home, Ed. Emmy's having her baby. I'm going for Nannie Taylor then I'll get Mrs. Knox."

Ed dropped his axe and took off without a word, and Eli turned back toward the Taylor place.

Not knowing which house to go to, Ed stopped at his father's first. Maggie was playing with Billy in front of the parlor fire. She was stacking brightly colored blocks that Jack had carved with the alphabet. As she stacked them, Billy would knock them over and both would laugh.

Ed burst into the room and without looking up the girl said, "Nobody's here. The boys went to the woods and Lizzie and Queen are at your place with Emmy. Coffee's on the fire if you want some."

Ed just looked at his baby sister. Always dependable, she was mature for your nine years. Ed had a fleeting vision of what she would be like as an adult.

Billy reached his little arms up and Ed's heart melted. He picked up his son and kissed him on top of the head. "Da, Da, Da," the boy kept repeating.

Maggie raised her head and smiled. "He hasn't ever done that before."

With tears in his eyes, Ed put the boy down and said, "Stay here with Aunt Maggie. I'm going to go see how your mama is getting on," and he ran out the door.

Ed recognized the buggies in the front of his house. They belonged to Nannie Taylor and Mrs. Knox. Dark smoke was coming out of the chimney and he knew that little one room house would be hot and stuffy, but he needed to see his wife.

As he stepped up on the porch, a scream tore through the glooming. The last time he heard a scream like that was the night Henry was born. Hesitant to open the door the need to see Emmy was stronger. Ed stepped into the room as Emmy's contraction peaked.

She caught her breath; looked at her husband and screamed, "Get out of here and shut that door."

Frightened and confused, he backed out and slammed the door. Standing there bewildered, he was startled when Nannie stepped out on the porch.

She smiled and took his arm and led him to the edge of the porch. "She's alright, Ed. The birthing room is no place for a man. Don't take her actions to heart. She'll be herself once the baby comes. Go get some coffee and one of the girls will come get you when it's time."

Ed walked slowly back to this fathers house in the darkening twilight.

"You look deep in thought, son," Eli said, as he set his axe on the porch. "How's Emmy?"

"Nannie Taylor says she's fine. But, Pa, I think the devils done possessed her."

Eli chuckled as Anderson and the others joined them on the porch. The older men lit their pipes and Mack spoke up, "What's Lizzie got for supper. I'm hungry."

Ed glared at his little brother, but Eli rocked harder and said, "Hush, boy. There's more important goings on here tonight. Your belly can wait awhile."

"But, PA! I'm hungry."

Watt spoke sharply, "Don't back talk your pa, Mack. You aren't too big to take to the wood shed. Here comes Lizzie and Queen."

The sisters approached the house, and Ed ran down to meet them. After a brief conversation, he took off at a run toward his home.

Watt saw the weariness on Lizzie's face. He stood and took his sister in his arms. She was trembling.

Queen was excited and started to babble. "It's a boy. A perfect little boy. Emmy is so brave. I wanna be just like her. Two beautiful babies in less than a year. And she's still so pretty and laughs so easy. Never angry or hateful."

Lizzie broke loose from Watt's hold and said, "Hush, Queen. Let's go get supper started. I'm sure Mack's hungry."

Christmas

After church services on Christmas Day, the family went home, followed by the Taylors.

Queen and Maggie looked after Billy and the baby while Emmy helped Lizzie in the kitchen.

Nannie had brought several dishes of vegetables and two pies. She directed Marthey, Callie, and Betsy where to place them on the two tables. Since it threatened to snow, the tables had been set up in the foyer.

It was a smaller gathering than some in the past. Neither Polly nor Sam was coming. Creed was visiting Sarah's family, and Ellen was celebrating with Joe's folks. The surprise had come when Jim Taylor announced he was spending the day with his sweetheart at her house.

The young people were disappointed that Jim was going to be absent and so was his fiddle.

The tables were laden with a roasted goose, which Mack had fed for months just for the occasion; a big smoked ham from one of Craig's Yorkshire/Duroc hogs; Lizzie's scrumptious sweet potato pudding and more pickles and relishes than they all could eat.

When everyone had eaten until they couldn't eat another bite, the women started to clear the soiled dishes but left the food for people to nibble on as they got hungry.

The men retired to the parlor and lit their pipes and discussed how to build the kitchen onto Emmy's house.

Before dawn, Watt and Ed had upheld tradition and cut a pine tree. It was sitting in the corner waiting to be decorated.

Jack had filled the walnut shells with beeswax and Lizzie had made gingerbread ornaments. Bits of colorful paper had been saved all year, and Maggie and Henry had cut out bright stars and bells and had strung some together to make a paper chain. Queen sacrificed a few of her hair ribbons to make bows and this promised to be the prettiest tree they had in years.

Before dinner, Lizzie and Nannie had made the eggnog. Lizzie beat the eggs until they were light and fluffy, then she stirred them slowly as Nannie trickled in a jug of her hard cider. It had to be done at a snail's pace so the alcohol would thoroughly cook the eggs. Thick, sweet cream was then added along with lots of molasses. The mixture had been sitting to allow the froth to settle.

Lizzie and Queen brought in the big bowl and set it on a side table and everyone was served.

Henry refused his cup. He had been spending a lot of time with Mack and the chickens lately and had recently declared he would no longer "eat anything that came out of a chicken's butt."

Emmy was holding her newborn while Billy sat in Ed's lap, playing with his beard, when Eli announced, "I think Billy should place the star on top of the tree this year." He walked over to Ed and handed the little boy the hand-carved star.

Billy eyed the shiny ornament and grasped it in his little hands then promptly put one of the points in his mouth.

Everyone laughed as Ed removed the star from his son's mouth and handed it back to his father. With laughter in his voice, he said, "Maybe next year, Pa."

"Then Henry gets the honor for one more year." Looking around the room, Eli didn't see his youngest son. "Now where did that boy get off to?"

"Probably went to the outhouse," Queen observed.

"Then Maggie would you like to place the star, sweetheart?"

"Yes, Pa. But I can't reach it."

Watt turned loose of Marthey's hand, which he had been holding for the past hour. He stood and lifted his baby sister high.

The little girl placed the shiny wooden star on the top branch of the tree and clapped her hands in delight.

The lamps were turned down low. Jack and Craig lit the many tiny walnut shell candles and everyone exclaimed how beautiful it was.

Little Billy's face was aglow in the flickering candle light, and he reached his tiny arms out to try to catch the flames.

Marthey started singing *Silent Night* joined by her sisters and then the rest of the group as they watched snow falling through the front window.

Jeff was standing next to Lizzie in the kitchen doorway watching the light flare across the back of her hair. He was fascinated by the changes in color from intense gold against the brown to flecks of red and glints of silver. Awakening from his trance, he realized the light was coming from behind her and the tree was in front of her. He looked over her head and saw the entire sky lit with flame.

"FIRE!" he yelled.

Everyone ran outside. Some ran out the front door, some out the back door. Except for Maggie.

She pulled a chair over to the tree and patiently blew out all the walnut shell candles. Lizzie had told her to never leave the tree candles burning. When she was finished, she too ran outside to see what was on fire.

Fire

"What in Hell?" Watt exclaimed.

The smokehouse was in flames and in true military fashion, Watt started giving orders.

"Ed, go get shovels. Jack and Craig, find as many buckets and pails as you can. Mack start hoisting the well bucket to the top."

Ed handed Billy to Maggie and ran toward the tool shed.

Emmy put the baby into Nannies care and went to help Mack at the well.

Lizzie ran back toward the kitchen pulling Queen behind her. "Get every pan, kettle, and big bowl you can find. Dump the eggnog and we can use that bowl too."

"No not the eggnog. I wanted more," Queen whined.

"Empty that bowl and do it now," Lizzie told her sister.

Jeff joined Mack at the well and Emmy started filling the buckets and pails and bowls as they appeared. Marthey and her sisters moved the vessels full of water along toward the burning smokehouse where Eli and Anderson threw them onto the roof and burning back wall.

The fire seemed to be concentrated on the back wall and hadn't spread to the remaining structure, and Watt and Ed were inside trying to remove and salvage as much of the family's meat supply as possible. "Watt, y'all get out of there. The roofs on fire," Jack yelled through the open door. "If the fire catches the grease, y'all will be cooked too."

Ed ran out the door with an armful of Black Pudding just as the back wall crumpled inward. Flames shot into the rafters and years of grease ignited.

Emmy dropped her bucket and ran to Ed who was stumbling from the percussion.

Smoke, soot, and ash billowed out the door and Marthey screamed as Watt crawled over the threshold coughing and gasping for air.

Anderson yelled, "Jeff, Craig, you boys start shoveling dirt through this door. And someone find some tow sacks to wet down."

Lizzie brought the sacks and got them soaking in a bucket of water with Emmy's help.

Tying wet handkerchiefs over their faces, Watt and Ed took the wet tow sacks back into the building to place over the salt troughs. Full of salted beef they wanted to keep them from burning.

Jack knocked as much of the burning back wall away as possible, and the bucket line continued to throw water on the roof and remaining walls.

As the flames died down, snow sizzled on the charred embers.

Nannie brought cups and the coffee pot out to the porch as activity slowed down. "Emmy, stop a while and come tend to your babies. You'll be no good to them if you get sick. Maggie's in Eli's bed with both of them, but the baby is getting fretful. I think he's hungry."

Cold, wet, dirty and exhausted, the women all poured coffee and took it to the men. Thankful for a break, the men gulped the hot coffee and tried to catch their breath.

Once Mack realized they could salvage some of the food, he jumped in to help transfer it to the springhouse to keep varmints away. He and Henry had put away the hams, bacons and sausages as Watt and Ed carried the pieces out of the burning building.

"We still need to empty those troughs. The salt and brine kept 'em from burning, but animals will get in 'em by morning," Watt said wearily as Marthey brought him a biscuit with goose meat between the halves.

"If you've got barrels, me, Callie, and Betsy can move the beef over from the troughs."

"But you're wearing your best dresses," Watt told her.

Looking down at her torn and soot stained dress, Marthey replied, "It's no longer my best dress." And she smiled and shivered as the snow continued to fall on her tangled hair.

"Alright," Watt said and yelled for his brother, "Jack get the barrels out of the shed and the girls will transfer the beef. Then we can make sure the fire's out and push the debris back farther."

Ed had been digging in the smoking and sizzling remains of the wall and walked around to where Watt sat on a stump. He held a shovel with a lump of metal on the blade.

"This was under the logs where the fire started."

It was a lantern. The chimney was shattered and the bail was bent. The blackened tank had embossed letters around the bottom.

"Bring a bucket of water and a rag," Watt called to Henry.

The boy brought the water and rag and after dousing the still-hot metal several times, Watt managed to wipe the soot from the lantern.

Eli and Anderson had joined them and Eli said, "Craig, you got good eyes. What does it say?"

Squinting at the letters, he read aloud, "Bra...dy..ville. Bradyville. Mer...can...tile. Bradyville Mercantile." Looking up he said, "Wasn't that Ruthie's store?"

"Yes it was. There must be hundreds of lanterns like that around these parts." Eli frowned.

"Why would anyone want to burn down our smokehouse?" Jack asked no one in particular.

Henry had been listening and spoke up, "I heard a horse in the woods earlier, when I went to the outhouse."

Startled, Watt stood up tall and took his baby brother by the shoulders. "Why didn't you tell me at the time? Why did you wait? Where was the horse?"

Sniffing and wiping his nose on his shirt sleeve, the boy's bottom lip started to quiver at his brother's anger. "I didn't know it was important. And it's Christmas and I was hungry. Don't be mad at me, Watt."

Pulling the boy into a hug, Watt patted the small back and said, "I'm not mad at you, Henry. Tell me where you heard the horse."

Henry pointed toward the woods behind the smokehouse.

Everyone started to move in that direction and Eli yelled, "Stop! Too many boots will cover any tracks. Me and Henry will go take a look. You boys finish up here." Turning to face his longtime friend, he said, "Anderson, thank you for your help tonight. Take your family home and get some rest. And Merry Christmas."

He took a lantern and, with Henry following close behind, moved off into the dark woods.

A few steps into the tree line Eli stopped. He had tracked game all of his life and it didn't take long to see something out of the ordinary. A boot print in the damp leaves. Where the next step should be was a round indention. Following the uneven prints to a small clearing, Eli had realized that the arsonist was someone with a peg leg.

Tree cover had kept snow from accumulating and covering the tracks until they got to the clearing. Here the snow was piling in drifts and he could not tell which direction the horse went. He could see where it had been tied to a tree branch but not much else.

Closer to the ground, Henry was looking hard and kicking snow and leaves around. "Pa, look here."

There was something sparkling in the moonlight.

"What is it, son?"

Henry bent and picked it up. He handed it to his father.

The leather scabbard was wet with snow but the brass crosspiece and pommel were bright and twinkled as Eli held the lantern high. The bone handle on the encased bowie knife was worn and yellowed, but the carved letters stood out plainly.

"L. P.," Eli read aloud. "Come on, boy. Let's go show this to your brothers, then get you to bed."

Land Grant

Recorded, 10th November 1871   221

THE STATE OF TENNESSEE,

To all to Whom these Presents Shall Come,--Greeting:

Know Ye, That in consideration of an Entry made in the Entry Taker's Office of Cannon County, dated the 10th day of September 1869, by No. 793

There is Granted by the said STATE OF TENNESSEE, unto W. R. P. Ownby a certain Tract or Parcel of Land, Containing Six hundred Acres by Survey bearing date the 5th day of November 1871, lying in S'd D. of same County. Beginning on a Blackjack oak the N.E. corner of R. Ownby's tract of land he bought of John Teal supposed to be 5 poles South of the old Peak corner thence South with said line passing a post oak at 163 poles supposed to be the Peak corner in all 260 poles to a stake in the Coffee County line, thence East with said line to the N.E. corner of said Coffee County on the Warren County line, thence North with said Warren Co. line 182 poles to a stake in a 5000 acre survey known as the Barrell land M. Hill acting as Agent, thence West with said line 550 poles to the Beginning.

With the Hereditaments and Appurtenances. To HAVE and to HOLD the said TRACT OR PARCEL OF LAND, with its Appurtenances, to the said W. R. P. Ownby and his heirs forever.

In Testimony Whereof, John C. Brown Governor of the State of Tennessee, hath hereunto set his hand, and caused the Great Seal of the State to be affixed at Nashville, on the 10th day of November in the year of our Lord, 1871, and of the Independence of the United States, the 96th

L. S.

BY THE GOVERNOR:

T.W. Butler
John C. Brown

CHAPTER 7

A TIME TO MOURN, 1870

A Cookie for Ed

"I hear a fella named Clyde Overton in Jackson is selling out and has some prime livestock to get rid of. Gonna be an auction on the 21st. Ed, you and Jack wanna go?" Watt said at supper one night in mid-January.

Ed glanced at Emmy with a questioning look. She smiled and bounced her baby in her arms and nodded. Ed had hardly let her out of his sight since little Andy was born and had been especially protective since the smokehouse fire.

They all were. The men carried a rifle or pistol everywhere and one of them accompanied Lizzie, Emmy, and Queen anytime they left the property.

Eli decided he needed a walk every morning and afternoon so he walked Mack, Maggie, and Henry to and from school.

The threat of L. P. returning seemed very real.

"You sure you don't need me to stay and help around here?" Ed asked.

"You don't do anything when you're here, you useless lump of lard. The smokehouse is repaired and it's too wet to get into the woods to cut timber. Me and Craig can handle the chores that need tending, so you and Jack go give this livestock a good look over. Try to get us a good team of mules. And anything else you think is useful to our production."

With Ed on Scout and Jack riding Storm Cloud, the men headed west on a bitter cold morning a couple of days later.

The weather stayed clear but cold and the men made good time. They stopped at night and made camp and were on the road before dawn each morning.

On the third day, they were a few miles west of Lexington when Ed halted Scout and motioned for Jack to do the same. He cocked his head and whispered, "Do you hear that? It sounds like a woman crying."

Jack listened and pointed to the north. "Coming from that a way."

The men dismounted and leading Scout and Storm moved as quietly as possible toward the sound. The crying got louder and a man's voice could be heard.

Through the trees, Ed saw the back of a very large black man with his arms in the air. An old black woman was on the ground holding a baby and surrounded by stair steps of children. Three horses were tied to a tree branch and a campfire burned in front of a rough lean-to made of branches.

"Where'd ya steal them horses, nigger?" a voice said. View of the voices owner was obscured by the bulk of the big man.

A woman's voice broke in sobbing. Ed recognized it as the sound they had heard earlier. "Don't hurt us, mista. Take the horses and leave us alone. We won't tell nobody."

Ed motioned to Jack to stay put and that he would move to the other side of the clearing. Putting his hand on Scout's nose, he signaled the horse to stay and moved off into the woods. He circled around to the front of the captive and had a clear view of the entire scene.

"I asked you a question, nigger. Are you deaf and dumb? Or do you just let your woman do your talking for you.?" He was holding a younger woman by the hair with one hand and held a knife to her exposed copper colored neck with the other.

The man's voice was familiar to Ed, but he couldn't place it. Seeing only the back of the man's head, he searched his memory for a recollection.

The woman twisted and jerked loose, knocking the man off balance. As he fell, Ed saw a wooden leg extended from the trousers.

94

The woman crawled through the dirt on her hands and knees until she reached the old woman and children. Sobbing, she took the baby and gathered the younger children into her arms.

"Stay down, Peterson," Ed growled as he stepped into the clearing with his pistol drawn.

Luther Peterson looked up from his position in the dirt at what appeared to be the Wrath of the Devil.

"Well, well, well. If it isn't one of the damned Ownby boys. Which one are you? As if it matters."

Ed raised his pistol and pointed it at Peterson.

"I'm the one that's going to send you straight to hell. None of us will get a moment's rest until you are no longer above ground."

"Your family has already cost me everything. You and your brother ruined my military career when you escaped from Camp Butler. Your sister stuck me in the ass with a pitchfork. Your family forced me to leave a prosperous business and because I was afoot and bleeding from the pitchfork, I lost my leg to a mountain cat that night. All because of you spawn of Satan."

The black man checked on his family then walked toward Peterson and Ed.

Jack stepped into the clearing with his pistol drawn. "You low life scum. You tried to burn us out, and now you're trying to steal from these folks who have nothing to steal." He looked around at the meager belongings of the family and turned back to Peterson. He aimed the pistol at Peterson's head and pulled the trigger. The pistol clicked and misfired.

Peterson scrambled to his one knee and reached into his waistband for his own gun. But the big man was quicker. He threw himself at Peterson and when the scuffle was over the big man stood and Peterson lay limp. From the angle of his neck, it obviously broke in the ruckus.

"It was an accident. I didn't mean ta kill 'em." The black man said in distress as Ed bent over the body.

"Them boys knows that, Silas. Them's some of Mista. Neddy's boys. Cain't you see the resemblance? Them boys won't hurt you, son." The old woman spoke for the first time. "Come git your mammy up out of the dirt so I can hug my boys."

Ed and Jack both rushed to help the woman while the children scattered to their mother.

They lifted her to her feet and she squinted at one face and then the other. "Who you boys belong to? Eli or my little Jeremiah?"

"Mammy Bess! Silas!" Ed cried out as he looked around the camp. "Where's Josiah?" He grabbed the old woman in a hug and shook Silas' hand.

Jack had never met the old woman but remembered her oldest son. As a child, he would follow the big man around Neddy's farm, getting in the way.

"We're two of Eli's sons. I'm Ed and this here is Jack. Watt told us that he saw you at Granpa Neddy's place, Silas. Is this your family?"

Silas nodded and introduced Penny and his eight sons then proudly presented his baby daughter, Tabitha Elizabeth.

Ed was solemn as he said, "Uncle Joe wrote us about you leaving. It seems like Granma Laurie's new husband is a man with few principles."

"No Mista Ed, Mr. Coble has no principles. He refused to pay me and Penny and even wanted to charge us for staying there. Said we needed to pay rents and that the chillun ate more than they were worth. So we left and went to stay in Lexington. Pappy died last month and Mammy here had a hankerin' to move to Arkansas where one of my brothers is. So that's what we're doin'."

Jack interrupted and asked, "What are we gonna do about Peterson here? If Silas is caught with the body they'll hang him for sure."

"Don't let 'em hang my boy," Mammy Bess cried out and Penny ran to her husband.

"I'll take care of it," Ed said and walked over to the dead man. He pulled out his pistol and shot the corpse in the head. "There. I shot him, not you Silas. He must have broke his neck when he fell. Did he have a horse?"

"I never seen one," Silas grinned.

Ed whistled and Scout came through the woods followed by Storm Cloud. Scout nosed the back of Ed's head and stood waiting for instructions.

"Let's get this piece of trash onto Scout's rump and we'll take him to the sheriff in Jackson. Silas, don't worry about anything. We won't mention your name. Ya might oughta bypass Jackson on your way west, though."

Bending over, Silas lifted the body effortlessly and placed it gently across Scout's backside.

Jack, with help from the older children, secured the body with rope while Ed picked up Peterson's pistol and knife from the dirt. Peterson had replaced his lost knife with an old and rustic hunting knife but still had his Yankee service revolver.

"I wonder who he stole this knife from? There's no markings on it." He handed both items to Silas, but the big man refused the gun.

"I have no use for that. A nigger caught with a shootin' iron is sure to be hung or worse. The pig sticker will come in mighty handy though."

Ed turned to Mammy Bess to hug her one last time and whispered in her ear, "I can still taste your molasses cookies. Sure wish I had me one right now."

She placed her hands on each side of his face; looked into his eyes and said loudly, "Little Josiah, bring me that brown sack from out of the lean-to."

The young boy did as his grandmother bid, and she handed the sack to Ed and said, "Now you be sure to share with your brother, and don't eat all of these at one time. You boys be careful and go with the good lord."

Ed slipped her some coins as he took the sack; mounted Scout and said "Come on little brother, let's ride."

One of the smaller boys opened his hand to show his father and said, "Mista Jack gave me these but I ain't never seen anything like 'em. They ain't pennies, Pappy. What are they?" In his little hand were five bright shiny dimes.

After the brothers left the little family at their campground in the clearing, Ed opened the sack and whistled.

Jack asked, "What is it, brother?"

Pulling out a big brown cookie, Ed took a bite; handed the sack to Jack and mumbled around a mouthful of cookie, "Get ready for a little taste of heaven."

Easter

Ed and Jack rode down the main street of Jackson and stopped in front of the Sheriff's office.

The big Appaloosa stud with a body on his rump drew a crowd which Ed and Jack walked through and ignored.

Opening the door to the jail Ed said, "Sheriff, names Ownby. I'm Ed and this is my brother Jack. We came from over Woodbury way to your fair city for the Overton auction tomorrow. Got held up on the road by a Yankee scoundrel named Peterson."

The sheriff stood and shook their hands and rubbed his chin whiskers. "I hate to hear that boys. Where is this Yankee now?"

"Well, sir, he's out front draped across the back of my horse. Ya see he pulled a gun on us and I had to shoot him."

"Did ya now? What did you say his name was? Peterson?" Taking his hat of the hat rack, the sheriff put it on his head and said, "Let's go have a look at this fella."

The crowd had grown in the street and Scout was getting restless and didn't like the men crowding him.

"Easy boy," Ed said as they stepped off the boardwalk.

"Sheriff," one of the townsmen said, "that there's the feller that cut Ruby last week down at the Traildust. Just 'cause she wouldn't go out in the alley with him, on account of he couldn't climb the stairs to her room."

An uproar from the crowd made Storm jittery and Scout whinnied.

The sheriff addressed the crowd loudly, "Ya'll go on about your business, and someone go tell Miss Ruby that her honor has been avenged."

The crowd grumbled and started moving away, but one man held back and approached the brothers. "I'm George, the bartender over at the Traildust, and Ruby's one of my best girls. That piece of shit hurt her bad. You did a good thing killin' him. Drinks are on me as long as you boys are in town."

Ed nodded. "Thank you, mister, but we're just here for the auction and will be leaving right after. Hope Miss Ruby gets better real soon."

Camping near the auction site the brothers talked about going back into town to visit the Traildust but both fell asleep during the discussion.

Noise from wagons and horses and many people gathering woke them early the next morning. The auction promised to be a lively event.

Ed examined the stock while Jack looked over the tools and implements. They each knew exactly what they wanted to bid on.

The auction was well organized and the bidding went quickly and with precision.

Ed got excited by a matched team of mules and overbid but won and made up for the overage toward the end of the auction with a little roan filly which was worth far more that what he bid.

Jack bought several hand tools to replace worn or lost items for the carpenter shop and bid low and won a two man tree saw. One handle was broken so no one else showed an interest but he knew he could replicate the handle with ease.

The next morning the two men headed east leading four mules and a roan filly. All of the animals were loaded down with farm and kitchen tools including an almost new iron kettle for Emmy.

The filly had the lightest load. Mrs. Overton had offered for auction several of her nicer dresses and bonnets and with only minor discussion, the brothers decided their sisters and Emmy deserved something pretty. So the filly carried little weight but much bulk with several muslin wrapped packages.

One hat, a pretty purple confection with a long yellow feather wouldn't wrap well, so Ed tied the ribbons around the filly's neck to make the trip home.

A few miles down the road Jack observed, "She looks like she's wearing her Easter bonnet."

Ed laughed and said, "That's what we'll name her. Easter."

Influenza

The weather continued wet and cold into the spring. Influenza was at epidemic proportions across the state.

Lizzie kept soup on the kitchen fire and the men and boys chopping and hauling wood so the house stayed warm. She insisted that Ed, Emmy, and Billy move to the main house and when anyone started feeling ill or developed a fever, she isolated them in Emmy's house.

Eli and Henry both came down sick the same morning. The oldest and the youngest woke with a cough and a fever. Lizzie quickly moved them to the cabin and proceeded to scrub Emmy's home until the already neat and clean household was shiny as a new penny. She tucked her father and littlest brother into the bed and instructed Queen to feed them chicken soup that was simmering on the hearth.

Eli caught her hand as she moved away. "Tell Ed to walk Maggie to school today, since I'm not up to it."

"Yes Pa, I'll tell him." She patted his hand and smiled.

As Lizzie was leaving to go check on the rest of the family, she sternly told Queen, "And do not use the same rags to wash their faces and their bodies. You use separate rags to clean them. You take the ones used on their bodies and you put them in the burn pile. We can't have that nasty body dirt on our faces."

Patiently and not too sweetly, Queen responded with a sigh, "Yes, Lizzie, I know what to do and how to do it. You have told me often enough. I promise I will keep the rags separate. Go home and see to the others. I'm sure Emmy needs your help."

When Lizzie got back to the house, she found Ed in the kitchen. "Pa says for you to walk Maggie to school today since he can't, and to take your rifle with you."

Watt looked up and smiled at his brother. "That's a good chore for you, you lump-of-lard."

Craig ducked his head and looked sideways at his brother.

Ed grinned and said, "There's no need to be on the lookout for that Yankee scoundrel. I hear he met his maker a while back. We can all forget about him. But I did forget to tell you that we ran into Mammy Bess on the road. Josiah died and she and Silas are moving to Arkansas." He sipped his coffee and looked at Watt seriously and said, "I'll tell ya all about it later."

Within a week, both Eli and Henry were back in their own beds and the whole family was well and strong.

Sadly, Sarah Ann Taylor wasn't as fortunate. Nannie and her daughters nursed Sarah Ann through the worst but she had not been strong since her last child was born. One morning Creed awoke to find his wife dead beside him.

The day after Sarah Taylor's funeral, Craig returned from town and ran up on the porch.

"Pa, ya got a letter from Uncle Joe. Want me to read it to ya?"

Eli was rocking in his chair and humming "The Bonnie Blue Flag" to little Andy who was napping in his lap.

Emmy came out the door when she heard Craig ride up. "Let me take the baby. I'm sure he's hungry."

"He needs changing too," Eli chuckled, handing the baby to his mother.

"Now let's see what my baby brother has to say."

Craig carefully unfolded the paper. Letter reading was usually reserved for Watt, but Watt wasn't here and Craig recognized the honor his father was giving him. He cleared his throat and began:

Carroll County   May 3, 1870
Dear Brother and family,
I'm afraid I bear bad news. The influenza hit Carroll County with the vengeance of the Lord. Nearly every family here bouts was effected.

We are all in mourning for Deliah. Everyone in the house was ill but she had it worse. After nursing us through the sickness she came down with it and died. Will is devastated

Craig stopped to see his father's reaction. Eli had tears in his eyes but made no comment so Craig continued.

Mother comes over daily with her little girl. Minnie was a year old last month and is cute as can be.

Will's baby boy, Geofffrey is only seven months old and our housekeeper isn't able to care for the house, cooking, Tabitha and an unweaned baby.

So Mother hired a wet nurse out of her household allowance, from Mr. Coble. I don't think she's told him.

Eli spoke for the first time. "I knew that man was no good. He better not cut into Tabby's income."

Craig swallowed hard and continued:

I was glad to receive your letter last month with the news of Silas and Penny. It's good to know they are all healthy and starting a new life in Arkansas.

K and his family are good. They all had very mild cases of the sickness. K tends to neglect the farm and spends most of his time in town at his men's club. The Ku Klux Klan as they are called, opened a branch here in Huntingdon and he was one of the first members. He's tried to convince me and Will to join but we are both too busy trying to get crops in the field.

I confide in you brother, I think no good will come from this association with K's group of friends.

"What does he mean, Pa?" Craig asked

"He means my brother K is weak and easily influenced. He will lose everything if he's not careful."

My hand is tired and my eyes are weary, brother, so I'll close for tonight. Tabitha sends her love to you and your entire family and so do Will and I. Please write soon.
Your baby brother
Joe.

Corn Shucking

The harvest was in and Ed's five acres produced a bumper crop of sorghum so he and Watt put their heads together to see why it was more productive than the others.

The corn was cut and stacked in the field. Watt and his brothers were busy moving the shocks, while Sassy and several of her offspring waited eagerly. Each time one of the shocks was tipped over, fat field mice went scurrying with cats and kittens chasing them.

Lester and Baxter earned their keep by hauling the corn to the new barn Jack had constructed during the summer. With the corn piled high in the center of the barn they were ready to have a corn shucking party.

Lizzie and Queen had been busy in the kitchen for two days, even though all the invited guests would bring food and drink. Mack,

Maggie, and Henry were extra excited. This would be the first big shucking bee they could remember.

The Taylors were the first to arrive mid-afternoon. Nannie and her daughters went straight to the kitchen while Anderson and his sons headed to the barn.

Soon the other neighbors started to arrive and it was time for the shucking to begin.

The young men lined up on one side and the young women on the other and they started shucking the ears of corn. Fifteen minutes into the process a young man yelled, "Hurrah, look what I found," and he held a solid red ear of corn aloft. He jumped up and ran around the corn pile. He stopped next to Queen, grabbed her hands, pulled her to her feet, and roughly kissed her on the mouth.

While the entire party laughed and hollered, Queen gasped, spit, wiped her mouth with the back of her hand, and said, "How dare you, Jamie Godwin!" and she ran out of the barn toward the house.

Embarrassed by her reaction, the young man slunk out the door and didn't return that night.

Soon, everyone was laughing and the incident was forgotten by most.

Jeff Taylor was sitting quietly with a red ear of corn in his hand when the youth next to him noticed and said loudly "Hey, Taylor. Who you gonna claim a kiss from? Bet I know who."

Jeff glanced across the pile at Lizzie with a questioning look. She nodded and rose to her feet. He climbed over the pile and put his arms around her. He kissed her long and hard. The crowd started hooting and hollering and finally brought them both back to reality. They separated with faces as red as the prized ear of corn.

The pile was shrinking as the older guests and children put the shucked ears into a pile in the corner and placed the discarded husks in a wagon out the side door.

Lizzie went to the house to make sure the food and drink table were set up on the porch. She spotted Queen on the far end of the porch and went to her. "Are you alright, little sister?"

"Yes, I'm fine. Jamie just took me by surprise. I wasn't prepared for him to kiss me. I didn't want him to kiss me. I only want John to come back and kiss me like a grown woman, not a little girl." The sixteen-year-old Queen broke down in heart-wrenching sobs.

"Oh, Queen. I didn't know you still carried a torch for that man."

"Lizzie, I've loved him since I was six years old and I always will."

Laughter and loud voices from the crowd of hungry corn shuckers interrupted the sisters.

Lizzie pushed her little sister into Eli's bedroom and said, "Wash your face, young lady, and regain your composure. Jim brought his fiddle and the dancing will start soon. You will go out there, with your head held high, and pretend to have a good time tonight."

Bobby Lee

After school one cool afternoon in October, thirteen year-old Mack ran ahead of his brother and sisters in order to beat them to the house. He had important news and he wanted to be the first to tell.

"Lizzie, Watt, Pa!" he yelled as he took the steps two at a time and landed on the back porch with a loud thud.

Lizzie came out of the kitchen wiping her hands on her apron; Watt stuck his head out of the tool shed; Eli came out of his bedroom and a breathless Queen stepped up on the porch behind her little brother.

"Robert E Lee died!" Queen blurted out before Mack could break the news.

Mack turned and gave his big sister a hateful look and pouted. "But I wanted to tell 'em the news, you big bully."

These two had been squabbling since Mack said his first words. Born less than two years apart, Queen always stressed the point that she was older and therefore, smarter.

"You would get it wrong, you silly little boy," she said and raised her head with a haughty toss of her curls.

Losing patience with both of them, Lizzie looked at calm and collected Maggie and asked, "Is this true. Did General Lee die?"

With tears in her eyes, Maggie nodded.

Eli took his youngest daughters hands, squatted down to her level, and asked, "Where did you hear this news, dear?"

Watt and Ed had joined them on the porch, and Maggie looked at her brothers and swallowed hard.

Queen opened her mouth to speak, but a look from Lizzie made her close it again.

"Tell us, sweetheart," Eli coaxed the shy Maggie.

"The teacher had a newspaper from Nashville, and it said that General Lee took sick a couple of weeks ago and died yesterday. It said he was smitten with paralisasis and couldn't move.

"That's paralysis." Mack poked his little sister on the arm.

"Well however you say it, he couldn't walk or talk or anything and then he died." Maggie broke into sobs and ran up the loft stairs leaving everyone staring after her.

Lizzie turned to Queen and said, "What got into her? She didn't know the man."

Contrite, Queen hung her head and told the assembled family, "During the war, when life was really bad and the Yankees had been here, Maggie would be frightened and would hide under the bed. You were always too busy, to notice, Lizzie. I would find her and coax her out by telling her that Watt, Ed and Sam were fighting with General Lee and they would send those Yankees packing and we would be safe. He kinda became her hero, I guess. I'll go talk to her."

CHAPTER 8

QUESTIONS OF LIFE, 1871

Fanny Winstead

Chestnut Ridge, Tenn
April 7, 1871

Eli and family,

It's with a sad heart I write you these lines to inform you of the death of my dear mother who died four days ago after a long suffering. She was burried the next day at the Mount Herman graveyard next to Pap. She had not been well since January and had suffered a sight since then. She craved so much to be out of her misery and to see Pap, Carol and Rufus in heaven. She had a smothering spell for a long time before she died. John was sick and wasn't able to come be with her before she died but he got out of the bed and came to the burriing.

Well I will say goodbye and am hoping to hear from you soon.
Your sister in marriage
Lauretha Phelps.

After supper Eli asked Watt to share their aunt's letter with the rest of the family while he sat on the porch and smoked his pipe. He had been fond of his mother-in-law and wanted to reflect on her life and family. Both Fanny and Sam Winstead had been good simple people. They had treated him fairly, and he would ask the preacher to offer a prayer for Fanny's soul at Sunday service.

While Lizzie and Queen cleaned up after supper, the men went about their evening chores.

As Watt passed the henhouse, he heard sobs. Big breath taking sobs straight from the heart. He quietly stuck his head around the door frame and to his surprise found Mack.

The big adolescent was bent over with his hands on his knees gasping for breath.

Concerned, Watt rushed to his brother, chickens scattering out the door and up to their roosts. "Mack, what's wrong?" he asked as he put an arm across the boys back.

"Grandma Fanny is dead," Mack cried.

"Don't be sad, Mack. You're old enough to understand that we all have to die. She's with Mama now and Granpa Sam and Uncle Rufus. She's happy."

"I know that, Watt. But nobody makes fig preserves like she did and now we won't get any more."

Old Ned and Lady Blue

Old Ned limped into the yard in the middle of the night and laid at the bottom step whining.

Lady Blue left her newest litter under the porch and sniffed his face and licked a bad wound on his side. When he didn't get up, she started baying.

Lighted lamps appeared in both lofts and Eli's bedroom.

Lizzie was the first out the door with everyone else following closely in their night clothes. Eli and Watt both carried rifles.

Watt carefully lifted his blue tick hound and carried him into the foyer. The old dog had a deep gash in his side and his back left leg jutted at an unnatural angle. His face and neck were scratched and bloody and one floppy ear was torn.

Lady tried to follow her mate into the house, but Lizzie pushed her back under the porch with her pups. Then she went to make coffee and boil some water to clean Ned's wounds.

"It appears he tangled with the wrong bobcat, son." Eli tried to comfort Watt.

Queen brought a basin of warm water and some cloths and Watt cleaned and bandaged Ned's wounds, but he didn't think he could fix the leg.

"Henry, go get Ed. He has a way with animals. Maybe he can fix Ned's leg," Eli told his youngest son.

When Ed arrived hastily dressed and still half asleep he looked at the leg and manipulated the joint while Ned looked at him sad eyed and whining.

"It'll be fine, old boy. I won't hurt you, I promise."

In one smooth move, he pulled and pushed and the hip joint moved back into place. "It was just out of joint. He'll be fine." Then rubbing the dog's uninjured ear said, "Won't ya, fella?"

Lady was scratching and howling at the door. Eli opened it and she dashed into be by Ned's side. Eli nearly tripped over the eight puppies. Lady had moved them up the steps and onto the porch.

Lizzie allowed Lady to stay with her mate and made the pups a bed from an old crate that Craig found in the barn.

They nursed the sick hound for two days, but his wound became infected and he never regained his feet. On the third day, Lady started to howl and when Lizzie went to check she found Old Ned lifeless.

That evening Watt led the family in a procession to Ned's favorite napping tree down by the creek. With much pomp and circumstance, he gently laid the old dog in the ground. Tears flowed and even little Billy seemed saddened by his first experience with death.

Lizzie called Lady to come back to the house but she wouldn't leave her mate.

Watt picked her up and carried the howling dog back to the house and her hungry puppies.

As soon as the door was opened the next morning, Lady bolted, leaving her pups behind.

Watt picked up the crate and carried it to the creek where he found Lady Blue laying across Ned's grave. He placed the pups next to their mother and for four days, Lizzie carried food to her mourning dog.

On the fifth day, she found the pups whining loudly and Lady Blue peacefully and permanently asleep.

Puppies

After burying Lady Blue beside Old Ned, Lizzie once again placed the pups in the old crate. At three weeks old, each pup weighed close to ten pounds. Ten pounds of ears and jowls and writhing, wiggly fur. They didn't stay in the crate long enough for Watt and Ed to hoist it aloft.

"Stop!" Lizzie yelled. "They will all break their necks. Leave the crate and everyone just take a pup. When we get home each of you can feed one of them."

It was early to wean but there was no other choice.

Every morning and every evening Lizzie made up a pan of oatmeal with lots of rich cream and bacon fat.

"This silly puppy won't eat," Henry complained as he wiped his messy fingers on his pants.

Queen, Mack, Maggie, Henry, and Lizzie were sitting on the porch in the middle of eight squirming, licking, whining puppies.

"Here let me show you how to do it," Lizzie told her little brother. She dipped her finger in the gooey mixture and holding the pup in one hand, rubbed the mess on his little mouth. The pup licked his lips then licked again. He whined then leaned toward Lizzie's fingers as she pulled them away.

Laughing, she put the puppy's head against her cheek and cooed, "You're a greedy little thing."

Henry tried and his pup was soon licking his fingers while the boy giggled, "That tickles."

Within three days, the pups scrambled to the pan as soon as Lizzie set it down.

Lizzie and Jeff

Jeff found Lizzie down by the creek, sitting between the graves of Ned and Lady Blue. She was sobbing loudly.

He quietly sat down beside her and took her hand in his. Then he scooted closer and put his arm around her. She buried her face in his shoulder and cried even harder. He patted her back and let her cry. When she took a deep breath and raised her head, her nose was running and her eyes were red and swollen.

Lizzie sniffed and Jeff handed her his not-so-clean handkerchief. To him she had never looked more beautiful, or more vulnerable.

After blowing her nose, she handed him back his soggy hanky and pulled the ever- present rag from her dress pocket and wiped her eyes.

"I miss her so much. She was the only thing I had to cling to during the horrible war years. She always listened when I had trouble or didn't know what to do."

"Did she give you good advice?" Jeff asked.

Lizzie raised her head and saw the grin on his face and laughed. "I don't know if it was good or bad. I never learned to speak hound dog." Pausing to take another deep breath, she continued, "I remember the day you gave her to me. It was nine years ago today. My twelfth birthday. She was such a tiny little thing. We grew up together and now she's gone and I have no one."

"That's not true, Lizzie. You have me. I'll always be here for you. I've loved you since we were children."

She raised her face and he kissed her. Lizzie put her arms around his neck and the kiss intensified until they heard a rustling in the trees. Turning toward the sound, Lizzie caught a glimpse of a skirt she recognized as Maggie's and the trousers legs of Henry's pants.

Giggling like a schoolgirl, Lizzie pushed away from Jeff. "Those scamps were spying on us. Guess we better get back before they send Watt after us."

Jeff stood and extended his hand to pull her to her feet. "But first I want to show you something." He pulled her out of the woods toward the back of Eli's farm. In a shallow valley surrounded by gentle hills, he stopped.

"Happy Birthday, Lizzie, where do you want the window?"

Looking around at the pretty valley she turned back to find Jeff on his knees. "What are you talking about, Jeff Taylor?"

"Marry me, Lizzie, and I'll build you a house with a window facing that hill over yonder." He turned her around and saw her mother's grave in the distance.

Breaking down in sobs again, she cried, "Jeff, I can't marry you. I can't leave Maggie and Henry. They are still too young."

"They are growing up and they have Queen and Emmy, to mother them. You know Watt and Marthey will get married before too long. Please, Lizzie. I love you and want you to be my wife."

Lizzie lowered her head as though in prayer, and Jeff held his breath as he patiently waited.

Finally, she raised her head and looked into his eyes. "Yes, Jeff. I'll marry you. But not until Watt and Marthey marry. Then I can turn responsibility for the children over to them."

Jeff smiled a smile that would light up the sky and kissed her long and hard.

Henry and Tag

"Noooo, you can't take Tag. He's my puppy," Henry cried as Watt loaded pups into an enclosed crate in the back of the wagon.

"Now, Henry, we talked about letting the puppies go to new homes. You want Tag to find a good family don't you?"

"He's got a good family. I'm his family," the young boy cried.

"You can't keep him, Henry. Lizzie is keeping two of his sisters and we can't keep the boy dogs," Watt explained to the sobbing boy. "We'll find him a good home and he'll be happy. You can keep one of the girls if you want."

Henry reached for the puppy one more time and Mack picked up the child and held him, squirming and wiggling and hitting with his little fists. "I want Tag."

"Tag can't stay here, little brother. He needs to go someplace else." Watt was losing patience. "Now, pick one of the girls or be quiet."

"NO. I want Tag. Why can't he stay with his sisters? We do."

Mack let go of the boy dumping him in the dirt, sobbing with his nose running down his dirty face. "You're such a baby," Mack remarked. "Don't you know anything?"

"That's enough, Mack. Leave the boy alone," Watt said sharply as he realized his baby brother needed to spend more time with the men and livestock. Stooping low, Watt picked his brother up out of the dirt and wiped the boy's face with his handkerchief.

"Henry, you know that it's wrong to marry your sister don't you?"

The boy sniffed and nodded with his eyes big and red.

"And you know that married people have babies?"

Henry nodded again, obviously confused.

At that moment, the neighbor tomcat decided to make a call on Sassy who was strutting across the yard with her tail held high.

The cats low screams started the pups howling as chickens scattered and ducks waddled for cover.

Suddenly a light went on behind Henry's eyes, and Watt knew the ten-year-old had grasped what Watt was trying to tell him.

Henry hung his head and slowly walked to the crate in the wagon. He stuck his fingers through the slats and Tag licked his fingers and whined.

"So long Tag. You're a good dog." Turning to Watt, "Promise you'll find him another little boy to play with?"

"I promise, Henry. Why don't you go help Mack with the chickens?"

"Come on, baby brother, I need to clean the roosts and you're just the right size to get in there and do it."

The boy thought a moment and turned up his nose and said, "Clean your own roosts. I'm going with Watt to find Tag a good home."

Laughing, Watt nodded and said, "Then you better climb aboard, baby brother."

Watt

During Christmas church service, Watt sat holding Marthey's hand. He wasn't paying attention to the service but was lost in thought about Christmas's past and what future Christmas' might bring.

Joe had written last week saying Will had remarried a woman named Minerva Grable and she was very attached to Will's son.

A baby's cry made him look around and he saw Emmy rise to feed her new baby girl.

Marthey squeezed his hand and he groaned; not from the pressure but at the realization that his younger brothers, Ed and Sam were both fathers of three. Will had a son and a new wife, while he was thirty years old and still slept in the loft with his much younger brothers.

After services, the Taylors hosted Christmas dinner. After the tree was lit and both families were singing carols and enjoying Nannies' eggnog, Watt asked Marthey to take a walk.

It was an unseasonably warm night and the full moon gave everything a silvery glow.

Followed by the geese who were hoping for a handout, the couple strolled leisurely around the grounds. Behind the big barn, Watt stopped and took Marthey in his arms. Her head fit just beneath his chin and as she wrapped her arms around his torso her soft breasts melded into his upper abdomen.

Watt groaned and Marthey turned loose and stepped back in alarm. "Did I hurt you Watt?"

He reached for her and pulled her tight against his chest. "You could never hurt me, dear. But I want you so badly and that hurts." He kissed the top of her head and she snuggled closer.

They stood entwined. Each cherishing the moment.

Watt turned loose first and as the cool air washed over them, Watt reached into his shirt pocket with one hand and took Marthey's left hand with his other.

"Soon I can make you my wife. You have been so patient, my love. I can't buy you a diamond but I do want to pledge you my vow," and he slipped a narrow ring on her finger. "I'll replace this with gold one day soon. I promise."

Marthey looked at her hand. A thin band of braided hair encircled her left ring finger. "This is you hair isn't it, Watt?"

"Some. But in the light you can see blonde strands also. I enlisted Betsy's help. She gathered your beautiful hair from your hairbrush. Queen braided the strands from yours and mine together to make us matching rings." He held up his left hand and a wider braided band adorned it.

"Merry Christmas, my darling," he said and kissed her again.

It was a kiss full of passion and promise.

Marriage Bonds

CHAPTER 9

JACK AND AGGIE, 1872

The Wrath of Watt

"Did you know Mack has been skipping school?" Lizzie angrily asked Watt, when she found him in the workshop, repairing a plow share.

He stopped filing in mid-stroke and looked at her in amazement. "He's done what?"

"Maggie told me after breakfast that she didn't have to go to school if Mack wasn't going. He hasn't been in a week and swore Maggie and Henry to secrecy. He wouldn't tell them what he's doing or where he is going. You need to take that boy in hand."

Watt stormed out of the workshop, his long legs striding toward the woods. His deep voice boomed, "Sterling McAlister Ownby, where are you?"

Lizzie walked back toward the house, glancing over her shoulder as Watt went in search of their scamp of a little brother.

Watt found Mack sitting on the creek bank. He had a fishing line in the water; a farm journal on his lap; his hat down over his eyes and was sound asleep.

"Why aren't you in school, boy?" Watt growled, low and quiet. His face was grim and his eyes were cold.

Mack had never seen this side of his big brother and it frightened him. He started stammering, "Well, I...uh...I...thought I'd...uh..." as he tried to scramble to his feet. He tripped over the fishing pole and tumbled down the bank and landed on his back in the creek.

He didn't see the tiny upturn at the corner of Watt's mouth. All he saw was his big brother, back lit by the sun, looking like the Wrath of God.

Watt walked down the creek bank and squatted at the edge of the water. He didn't offer Mack a hand but instead calmly said. "I will not tolerate you lying and sneaking around. Nor will I stand for you involving your little sister and brother in your deception. You WILL continue school for the remainder of the year. You will be fifteen by then and can stop. Am I clear?"

"Yes, sir."

"Any questions?"

"Uh yes, sir. I've been wanting to talk to you about the chickens."

Watt stood and extended his hand to help his little brother out of the creek.

Mack picked up his fishing pole.

Watt scooped up the wet hat and plopped it on Mack's head. He laughed for real as water dripped over the young man's face.

At the top of the creek bank, Watt clapped Mack on the back. "What about the chickens?"

Mack looked around and found the discarded farm journal he had been sleeping over and pointed to an article. "I've been studying this new breed called Plymouth Rock. If we put a few with your Dominickers, we can increase our egg yield by twenty-five percent in just a few months. I have the figures back at the house."

"I'll look at your figures and we can send Pa to find a couple of hens if you want to try them. But, you go to school tomorrow and the rest of the year. AND you apologize to your sister and brother for lying and shirking your responsibility."

"Yes, sir, I will."

Mack had learned something that morning. Being honest and forthright was more effective that lying and he would rather meet his maker than ever again see that cold, deadly look on his brother's face.

Maggie

The sun was breaking over the hills as Margaret Emily Ownby opened the barn door, unpinned her hair, and kicked off her shoes. Her hemline was wet with the early morning dew, and she had awakened that morning feeling out of sorts for no reason.

On her twelfth birthday last month, Lizzie had presented her with two new skirts in a longer length to emphasize her maturity. With the skirts had come a lecture about keeping her hair pinned up and a lot of other nonsense Maggie intended to ignore. Lizzie and Queen had never been secretive about what it meant to become a woman or what to expect. But to Maggie that was a long time off. She'd worry about it when the time came.

Eight kittens circled her legs and two began to climb her skirt as she made her way toward the back stall. Eloise the milk cow was waiting patiently.

Maggie set the pail down and pulled the stool up to the cow's side. Eloise turned her head to see what was happening and sniffed the girl's hand, then blew gently.

Like Lizzie, Maggie enjoyed milking first thing in the morning. The cow barn was warm and cozy and Eloise was cooperative and always seemed grateful when the milk pail was full.

The kittens were getting more insistent for attention. Sassy had died last year and the official title of Barn Cat had passed to one of her offspring. She originally named the reining queen of the barn Bossy because as a kitten she was the boss of the litter. Maggie tried to name the cat Lizzie, but Watt convinced her that Bossy would be less confusing.

Bossy was winding around Maggie's legs wanting some of the fresh milk, so Maggie poured some in a chipped bowl kept just for that purpose. As the cat lapped at the foamy milk, the kittens abandoned the girl and swarmed their mother.

Kittens and cat scattered as the barn door flew open and Henry bounded in yelling, "Lizzie needs the milk. She says to hurry and get it to her now."

"I'll be right there," Maggie told her little brother as she patted the cow's side.

"Hurry, Pa's gonna take me hunting as soon as breakfast is over. That means I don't have to help Watt in the field today."

"You take the milk pail. I want to give Eloise some fresh hay. Tell Lizzie I'll be along soon."

Maggie wasn't ready to go back to the crowded house full of noise and people.

She was confused. Born fifteen months apart, she and Henry had always been the babies of the family and treated accordingly.

The family all called her "baby sister" but now Lizzie was telling her daily that she had to act more grownup and ladylike.

As she threw fresh hay to Eloise, she rubbed her bare toe in the dirt, spit on a smudge on her arm, and wiped it with the hem of her skirt. When the cow was fed, she sat on the stool and laid her head against the warm massive rump.

She sighed, "I don't know what grown-up means, Eloise. Do you?"

Maggie sighed and re-pinned her hair so Lizzie wouldn't scold. As she bent to put her shoes back on, she felt a pressure in her private place. It wasn't like anything she had ever felt before. She put her shoes on and stood. Bending to pick up the milking stool, she saw something on the wooden seat. It looked like blood. Then she felt the trickle between her legs.

"Ohhhh, nooooo," she moaned. "Eloise, I don't want to grow up."

In response the contented bovine flicked her tail across Maggie's back. and the girl despondently left the cow to eat her breakfast in peace.

Fourth of July Fireworks

Woodbury was celebrating the 4th of July with a picnic, horse races, and fireworks. Everyone from miles around was crowded into the town square, which was decorated with colorful banners and flags.

Watt, Ed, and Jack had brought horses to race, hoping to win and gain some recognition for their stock.

Lizzie and Queen brought preserves to enter the judging and everyone was excited and ready for a fun-filled day.

Scout won the race and Ed was proudly basking in the glow and the well wishes of the crowd. Watt came in second, but Jack didn't place and was wandering around in a despondent mood. It was almost noon. The Ownbys and the Taylors were planning to meet under the big oak tree by the stockyard.

As Jack headed in that direction, he noticed a crowd of men surrounding a stage set up on the corner. There were girls and young women lined up on the stage. Each of them was holding a large picnic basket and there was a hand-lettered sign that said, *Buy Lunch and Benefit the Confederate Widows and Orphans*. It seemed there was an auction going on.

Jack stopped to watch as one by one the girl's lunches were bought, and the girls left the stage with the men who purchased their baskets. Most were bought by their beaus, brothers, and in one case the girl's father.

There was one young lady standing off to the side dressed all in brown which matched her hair and eyes. There was no color to the poor girl anywhere. She resembled a sparrow among a pandemonium of parrots.

Jack recognized her. She was Agatha Ann Willis who had been in school with him and had always sat in the back of the room and never had much to say to anyone.

Today, something about her struck a chord in Jack's brain as he watched the auction and Aggie. A hand pressed on his shoulder and he jumped.

Ed grinned and said, "What's got your interest little brother?"

"Ya got any money, Ed? Lend me a few coins," Jack said never taking his eyes off the stage.

Ed dug in his pocket and handed Jack some coins, mostly copper but one glint of silver sparkled in the sunshine.

With his eyes still glued to the auction, Jack said, "Thank you, brother. I'll pay you back one day."

"Yes, you are going to pay me with interest." Ed laughed as he walked away.

But Jack didn't hear him. He moved closer to the platform. And Aggie.

When the crowd had dispersed, she was the only one left on the stage. Jack raised his hand to the auctioneer (who was the preacher) and bid on Aggie's lunch basket. He paid a dime for the lunch but figured it was for a very good cause.

Jack helped her down from the stage and took the basket as they walked toward a shady spot on the courthouse lawn. "I remember you. You're one of the Ownby boys. Which one are you? You all look alike."

"Guilty, ma'am. I'm Andrew Jackson but they call me Jack."

"I saw your brothers and sisters earlier. Won't they be expecting you for lunch?"

Jack laughed and said, "I doubt they'll miss me; there's so many of us."

Jack spread the cloth from the basket and the young people sat on the edge as Aggie set out the meal she had prepared. There were crispy pieces of fried chicken, boiled eggs, sweet pickles, and buttered biscuits. By the time he finished two fried apple pies, Jack had decided this was the best meal he had ever eaten and the most interesting conversation he had ever had.

Aggie was simply shy. She was well read, articulate, and could converse on any topic from history to farming.

Ed joined the rest of the family and Lizzie asked, "Where's Jack."

"He's occupied elsewhere. I'm sure he'll be along before night fall." He winked at Watt and lifted Billy up on his shoulders while the little boy giggled.

Jack and Aggie stayed together the rest of the afternoon and at dusk, they settled in to watch the fireworks from a staircase attached to the side of a building. When the fireworks started, Aggie jumped and was frightened.

She threw her arms around Jack's neck and turned her head into his shoulder.

He hesitantly put his arms around her and held her tight. Her hair smelled slightly of roses and was silky soft against his cheek.

When the last of the fireworks faded from the sky, Jack walked Aggie to her family. He was afraid her father would be angry she was so late. But John Willis was smiling and helping his wife load their wagon.

Aggie introduced Jack to her four younger sisters and her mother. Mr. Willis shook Jacks hand and said, "It's nice to meet you, young man. I know your Pa and brothers. Saw Ed a while ago and he told me you were keeping my Aggie safe for the fireworks show. Ya know the crowd can get a little rowdy on the 4th of July. Thank you son, for taking good care of my girl. Now it's late and we better get these girls home, Ma."

He turned and climbed on his wagon and flicked the rein.

Aggie waved shyly from the back of the wagon as Jack watched it fade down the dark road.

His mind was awash with the scent of rosewater.

Jack was in love.

Nan Takes a Fall

One beautiful September Sunday, Emmy invited the family to her house for dinner. She wanted to christen her new kitchen. The men had finished it the week before. Creed Taylor set the last fireplace stone and declared it ready.

The men had harvested enough timber to finish out the loft room also and now the little house was really feeling like a home.

Sam and Ruthie brought their family, and the Taylors were all in attendance.

Lady's daughters, Princess and Countess, both had pups who were almost weaned. The children had a fun time chasing pups all over the yard.

"I got a filly about to foal and I'm not sure how she's gonna do," Sam told Ed. "Think you could come by tomorrow and take a look at her?"

"Watt can do without me for a day or two. Can't ya, you old sack-of-bones?"

"You're useless anyway, you lump of lard." Watt grinned.

"I'll just go home with you tonight and stay till your filly delivers."

Three days later, Ed rode up to Eli's house and as he tied Scout to the railing, his father asked, "Was it a colt or a filly?"

"One of each Pa. That's why she wasn't doin' so good. She had twins." Ed laughed and said, "They are both healthy and strong and she's feeding them, so Sam got a bonus."

At the sound of their father's laugh, Billy and Andy came running out the door with little Nancy toddling behind. Maggie was trying to catch all three.

Ed stooped low and caught all three and commented, "I suppose Emmy is here."

"Yes son she is. Maggie, go tell Emmy that her husband is home." He turned but the girl was already gone, and Emmy came flying through the door and nearly knocked Ed over.

"I think I'll leave more often if this is the welcome I get," Ed said as he hugged his children and kissed his wife.

Lizzie and Queen offered a more sedate welcome but it was obvious they were glad to see their brother.

"I do have some sad news," Ed said more seriously.

Waiting expectantly, the women stood still and even the children got quiet as Eli picked up Nancy and rocked her while she sucked her thumb.

"Don't dawdle, son, tell us what it is."

"One of Sam's twins broke her ankle day before yesterday."

"Oh my goodness!" Lizzie declared in alarm. "What happened to the child? They are only four."

124

"Sam and I were in the barn tending to the filly and the twins and Gracious were climbing on the wood pile. It shifted and a big log fell on Nan's ankle. Tennessee went for the doctor 'cause we could tell it was bad. The doctor says it's crushed and probably won't heal right."

"Poor little thing. Is she in a lot of pain?" Queen asked, almost in tears.

"The doctor left some laudanum for her so she sleeps a lot. Poor Gracious is shattered. The child won't leave Nan's side. She clings to the bed post if anyone tries to remove her from the room."

Ed chuckled. "Molly seems a bit envious of the attention Nan is getting. She keeps saying she's sick too. But Ruthie says she just wanting some pampering."

Emmy gathered her children close, recognizing the same fate could be theirs in a heartbeat.

"Lizzie, Emmy, let's go visit and cheer those babies up tomorrow. We'll have a little party with all the children." Queen started making plans before the other two women could respond. "I know let's make an almond pound cake. It was always my favorite as a child. We have the makings. Except for a lemon."

Smiling her prettiest smile, she turned to Ed, "Ed go to town and get us some lemons."

Ed looked at his sister then his wife.

Emmy shrugged and tried not to laugh, "Ya better get back on that horse, Edward Dallas, if you wanna be back in time for supper."

Lizzie took Queen's arm and pulled her toward the kitchen, "And you, young lady, had better get back to stringing those beans to hang if you wanna go anywhere. They'll ruin if we don't get 'em done today."

Farm Map

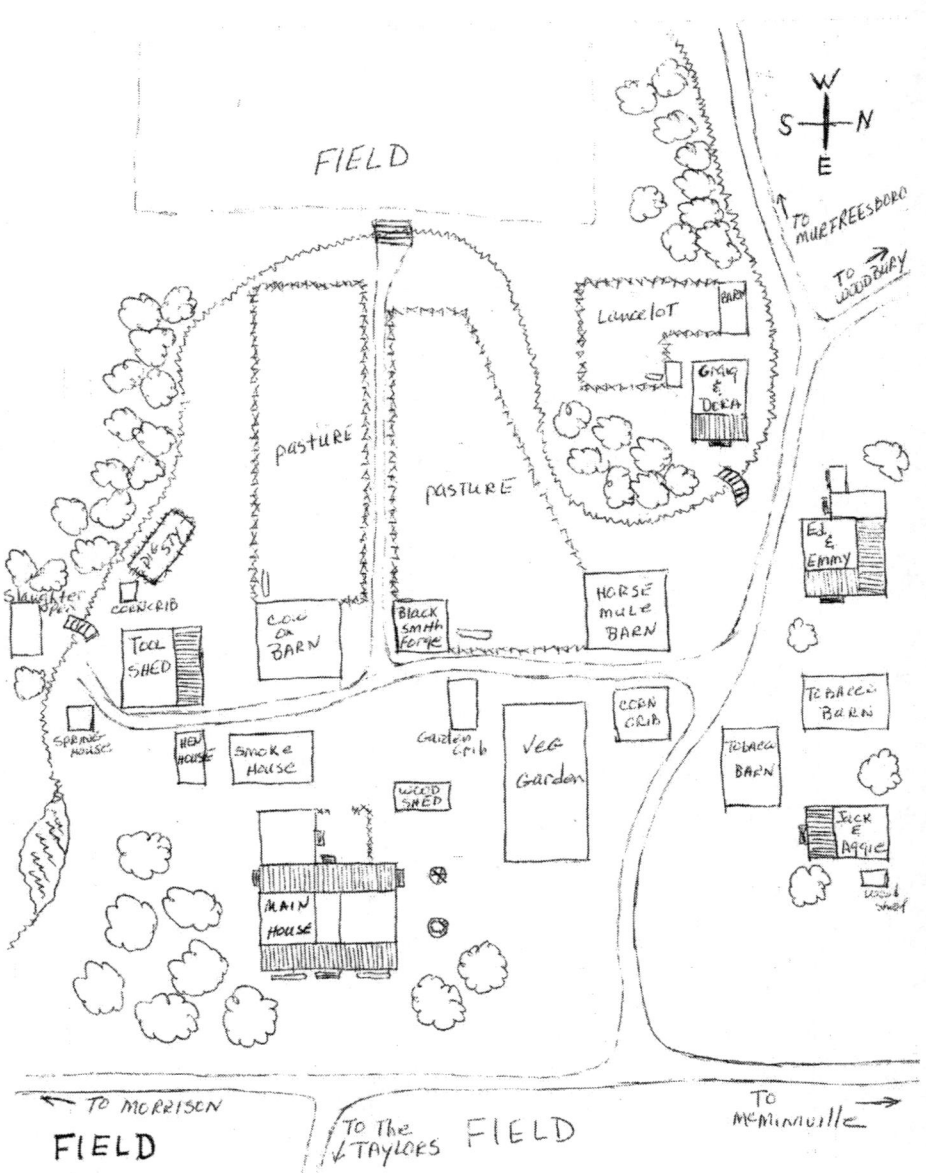

CHAPTER 10

A DOUBLE WEDDING, 1873

Joe's Inheritance

"*March 1, 1873*   Carroll Co. Tenn.*
    Dear Eli,
    I tell you brother, I'm as mad as an old wet hen. I just this minute returned from the lawyer's office in town where I expected to receive my inheritance.

    Joe stopped writing; laid down his pen and put his head in his hands. After a few moments, he raised his head and picked up a heavy glass paperweight. He turned it over in his hand and examined it closely like he had never seen it before.

    Suddenly he bent his arm back and threw the paperweight with all his might. It hit the doorframe and bounced into the hallway missing Will by inches.

    "Did you drop this, little brother?" Will asked as he stuck his head through the doorway.

    "No. I threw the damn thing," Joe snarled.

    "I take it the lawyer visit didn't go well. Are you all right?"

    "No, I'm not alright. I'm broke, Will. There's nothing left of Papa's estate. This house and the few surrounding acres." Joe slammed his fist on the desk and the ink well bounced but didn't spill.

    Will paced in front of the desk with his hands behind his back making Joe think of their father who would take that same position when deep in thought.

    "How did that happen, Joe? Papa always had sufficient funds for what ever he needed."

    "Mr. McNeil said Papa was land poor at the end of the war. He bought several pieces of property as folks sold out and had very little cash reserves. After he died, the taxes never got paid on the acquisitions.

Seven years they didn't get paid. So they were all sold at auction last year."

"Why weren't you notified?" Will raised his voice, enraged.

"Because I wasn't the heir last year. No one was required by law to tell me. So no one gave me a chance to save Papa's land."

"Damn, little brother. We might have been able to stop the auction if we had known."

"No one knew. It was kept private. And do you know who bought most of the acreage? Relatives and friends of Mr. Coble. If I thought for a moment Mother knew anything about this I don't know what I would do."

Will sat hard in the nearest chair.

Joe's face was red and he kept clenching and unclenching his fists.

Will stood and went to the sideboard behind the desk and removed Neddy's whiskey decanter and two glasses. There wasn't much of the dark amber liquid left but he poured what there was into the glasses.

"Here, little brother, drink this before you suffer an apoplexy."

Joe emptied his glass in one gulp; grimaced and looked at his unfinished letter to Eli.

He raised his eyes and they were sad. He quietly said, "I'm not concerned about me. Tabitha and her upkeep is what has me worried."

"You know that anyone in the family would help with Tabitha. Minerva loves living here with you and Tabby and doesn't want to move. I have some money put back and you are welcome to it. We'll work together, Joe. That's what Papa would have done. But I will make it clear to Mother Laurie that her husband is not welcome in this house."

Will downed his drink and slammed the glass down on the desk. "And I had better not ever find out that K was involved. I'll see you at supper," and he left the room.

Joe sat staring at the letter to his brother. He wadded it; threw it in the trash and reached for a fresh piece of paper.

Dipping his pen in the inkwell, he began again.

March 1, 1873   *Carroll Co., Tenn.*
Dear Eli,
I hope this letter finds you all doing good and healthy.
 Will's baby boy, Ernest turned eight months old yesterday and is the delight of the household,. Little Geoffery has adjusted to Minerva as his new mother and both children keep Tabitha entertained.
 I met with the lawyer today and signed the papers for Papa's estate. It seems the war depleted Papa's cash and there isn't anything left but the house and a few acres. Everything else went for back taxes.

Once again, Joe stopped writing and read over the letter. And once again he wadded it and trashed it. Rising from the chair, he mumbled to himself, "I'll write the damned letter tomorrow."

Two is Better than One

"Lizzie, your hounds just took off down the road. Probably have company coming," Eli called from his rocker on the porch.

Wiping her hands on her apron, Lizzie stepped through the parlor door and looked down the road just as a lone rider topped the last hill. The dogs were running along beside. "Who is it Pa?" she asked.

"Not sure, daughter, but you better throw another potato in the pot. He looks tired and is probably hungry. We'll know soon enough who it is." And he went back to rocking and humming the "Bonnie Blue Flag."

The rider dismounted by the horse trough and tied his horse to the railing as Eli stood then smiled widely. "Is that you, baby brother? My, but you've grown since I saw you last."

The men hugged long and hard and Eli stepped back with his hands on Joe's shoulders.

"Let me look at you, boy. You look more like Papa every year."

Joe laughed and sat down, "I look just like the rest of you."

Lizzie brought a cup of water and Eli said, "Lizzie, you remember your Uncle Joe. It's been a few years and both of you have grown up." He spotted Maggie peeking around the doorframe. "Maggie dear, come meet my baby brother and where did Queen get off to?"

"She's down at Emmy's, Pa. How do you do Uncle Joe. We enjoy your letters very much," Maggie said in her most ladylike manner. Then she blushed.

Lizzie pushed Maggie toward the door and whispered, "Go tell Queen and Emmy we have company. Now! Run along." She turned to leave as she told her father and uncle, "If you'll excuse me, I need to go tend supper."

"I hope you're making some of those heavenly biscuits Will is always going on about." Joe smiled.

"I think we can manage that," she smiled back and left muttering under her breath, "What does that damn Yankee know about biscuits?"

"Now, little brother, what brings you all this way? I know it wasn't Lizzie's biscuits."

Joe's face became serious and he leaned forward with his elbows on his knees. He lowered his voice and replied glumly. "No, Eli, it wasn't. I need some advice and who better to give it than my big brother? It's something I couldn't put in a letter."

"If it's woman problems, little brother, I have no advice to give you."

Joe laughed despite his anger and frustration. "It's more important than any woman, Eli. I can't consider women until I solve this puzzle."

"Tell me Joe."

So Joe told Eli about the estate being reduced and having no real inheritance. He stressed his concern about Tabitha and keeping her safe and healthy.

Eli listened; relit his pipe and took a puff. He blew a huge smoke ring and watched it dissipate then asked, "Have you talked to Tabby about this?"

"No! And I don't intend to. I don't want to disrupt her routine or her life."

"You underestimate our big sister, Joe. Tabby is more resilient than you think. I know Papa and your mother petted and pampered her these past few years. But don't forget that she grew up in a two pen house and helped take care of us younger children 'til we were almost grown. She's very capable and she's also intuitive about people."

"But Papa entrusted her care to me and he thought he was leaving adequate means to provide for her needs." Joe sobbed at the thought of disappointing his sister.

"Joe," Eli said quietly, "Tabitha knows she has a home with any of the brothers and sisters should the need arise. And so do you, baby brother."

Joe settled back in his chair and let out a breath he didn't realize he had been holding. "Will seems sure we can keep the house and land. We can grow enough food to keep from starving and there are many unnecessary things in the house I can sell if we need cash. But the style of living will be diminished. I'm so angry with Mother, I can't look at her. I haven't spoken to her since before I met with the lawyer. When she comes to visit I go to the barn or somewhere out of sight."

"Do you suspect she knew what her husband was doing?"

"I don't know. Will doesn't think so. He told her what happened and he said her surprise and shock seemed genuine. You know how she is. As long as she has a new hat or ribbons for Minnie's hair she isn't concerned about daily things. Will did tell her not to bring Mr. Coble to the house. And she hasn't."

Eli could see Joe was getting angry again. He said quietly, "Ecclesiastes says:

Two are better than one, because they have a good reward for their labor.
For if they fall, the one will lift up his fellow;
But woe to him alone when he falleth; for not another to help him up.

You aren't alone, Joe."

Joe appeared to take comfort from his brother's words and calm demeanor.

The men sat in silence listening to the pans and dishes rattling in the kitchen as the women prepared super.

The mood was soon broken.

"Hello, Uncle Joe," Watt said, coming through the foyer and joining his father and uncle on the porch. "Lizzie told me you were here. The others will be along shortly."

"How's the new calf, son?" Eli asked.

"She's fine, Pa. Having her supper right now. But Ed's watching Easter closely. Got her penned up. She's been off her feed the last couple of days and should foal tonight or tomorrow." He turned to Joe, "How's Uncle Will and Uncle K?"

"Will's good and so is his family." He chuckled and continued, "K? Well K never changes. He's still being K. He's disillusioned with that club of his. They failed to recognize what he calls his 'leadership abilities' and they elected someone else to be club president. Or Grand Dragon as he called it. If he would quit this ridiculous Ku Klux Klan he might could get his crops in the ground."

Watt laughed at the thought of his uncle leading anyone to accomplish anything. "I better go wash up before Lizzie comes after me with her broom. See you both at supper."

Wedding Preparations

The farm was recovering slowly but steadily. The horse pasture was full of colts with a total count of twenty horses including Belle, Scout, Storm, and Easter.

Craig's Duroc boar had indeed put fresh blood into Priney's litters and the smokehouse was full of bacon and hams. Craig was now studying cattle breeds to see if they wanted to take a different direction in breeding for both milk and beef.

Anderson and Jeff convinced Watt to purchase a few sheep. The wool was bringing decent prices so the return was good profit and the sheep could graze in the orchard and woodlands.

One night in October, Watt announced at supper, "It's time for me to honor my vow to Marthey. The harvest is in and we are getting married next week." He looked at Lizzie for her reaction.

"Then let's save time and make it a double wedding. I'll marry Jeff."

Queen jumped up from her chair; pulled Maggie to her feet and started dancing in circles.

"Oh, Lizzie that's marvelous. We have to make you a new dress and do something with your dreadful hair." She burst out with typical Queen enthusiasm.

"My blue calico will suit just fine, sister, and what in sam hill is wrong with my hair? It sits atop my head like the good lord intended."

Queen sat down, despondent and pouted, "Emmy talk to her. Convince her this is the most important day of her life and she must look her best."

"I think I hear Billy calling," Emmy said and left. She wasn't going to get involved in the sister's squabble.

The men all exchanged looks; rose in unison and exited the room together as Queen continued to chatter about dresses and hats and other girl things.

Once on the porch, Watt told his father, "I'm going to go see Marthey. She planned to tell her family of our plans tonight. I expect Jeff to be along soon."

Eli sent his younger sons to be about their evening chores and sat rocking, humming and smoking his pipe. He heard Jeff's whistle for several minutes before he saw the young man step onto the path to the porch.

"Good evening, Jefferson. Out for an evening stroll are ya?" he said with humor in his voice.

"Yes, sir. I mean, No, sir. I mean, I come to talk to you and to see Lizzie."

"What did you want to talk to me about? You've already convinced Watt to buy those dastardly sheep. What scheme are you planning now?" Barely able to carry on his teasing, he pretended his pipe was out and made a big show of relighting it.

"Well, sir, Mr. Ownby that is. You see Lizzie said she would marry me when Marthey and Watt got married, and, well Marthey told us tonight at supper they're gonna get hitched next week and I intend to hold her to her promise. That is if she's still willing."

Eli felt guilty about teasing the distraught young man. But couldn't resist just a bit more. "Are you asking me for my daughter's hand in marriage, son?"

"Uh, yes, sir. I guess I am. Do you think she'll marry me?"

Unable to control himself any longer, Eli burst out laughing,. "Why don't you go ask her, Jeff. She's in the kitchen. And yes, you have my blessing."

The next day, Nannie and Marthey came to visit with Lizzie and make plans.

As the mother of one bride and the surrogate mother to the other, Nancy Jane Canady Taylor intended to host the best wedding the two counties had seen in a while.

Queen was determined to get her way and insisted Lizzie have a new dress.

"A woman only get's married once and a new dress is in order. Tell her I'm right Marthey."

"Well," Watt's intended said with a smile. "I'm wearing a new yellow muslin with a pale green bonnet."

"See Lizzie. You simply must have something stunning to wear. Let's go to town tomorrow and find some material. I know Betsy and Callie will help me make you a new dress." She tugged on Marthey's hand and said, "Help me look through Mama's old clothes and see if there might be something in there we can use."

With a look of helplessness, Marthey followed her exuberant future sister-in-law out of the parlor.

Lizzie frowned but Nannie laughed and said, "That girl gets excited about everything. Her lust for life is contagious. But I'm glad they left us alone for a moment."

Nannie got a serious look on her face and took Lizzie's worn and calloused hand in her own. "Lizzie, you're mama was my dearest friend. I've considered you another daughter since she died. I want your happiness more than anything. But I also want my son to be happy. Tell me girl. Do you want to marry Jeff and spend the rest of your life with him?"

Lizzie broke down crying.

Nannies face fell. She had been worried that Lizzie didn't love Jeff.

"Oh, Nannie Taylor. Yes. I do. I've wanted to marry him for years. Ever since he first asked me. But the children needed me. Mama made me promise and I couldn't shirk that responsibility."

Nannie put her ample arms around Lizzie's narrow shoulders and patted her bony back. "Oh, sweetling, the children are almost grown. Why, Maggie's a young woman now and Henry will be a fine young man soon. Jeff loves you so much and he's fond of all your brothers and sisters."

"I love him. He always knows just what to do to make me laugh or smile when things are gloomy. I'm looking forward to being his wife and your daughter."

Nannie gave a huge sigh of relief and hugged the girl harder. "Now, dry your eyes before Queen comes back and starts asking her nosy questions. We have a double wedding to plan for."

Fountain Spring

Two days before the wedding Watt told Eli, "I'm going to town to get Marthey a ring. I'll be back by noon."

"No need, son. I've got something for you." He reached into his picket and pulled out a shiny gold band. "This belonged to you mother. I placed it on her hand thirty-four years ago. She asked me to give it to you when you needed it."

"But, Pa, shouldn't Polly or Lizzie have Mama's ring?"

"No, son, at the time Polly already had her own wedding ring. Your mother knew Marthey would cherish this symbol as she did. It's yours to give to your bride."

The tiny narrow band was dwarfed by Watt's large, rough hand. He gently turned it over a few times in his hand, then pulled his bible out of his vest pocket and inserted the ring between the pages. With tears in his eyes, he put the cherished book back in his pocket and he looked at his father. "Thank you, Pa. I know Marthey will love it."

The two couples were required by law to file for a marriage license in the county where the bride resided.

Eli went to Woodbury with Jeff and Lizzie to file the security bond in Cannon County, while Anderson went with Watt and Marthey to the Warren County Courthouse in McMinnville. Watt's best friend, J. E. Turner went with them and signed the Marriage Warranty Bond.

October 16, 1873 dawned clear, warm and glorious.

Both families performed their morning chores quickly and cheerfully. There was celebration in the air that even the livestock seemed to feel.

Friends and neighbors from both counties were planning to attend.

Polly had arrived two days before, with her children, Roy would be there in time for the wedding.

Sam and Ruthie had come yesterday with Tennessee and all of the children.

Emmy and Ruthie offered to stay at the Taylor homeplace to greet party guests while Nannie attended the ceremony.

Instead of the church or courthouse, both brides had embraced Nannie's stories of Celtic tradition by having the ceremony performed outdoors under God's canopy of sky and trees.

There was no more perfect place than the grove of trees surrounding fountain spring. Located on the back acreage of Anderson's property, fountain spring bubbled up from the bottom of a shallow rock lined pool.

Today the spring was truly a fountain. The water rose four feet in the air.

Watt and Jeff stood with the Reverend near the edge of the pond. Birds were singing and the spring bubbled in accompaniment.

Anderson escorted Marthey, who looked radiant in her pretty yellow dress. The green of her hat perfectly matched the ribbons decorating her skirt and bodice. But no one was looking at the dress or bonnet. Her smile outshone the sun.

After placing his daughter's hand in Watts, Anderson moved to his weeping wife's side and put his arm around her shoulders.

Eli stood tall and proud and stepped out of the woods with the tiny Lizzie on his arm. She had found the perfect dress in her mother's things. It was a sky blue that mimicked the color of her big round eyes. Her future sister-in-law had cut it down and made it fit her slight build. Refusing to wear a fussy hat, Queen had insisted on dressing Lizzie's soft brown hair with ribbons to match the dress.

Jeff's mouth gaped open as his bride approached with her father. Watt elbowed him in the side and he closed it. Jeff had never seen Lizzie look so beautiful.

A slight cloud cover had dimmed the sun, but the ceremony went by as if all the participants were n a dream. Vows and rings were exchanged. Marthey's plump hand was adorned with the narrow gold band belonging to Carol. Lizzie's thin, long fingered hand felt awkward with the widest and heaviest ring Jeff could find in two counties.

Lizzie looked into her groom's eyes and the clouds parted.

Nannie saw Lizzie shiver and experienced a chill up her own spine as the preacher said, "Husbands you may kiss your brides."

Amid much laughter and back slapping, Anderson whistled loudly.

"Food and drink is ready at our place. Let's go eat. I'm hungry."

Nannie seemed to think that a double wedding required double food. There were two identical tables. Each had a white bride's cake surrounded by autumn leaves. The neighbors and friends all contributed food, and Ruthie brought gallons of apple cider. There were baked pumpkin, fried apples, and many delicious foods for everyone to sample.

Eli and Anderson had slaughtered a pig and it was roasting on a spit in the side yard. Mack was in hog heaven. The boy sat watching it cook with his mouth watering.

Jack escorted Aggie to the wedding and to no one's surprise, he got the ring from Marthey's bride's cake. Watt got the darning needle, which signified blessedness but Marthey's piece of cake was empty. She was relieved. At least she didn't get the button for fickleness.

Lizzie laughed loudly when she bit into the coin for prosperity and Jeff didn't care that his piece was empty. He had all he wanted standing beside him.

Ellen pulled out one of her mother's quilts and Betsy found the orange marmalade house cat, Sweet Pea, who had been allowed to attend the weddings because she would bring good luck.

The young single women lined up around the quilt and Anderson tossed the cat in the middle. The cat seemed content to be there and laid down to take a nap. After several shakes of the quilt, it appeared the lazy cat wasn't going to move. So with much laughter, Watt, Jeff, Ed, and Sam each took a corner of the quilt and shook it as hard as they could. The big orange cat dug her claws in and refused to let go. Trying again, they shook the quilt six feet in the air. The quilt settled back down and with a tremendous squall Sweet Pea dashed off the quilt and hid behind the corner cupboard. In her beeline for a safe haven, she brushed against Aggies's arm.

Aggie shyly looked up into Jack's eyes and saw the twinkle there.

Proud as two peacocks, Eli and Anderson sat on the porch, smoking their pipes and listening to the music from Jim's fiddle and the stamping of feet as first one reel then another was played.

"Welcome to the family, Taylor," Eli said with an unfamiliar joy in his voice. Then with a knot in his throat, "I hope Carol is smiling in heaven as she sees our families united. Not once but twice."

With his own emotion showing in his voice, Anderson responded, "I'm sure she is, Eli."

Lizzie, along with Lady's daughters, Princess and Countess, moved in with Jeff and the Taylors until their house was finished.

Marthey moved into the Ownby household.

The two women had been in and out of each other's homes so often through the years that it felt natural.

Eli moved his personal things to the loft and gave the newlyweds his bedroom.

Queen and Maggie still occupied the left hand loft and Jack, Craig, and Henry, the right. Now Eli slept with his sons and it felt right.

Elopement

Overwhelmed by the Ownby-Taylor double wedding, Aggie didn't want a big celebration or a lot of attention. So, one day in November, Jack slipped away from the farm and the couple quietly went to get their license and got married.

That evening close to suppertime, the newlyweds stepped into the parlor and asked Eli to please assemble the family. Once everyone was there, Jack presented Mrs. Andrew Jackson Ownby, while Aggie blushed.

Emmy and Marthey were delighted. They loved the shy young woman and knew she would be a good wife to Jack. Ed and Watt teased Jack until his face turned scarlet.

Queen jumped up and hugged her new sister until Aggie couldn't breathe and then turned to Henry and said, "Run, get Lizzie and Jeff. They need to be here, too."

Thirteen-year-old Maggie was a bit confused. A lot had changed in her home lately but she showed grace and charm in welcoming Aggie to the family. Aggie sensed a kindred soul and an innate shyness in the girl and put her arm around her and hugged her tight.

"What are your plans, little brother?" Watt asked with a smile.

"We haven't really made any. Aggie's Pa said we can stay there until we do."

"I won't hear of it. Aggie you pick out a place here on the property, and I'll go tomorrow and file with the clerk," Eli thundered.

Lester and Baxter were put to work the next day. As the brothers cut trees, Jack fashioned logs to build the floor for his own home.

There would now be two smaller houses in addition to the larger farmhouse.

Eli found an old bed and moved it to the tool shed for the newly weds.

"It's not fancy," He told the couple, "but it's dry and warm and most of all it's private."

Aggie blushed and Jack said, "We'll be fine here, Pa, until our house gets finished."

Eli left them alone and Aggie proceeded to try to make the tools shed homey.

Jack stepped out the door and his toe kicked something hard. A pile of rocks was stacked in the door opening.

He heard a childish giggle and spotted Henry running away.

"Come back here, Henry McGrew Ownby."

"There's your rocks, Jack. I'll bring ya some more," the youngster yelled over his shoulder.

He remembered the fun at Ed's wedding.

Family for Christmas

Polly came from Shelbyville with her family to celebrate Christmas. A foot of snow had fallen and as Roy pulled the buggy up into the yard, Polly smiled to see a pup chasing a half grown calico cat through the snow and up the large oak tree in the front yard. She turned to Roy, laughed, and commented, "Nothing changes here on the farm."

When Sam and Ruthie arrived on Christmas Eve Day with their children, Eli's entire family was under one roof for the occasion. All eleven children, their six spouses, and all nine grandchildren were together.

Pallets of quilts filled the corners, and every bed was crammed to capacity.

Little Nan's ankle had never mended properly. She used a crutch and couldn't navigate the loft stairs. Eli made a big show of carrying the little girl up the stairs so she could sleep with her cousins.

The fires were burning down to coals and the candles and lamps had all been snuffed. Eli made slow progress through the house quietly waking everyone sixteen years old and older. It was time to go to the barn.

Jack and Polly had already told Aggie and Roy about Eli's tradition and they were awake and dressed and waiting by the front door.

Watt had difficulty convincing Marthey to exchange their warm bed for the cold snow outside.

Craig and Queen came down the loft stairs together and Craig grinned at Watt, "Henry's nose is out of joint because he can't come with us, but Mack's snoring is rattling the rafters."

Queen reported, "Maggie said she will keep an eye on the little ones until we get back."

"That's nice of her." Sam said. "That means that Tennessee can come with us."

Ruthie was big with her seventh pregnancy and Tennessee refused to leave her side.

141

The group left the house and trudged through the snow following Eli's footsteps.

Ed and Emmy were already seated in the hay.

Eli dozed in a corner.

The quiet night was shattered by the jingle of sleigh bells.

Watt opened the door and exclaimed, "It's snowing again. Here's Jeff and Lizzie and Anderson and Nannie are with them."

Jeff helped Lizzie down from the sled and told Watt, "When Lizzie told us about listening for the animals to talk, Ma and Papa wanted to come too."

Eli stepped around his oldest son and beamed, "Glad to have you, Anderson. Maybe this will be the year the animals bless us by speaking."

The newcomers entered the barn, and Nannie and Lizzie spotted the women all grouped together in an empty back stall.

Eloise was lowing softly and swishing her tail.

Nannie headed for the stall with Lizzie right behind just as Emmy came out putting on her cloak.

"Keep your coat on, Lizzie. We need to go boil some water and find some clean rags. Ed, you and Watt come with us to help carry supplies."

Ruthie was in labor and too far along to go back to the house.

Eli was ecstatic and the other men gathered around Sam to give him support while the groans and soft-spoken words came from the back stall.

Steaming hot water was brought and the kettle disappeared in the stall behind seven skirts.

"It's midnight. Christ's birthday," Eli said from the door as he surveyed the snowy sky.

His proclamation was accentuated by a loud "Moooooo" from Eloise and loud grunts from Lester and Baxter.

Then came a loud baby's cry and Tennessee's low contralto:

"Go tell it on the mountain

over the hills and everywhere.
Go tell it on the mountain
that Jesus Christ is born."

Polly held the tiny infant wrapped in a warm blanket and smiled as she handed her brother the bundle. "Here's your new daughter, Sam."

Sam examined the infant. His face appeared spellbound. Childbirth still awed him.

Looking to his father with tears in his eyes, he quietly said, "Pa, may I introduce Anna Jane Ownby?"

Christmas Day

The procession of buggy's and buckboards was impressive Christmas morning as it rolled into the churchyard. The only family members missing from the Ownby clan were Ruthie and little Anna Jane.

Ruthie wanted to attend, but Tennessee insisted she stay in bed and not expose the new baby to the wintery air.

Sam took Gracious along with the other children.

Anderson and Nannie arrived shortly after the Ownby's with Callie and Betsy. Ellen and her husband Joseph were in the buggy behind and Lizzie and Jeff brought up the end of the Taylor procession. Creed and Jim were staying home with their wives and children.

The Taylor clan was invited to Christmas Dinner at Eli's home after services.

Watt, Ed, and Sam had gone early that morning and brought back a huge Cedar tree which was already installed in the parlor, ready to be decorated.

After a moving Christmas service, the two families made their way back to the farm.

Queen went straight to look in on the new mother and baby.

The other women went to the kitchen while the men took the children to decorate the tree.

"Why is you backside so big?" Maggie asked Polly as they were carrying dishes of food to the table.

Polly laughed loudly, set her dish down, and hugged her baby sister. "That's the latest fashion, dear. It's called a bustle."

"Why?" Maggie insisted.

"Because it is stylish and sets her apart, you silly little girl," Queen said with distain, then pouted her best pout. "I asked Pa to buy me one but he refused."

Still pouting she flounced out of the room.

After sundown, their guests had left and the Ownby's were still digesting the tremendous meal they had devoured.

Eli was sitting in front of the parlor fire surrounded by his grandchildren.

In her position as Woman of the House, Marthey signaled to Watt that it was time to open the presents. The children had been begging for an hour and the youngest were starting to nod.

Ruthie had already taken little Anna to feed in Marthey and Watts room.

Everyone had a present from someone. After the men opened their shirts and handkerchiefs; the boys their whistles and toys; the women their Sunday hankies and the girls their hair ribbons, Polly asked for everyone's attention.

Roy stood next to her with his arm around her waist.

"Roy had an exceptional crop this year and did very well at the horse market in Nashville. While we were there, we decided to share our good fortune and bring presents to everyone for Christmas. The years have been difficult since the war," Polly choked and turned her head as tears filled her eyes.

Roy cleared his throat and said, "Enough doom and gloom. John, you and Henry start bringing in those tow sacks from the back porch, and let's get this party started."

The boys brought in two large burlap bags and went out for more as Roy and Polly handed out gifts.

Starting with the youngest there were fashionably dressed dolls for the girls under ten and fancy painted wooden horses for the boys.

Gracious had not been forgotten and hugged her Rag Mammy Doll the rest of the night.

The older boys were excited by the shiny new Jack knives and almost wore them out opening and closing them to see how they worked.

For Ruthie's daughter, Mary Smith, there was a small bolt of lace and for Maggie a lovely fur collar that matched her dark brown hair.

"Oh my goodness!" Queen's scream drew everyone's attention. "Thank you, big sister."

She could barely be seen in the crowded room as she pranced up and down with what appeared to be a wooden rabbit trap bouncing on her posterior.

Shocked, Polly exclaimed, "Queen, you are supposed to wear the bustle under your skirt not out in public view!"

The men had congregated on the porch where they were examining various tools and implements that were their gifts. A large roll of thick leather for harness repair for Watt; a new anvil for Ed's forge; brass hames for Sam and Jeff; a set of steel lathe tools for Jack and Springfield carbines for Craig and Mack.

Queen's squeal brought them back into the parlor.

"Why, sister, there's just family here. What harm can it do?"

The men laughed out loud and the women hid their giggles behind their hands. The children didn't care and went on playing with their new toys.

They soon lost interest in Queen's silliness, and the other women showed off their presents.

Ruthie held up a beautiful silk parasol with an ebony handle. The silk was the color for a summer sky.

Aggie received crimson stockings and her face almost matched the color of the yarn.

Marthey charmingly fluttered her lashes behind a pale yellow fan and Emmy inserted a carved tortoise shell comb in her chestnut hair.

"Open yours Lizzie," Queen prodded her sister. "Let us see what you got."

Lizzie slowly opened the small package and lifted out a shiny bauble. As she held it in her hand, she was speechless and blinked back tears.

It was a delicate Chatelaine brooch.

Made from brass, it had an intricate pendant depicting cherubs in a garden. Suspended from the pin were five linked chains. Each chain held a useful housekeeping tool. There was a tiny pair of scissors, thimble, pincushion, vinaigrette and a tiny mesh coin purse.

"Oh Lizzie how elegant that is," Emmy cried out.

Lizzie looked up at her big sister with questioning eyes. "This is too extravagant, Polly. You must take it back."

"You deserve something extravagant, little sister. Wear it with pride for all you have accomplished with this family."

Eli had reclaimed his rocker by the fire and was watching his family with his heart full of love.

Roy approached and laid a long narrow parcel on Eli's knees.

Surprised, Eli slowly peeled away the cloth to find a Sharps Sporting Rifle, unlike the carbine he was accustomed to.

Ed took the weapon from his father and sighted down the long barrel. He looked at Watt and said, "I wish we'd had these during the war. Even a sack-o-bones like you could have hit something."

CHAPTER 11

MOTHERHOOD, 1874

Flooding

"Get up, you lazy louts!" Watt yelled through the loft door. "The creeks almost out of it's banks."

Craig jumped out of bed and started for the door to go check his beloved pigs.

"Put your pants on first, brother." Watt laughed in spite of the seriousness of the moment.

"Henry, go wake Ed and Jack and tell them to meet us at the pig sty. We need to get those hogs moved to high ground. Mack you come with me."

Eli woke from his bed in the corner. "What can I do, son?"

"You stay here in the dry, Pa. Marthey has breakfast started and coffee is on. Later you can gather the eggs since Mack is going with me. Let's go boys, we got work to do."

It was only two in the morning, but Watt had been unable to sleep. It had rained off and on for two months and the ground was saturated and creeks and ponds were full, leaving the water nowhere to go. When this thunderstorm started around midnight, Watt knew the creek was in danger of overflowing, so he went to check the livestock. For the first time in his memory the pig sty was filling with water.

Ed and Jack were already at the sty when Watt and the others arrived. All but one high corner was already flooded and the fence had washed out closest to the creek. Lanterns were hung in the trees giving very little light.

Ed was trying to rope a section of fence that threatened to topple over and wash downstream. They needed whatever they could salvage to contain the hogs in the dry corner.

Craig despondently told Watt, "The sows are all here but there's only four pigs left. The others must have drowned and floated away."

"Mack go help Ed and Jack get that fence in place. And be careful, don't fall in the creek."

Through the thunder, Watt heard a yell and a splash.

"Mack's in the creek," Ed yelled and grabbed the rope and jumped in to help his little brother.

Jack and Craig secured the other end of the rope to a sturdy oak.

"I have him," Ed hollered. "Quit fightin' me, boy."

Watt strained to see what was happening but the rain was falling too hard.

"Pull us in," came the call from the creek, and they heaved on the rope, pulling two dead weight bodies against the raging water.

Henry brought a lantern down close so they could see. Ed was holding a limp Mack in his arms and trying to keep them both above water.

When Ed and Mack were finally dragged into the mud of the pig sty, Watt asked, "Is he alive?"

Panting heavily and spitting out floodwaters, Ed said, "He's breathing. I had to knock the dumb pie eater in the head to keep him still."

Jack rolled Mack over on his stomach, and coughing raggedly the big teenager sat up then vomited creek water on Jacks boots.

Jack jumped back and fell on his backside in the mud.

Mack glanced around and saw the worried looks on his brothers faces then spotted the sows high and dry and secure.

He looked at Watt and smiled, "Reckon Marthey's got breakfast ready yet?"

Watt laughed and took his little brothers hand and pulled him to his feet. "The hogs are secure. Come on y'all, let's go feed this boy. Then I think we all need a bath."

Twins for Will

In April, the rains finally stopped and the fields dried enough to get the crops planted.

A rider rode up to Eli's door one day as Queen as helping Marthey with the wash. The wet weather had set back springhouse cleaning by a month and everyone was ready for sunshine and clean curtains and bedding.

Queen removed her bonnet and tucked a loose strand of hair behind her ear as she went to the front of the house to greet the visitor.

"Hello," she said pertly.

"I have a telegram for Mr. Ownby," the young rider blurted out.

"Oh, my. A telegram. Which Mr. Ownby are you looking for? We have several. There's my Pa and four of my older brothers and then there's Mack and Henry if you wanna count them."

"Mr. E. C. Ownby. It's from Huntingdon over in Carroll County."

"That's my Pa. He's helping in the fields today. I can take the telegram for him."

The young man snarled, "I need someone to sign for it so I better go find your Pa or one of your brothers."

Queen's eyes flashed fire. Every hair on her head stood out. She put her hands on her ample hips, and the horse stepped back and whinnied.

"How dare you say such a thing to me, you fool! I can sign for the ridiculous telegram. I can read and write, perhaps better than you can. Of all the nerve." She stepped up and ripped the telegram from the rider's hand. "Now what do I need to sign?"

Dumbstruck and a little frightened the man handed her a clipboard and a pencil. "Sign right there on the first empty line, please, ma'am."

149

So in her best penmanship she wrote *Queen Ann Matilda Ownby*; handed him the clipboard and pencil; stuck her tongue out and flounced into the house.

She placed the telegram on the foyer table; retied her bonnet, and went back to help Marthey hang out the wet washing.

The telegram laid there for two days before Eli noticed it. He broke the seal with trembling fingers. Telegrams never brought good news, only bad tidings. With his heart beating in his throat, he remembered the last one he received. In 1864; telling him Watt had been captured and sent to Camp Chase prison.

Heart still thumping erratically, he opened the folded page and smiled a huge smile as Watt joined him in the foyer.

"Why so happy, Pa?"

"Your Aunt Minerva gave birth to twins last week. A boy and a girl and all are healthy. Your Uncle Will is a lucky man."

Tomatoes

In August a few days after Queen's nineteenth and Henry's thirteenth birthday, Lizzie was gathering tomatoes in her garden.

Jeff refused to start with a one-pen house and had built an impressive two-pen house with foyer and loft as well as the detached kitchen. He had kept his promise and the doublewide window in the kitchen overlooked the hill where her mama was buried.

During construction, Lizzie couldn't get an answer from Creed regarding the extended hearth and stone wall adjacent to the cooking fireplace and brick oven. But the question was answered when to her surprise Jeff bought a cast iron wood stove.

She had refused to use the "contraption" as she called it, when it was first installed. But every day she discovered that it was more convenient and versatile than cooking in an open fireplace.

They had moved into the house in early spring, and Lizzie had a full garden as well as a small patch of herbs by the back door.

She stood and rubbed her lower back. Her extended abdomen looked almost grotesque on her tiny frame.

"I've been a mother to the children for twelve years," she lamented to one of the speckled pups who were never far from her feet, "but I don't know if I can face this now."

The pup just cocked her head, whined, and rolled over for a belly rub.

Lizzie laughed at the puppy and bent to pick up the basket of tomatoes and patted the pup's head, when the pain hit. She screamed. The puppy squealed and bolted. The tomatoes spilled in the dirt. Then it was over.

Breathing deeply, she retrieved the dusty tomatoes and slowly walked toward the house. Sitting the basket on the table, she sat in a chair and wiped her brow and hoped someone came by soon.

She was seldom alone these days. One of her sisters or sisters-in-law came to check on her everyday. Where were they now?

Another contraction doubled her over in the chair. These were different from the small pains she had been having for the past week. She knew how the process went, after helping so many babies and mothers the past few years. But no one had explained how it felt.

As she watched her belly become rock hard, she took another deep breath and rubbed her stomach and crooned, "Mama will hold you soon, my little one. All in good time. But let's wait for help to come."

A horse neighed as the contraction ended and Lizzie rose to look out the door.

Henry was getting down from his pony and said, "Morning, Lizzie. Marthey and them are picking beans this morning and sent me to check on you."

Then he noticed her pale face and the sweat on her forehead. "Are you alright, Lizzie?" He started toward her, frightened.

"Get back on that horse, Henry. Go tell Nannie Taylor it's time. Then go tell Queen and Marthey. And find Jeff. He's cutting wood near the north pasture. Go, little brother. Hurry."

Lizzie had rinsed the tomatoes and laid them on the windowsill and was wiping off the table, when Nannie and her daughters arrived in a rush.

"There's a kettle of water heating and a clean stack of rags by the bed." She told her mother-in-law.

Nannie burst out laughing. "I swear, girl. Are you sure you need our help?" she said as Queen, Maggie, and Emmy stepped on the porch.

"Of course I do. Those tomatoes aren't going to cook themselves. Queen, you and Maggie get them stewing in the pot so they don't ruin."

And then the pains started in earnest and the kitchen floor flooded.

Four hours later with very little fuss and muss, Lizzie presented Jeff with a son they named Maurice Lester and eight quarts of tomato catsup.

Maurice and Carol

In September, on Lizzie's twenty-fourth birthday, she took her son to visit her mother's grave.

"Mama, I'd like you to meet, Maurice Lester Taylor. He's the very best birthday present I've ever had. He's a good baby and sleeps peacefully in the new cradle Jack made for him. I was so scared before he came. Not of birthing him but afraid how I would feel about him and Jeff. We haven't been married a year, yet and so much has changed. Jeff and the family built us our own house and it was odd with just the two of us at first. But Nannie Taylor and the girls come by almost every day, and I visit Pa and the others often."

She chuckled, "Queen comes every morning to check on the baby. The hardest thing has been eating supper at the Taylors instead of cooking for the family at home. Nannie is so accustomed to cooking for her family and lives close so it makes sense to help her in her kitchen. But it's so different."

Lizzie sighed and looked around at the lovely hill her mother was buried on.

"I love the Taylors and Marthey is happy being Watt's wife. She manages the house well and gets on good with Queen, and Maggie and the boys all respect her. Everyone is doing good. Maggie and Henry are still in school. Mack stopped last year when he turned fifteen. Him and Queen are still hungry all the time. Watt and Ed tease them about it, but they don't understand how hungry those two were during the war. Pa is good too. He lets Watt and Ed run the farm, and Jack has more responsibility since he married Aggie."

Maurice started to whimper. Lizzie unfastened her dress to let him nurse as the sun shone on them both.

"I didn't mean to stay so long, Mama, but I wanted you to see my baby. I loved Maggie and Henry when they were babies and I would do anything for them, but now I understand how you loved all of us so much, and why you kept having us."

Craig and Dora

Eli was feeling ill so Craig took the newest litter of pigs into market. He had them caged in the back of the buckboard and was glad the mules were in no hurry to get to town. It was a beautiful, crisp, September day and at the moment there was a lull in the harvest chores. Knowing this respite wouldn't last, and there would be no time to himself for the next couple of months, he was enjoying the slow ride into town.

At the crossroads, he heard a rumble. He looked up to see a horse and buggy running straight toward him at break-neck speed. He stopped the buckboard in the middle of the intersection hoping to slow the runaway. The big wagon accomplished its purpose and the beautiful Tennessee Walker slowed enough for Craig to throw his leg over the horse, grab the driving line, and pull the horse to a stop in one smooth motion. The walker snorted and pranced but stayed in place.

Seated in the buggy was a pretty young woman wearing a pale green dress, the same color as her eyes. A large, floppy, straw hat with matching ribbons sat atop her ash blonde curls. She was flushed and breathless, holding one end of the broken driving line. Craig was angry and yelled, "What do you think you're doing? Trying to kill me, yourself, or this horse?"

Trying to straighten her hat and regain her composure, she looked over the buckboard and saw the mules and the pigs. She retorted, "I'll have you know, Lancelot is very well behaved. He was spooked by a rattlesnake back up the road, and I lost the reins. What would a pig farmer know about horses, anyway?"

Craig took out his knife and made a slit in the end of the broken line and reached up and tried to remove the other end of the line from her frozen fingers. She resisted but he yanked it from her hand. He made a slit in the end of the free leather piece and looped the uncut free line through both slits, splicing the two ends together and forming a temporary drive line.

Finished with his repair and not in the least insulted by her remark, Craig removed his hat and chuckled. "Let me introduce myself, Eli Craig Ownby, Jr., the best pig farmer in these parts. My Durocs are sought far and wide, ma'am, as well as my family's horses, cows, and chickens. I've not seen you in town before. What's your name?"

"My name is Madora Turner. Now, if you would be so kind as to move your pigs out of my way, I have a dressmaker's appointment in town."

Smiling to himself, Craig handed her the repaired line, replaced his hat, and said. "You're J.E.'s little sister aren't you? I'll send your father a bill for the repair." Then smiling broadly, he climbed up on the buckboard and started the mules back on their trip to town. Still at their easy pace, the big slow wagon blocked the road. The buggy containing the feisty little lady was forced to follow along at the mules pace. The last time Craig had seen her, she was in short skirts and pigtails.

When the road widened at the edge of town, Dora whipped up the walker and passed Craig with a cheery little wave of her gloved hand.

He could only scratch his head and stare in admiration. She really did know how to handle Lancelot and she sure was a pretty sight to behold.

Queen Pines for John

Near Christmas, Eli received a letter from John Christopher wishing everyone a wonderful Christmas. He was living in Arkansas; married and had a baby son. They had a nice farm on Arbuckle Island in the Arkansas River, but he was considering moving. Some of his cousins had moved to the Red River in Texas and the area sounded promising. John closed his letter with best wishes for everyone and a special regard for the "little Queen of my Heart."

After the letter had been passed around and read by everyone, Queen snuck it in her pocket and slipped out of the parlor and quietly climbed the loft stairs.

Lizzie and Jeff had come for supper, and Lizzie saw Queen leave.

Once in her room, Queen lay down on her bed and re-read the last sentence of the letter, "to the little Queen of my Heart," and her eyes filled with tears.

Remembering that hot summer day twelve years ago when the dashing cavalry lieutenant rode into the yard. Eli had introduced her as Queen Ann Matilda Ownby.

His brown eyes twinkling, Christopher squatted on the porch to bring himself face to face with the six-year-old Mattie. "It's very nice to make your acquaintance, but that's too many names for such a little girl. What shall I call you? I know. I'll just call you Queen, because you are the Queen of my heart."

Mattie had died that moment and Queen was born.

A year later, during the darkest days of the war and surrounding battles, he had returned. Like a hero from a storybook on his tall grey stallion.

Queen dozed and dreamed she was a grown woman, riding Shadow Dancer nestled in John Christopher's arms.

Lizzie opened the loft room door and found her sister asleep with the letter lying on her breast.

Queen awoke with a start and stuffed the paper under her pillow.

"What was that?" Lizzie asked.

"Nothing important. Just a list of things for Pa to get in town," Queen said trying to hold back her tears. The tears won.

Lizzie removed the letter from under the pillow and sat on the edge of the bed.

"Oh, Lizzie, why couldn't he come back for me instead of going off and getting married?"

Her heart breaking for her sister, Lizzie reached out to take her hand. "You were just a child, Queen, and he was a grown man, being nice to a little girl. Did you really think he would come back for you?"

"I always dreamed about it. From that first day when he called me Queen of his heart."

Lizzie's practical side came through and she lost her patience. "Well, he's married now and has a family. So you had best forget about him and find someone else to dream about."

"But Lizzie, wives die. All the time. So I can still dream. Besides, she's probably just some squaw or bar trollop."

CHAPTER 12

CRAIG AND DORA, 1875

Wedding Feast

In January of 1875, Martin Turner spared no expense in celebrating the union of his daughter and the "Pig Farmer."

At twenty-three, Craig was fully grown and equaled his brothers in height. Wearing his first ever, store bought suit he stood tall, proud and handsome next to his beautiful bride.

Dora's gown had been made by the best dressmaker in Woodbury from ivory silk satin. The full skirt had a pleated flat front with a very large bustle back. The bustle was exaggerated by rows of fine lace. Falling from the pseudo backside was a five-foot train trimmed around the edges with the same lace.

The deep square neckline highlighted Dora's snowy white bosom and the front lacing emphasized her tiny waist.

Together they made an impressive couple standing in front of the massive marble mantle in the Turner's opulent parlor.

The music was lively; food was abundant and champagne flowed freely.

Tennessee offered to help serve and little Gracious watched the crowd from a quiet corner.

Watt took a glass of champagne from Tennessee's tray and offered it to his sister. Lizzie put out her hand palm forward and turned her head. It was her first experience with the bubbly wine and she vowed it would be her last. "No thank you, Tennessee. I'll have some plain cider though."

Watt laughed and kept the glass for himself.

Hearing Queen's girlish giggle, Lizzie frowned. "You should warn Queen about that wine. She's making a spectacle of herself!" she said with distaste.

"She'll be fine, little sister," Watt replied, looking out over the crowded room. "At twenty, she's too old for you to mother."

Watt noticed Lizzie shiver. "Are you cold, sister? Want me to go find your wrap?"

"No, I'm not cold. I just saw young Wilbur giving Gracious a cookie in the corner and was overcome with memories."

Before he was old enough to talk, Wilbur had been found in the woods along side his dead mother and infant sister during the war. He had been taken in by the Hoppers who owned the Mercantile in Woodbury. When he turned fourteen, the Hopper's allowed him to earn extra money by serving at parties and town functions. No one knew his story or that of his parents. It was assumed they were runaway slaves from down south.

Lizzie shivered again. "Have you noticed Wilbur watching us?" she asked.

"I can't say I have," Watt observed as he spotted the young man pouring Queen yet another glass of champagne. "Relax, Lizzie. The boy doesn't remember anything about that day. He was too young. Smile! This is a happy occasion."

Lizzie scowled at her brother, hiccupped and snapped, "I can't relax, nor can I forget that day. I'll never forget the sound that man's head made when it hit the floor, or the smell of that poor woman's back where it had been torn by the whip. I can't forget the damn Yankee soldiers laughing as they poured honey on the stair case. I don't understand how you can forget so easily." She hiccupped again and walked away, her shoulders slumped and tears in her eyes.

Watt stood watching his little sister; wishing he had the power to remove some of her pain when he saw her facial expression change. Jeff was approaching with little Maurice in his arms and the radiance of Lizzie's smile dulled the chandelier in the parlor. Watt was happy and thankful his sister had someone to help her heal.

He scanned the room looking for Marthey. He finally spotted her in a huddle of women surrounding Aggie who was expecting her first child at anytime. Seeing the group all together, he frowned; hoping his sister-in-law wasn't ill or in labor.

Marthey separated and moved toward her husband just as Ed claimed Emmy's hand and danced her across the room.

The shy smile and faint blush to Aggie's cheeks made Watt think the women had simply been teasing Aggie about her upcoming motherhood.

Marthey joined him and as they moved onto the dance floor, Watt spied Eli in serious conversation with Dora's father and he assumed it was about the property Eli was giving the newlyweds.

As the music faded, Queen's laugh rippled through the crowd. She was holding court, surrounded by young men, all taking delight in her charm.

Another toast was in order and Jack held his glass high to deliver it. "As the youngest of the four older brothers, I was always the one assigned the chore of keeping the wood box full. I think I was about twelve before I knew my name wasn't 'Get Wood.' When I left home and got married, I knew that chore would go to the next oldest brother. So here's to my little brother, 'Get Wood the fifth', and his lovely bride Madora."

Applause and laughter swept the room as Craig raised his glass and made eye contact with Mack. "And here's to 'Get Wood Six'."

Babies

The next morning Craig and Dora arrived at Eli's home and found everyone busy with chores, except a very subdued Queen. She was sitting in the parlor with a wet rag on her forehead. "I think I danced too much at your celebration last night," she said quietly, "but what a lovely time I had."

Craig held back the laughter that bubbled to his lips and said, "Yes, sister, it must have been the music and dancing," as he exchanged a knowing look with his new wife.

Dora and Craig accompanied Eli around the property and Dora admired Emmy and Aggie's homes. They were modest compared to the substantial Turner home, but Dora remembered her childhood home which hadn't been so opulent. She had been content as a child and knew that it was the people who occupied a house that made it happy or sad.

As they walked along the creek near the very back of the property she spotted a lovely clearing across the creek. "That's where I want our house," she cried out. "In those threes and Lancelot's stable and paddock can go right over yonder."

"But sweetheart," Craig said with caution, "It's on the other side of the creek."

"So," she answered, "build me a bridge."

She then sat on the ground and removed her shoes and stockings; hiked up her skirts and waded across the shallow water. She stood in the clearing with her arms out wide and turned in circles. "Yes," she called across the creek, "this is the place."

Eli laughed and called out to her, "It's yours, Miss Dora." He turned to his son and said, "Know when to give in son, and you'll always be happy. Let's go make it legal and put Jacks skills to work building you a bridge."

Dora rejoined the men and put her shoes back on and they strolled leisurely back toward the main house. Maggie came running up out of breath.

"Aggie's having her baby. Jack's gone for Mrs. Willis. Craig, go get Nannie Taylor and Lizzie."

Eli said, "Son take your bride back to her mother's, I'll go for Lizzie and Nannie."

"Don't be ridiculous, Mr. Ownby," Dora said, not at all maidenly. "I've helped foal too many mares to be shocked by a birth in my own family." And she strode purposefully toward Jack and Aggies's house.

The other women were glad to have Dora's level head in attendance. Although all of the women were experienced in birthings, each one was different and there was comfort in numbers.

Aggie had an easy delivery and little Debra was presented to her father who announced her perfect in every way before he laid her in the fanciest cradle any of them had ever seen. The canopy was carved inside to resemble clouds so the baby had something to focus her eyes on. Once they could focus.

Craig and Dora moved into their new home at Easter time. Fruit trees were starting to bloom and the fields were sprouting green.

Mack went to town the day after Easter and brought back a postcard from Polly in Shelbyville;

Dear Pa and family,
March 28, 1875

Delivered safely a baby girl yesterday morning. She's beautiful and we named her Beluah. Will write soon.

Your loving daughter and sister
Polly

Eli was delighted with the news of his twelfth grandchild. He was unsure why, but it had been twelve years since the birth of Polly's last child and this baby girl seemed like a special blessing.

Spring and early summer were extremely busy as the women worked their gardens and preserved the fruits and vegetables as they ripened. Maggie had finished school in the spring and tended the children while their mothers worked separately or in groups.

Queen and Marthey were cutting cucumbers for pickles one hot July day and Queen was talking incessantly about the latest fashions she saw in a magazine in town.

"Go fetch my Ma." Marthey nonchalantly interrupted Queen while she continued to peel a cuke.

Queen stopped in mid-peel and said, "Why? We know how to make pickles."

"I don't need her for the pickles." Marthey smiled, then just as quickly frowned and stopped her peeling. She laid the knife and the cucumber in the bowl and looked at Queen. "It's time."

"Oh my goodness gracious. Of course. I'll go get her and Betsy and Callie and Lizzie, and I'll stop to get Emmy and Aggie and..."

"Stop talking and just go, Queen," and the prospective mother picked up the knife and resumed her peeling.

Watt and Marthey had discussed names for the baby the night before. Tradition called for the first born to be named for the grandparents. A baby girl would be easy. Since both grandmothers were named Nancy, it was a forgone conclusion the child would be named that.

But a boy child was more complicated. Eli Craig and Anderson Lafayette were harder to put together.

Before mid-night, July 9, Anderson Craig Ownby slid into his grandmother's waiting hands but had to wait to be introduced to his two anxious namesakes, until his father had examined him thoroughly.

Letter from Texas

12 August, 1875

To my own cousin, Eli,

I received a letter from your half brother Joe last week and he gave me you're address. I haven't heard from you since we moved to Texas.

Pa and Uncle Neddy wrote each other often but with both of them dead we don't hear much about you anymore.

My brother Doc, writes occasionally. He sees Joe, K and Will now and then. Pa choose a good place for us to settle here in Lamar County. It's right close to the Red River in a nice little town called Paris.

I was the jailer here for a while, but after Pa died I went into business with my brother John in his carpenter shop. Our littlest brother Bart, married a girl from here and has started working with us. The town is growing and there is plenty of work.

Joe writes that things are bad in Tennessee. He says the carpetbaggers are controlling prices and that times are hard for the farmers.

I want to tell you, cousin, that Texas is still free and a man can live and raise a family without government interference.

I hope to receive a letter from you soon.

R. D. Ownby

Watt read the letter to Eli without interruption. He thought his father had dozed off into one of his many naps. Folding the letter quietly he rose to leave Eli in peace.

"Sit back down, son. It's time we talked about the future," Eli said with his eyes still closed.

Watt sat back down. He had learned to be patient with his father. Jack had told him about Eli's injuries at the hands of the Yankees, and Watt understood how the loss of a portion of his manhood could play havoc with his mind. Eli had periods when he seemed to be out of touch with his surroundings and disconnected from whomever he was talking to.

The spells were brief and never violent and each family member took them in stride.

Eli opened his eyes and they were clear and bright blue. "The family is growing, son. We need more room if you boys are going to prosper. This part of the country is being beaten down by the government."

Watt sensed that his father was getting his dormant wanderlust stirred up again. Eli had the same expression as when they moved from Marshall to Cannon County.

"What do you have in mind, Pa?" Watt asked cautiously.

"Nothing in particular, son. But R.D.'s letter got me to thinking. Texas is still open country. Your mama and me talked about going with R. D. and Uncle J.J. when they moved before the war." Eli stopped and lit his pipe. Watt did the same and both men took the time to get the tobacco glowing red.

Watt broke the silence. "Why didn't you?"

Eli chuckled and said, "Your mama wouldn't hear of it. That was the only time she ever refused me anything. She said she wasn't moving across the country away from civilization to be killed by a bunch of Indians. So she agreed to move here."

Watt laughed at the thought of his gentle mother arguing with her husband.

Eli looked his son square in the eye and said clearly, "But I've still got a hankering to go to Texas."

Dora

The autumn sun was weak and the day was brisk as Maggie helped Marthey make lye soap in the side yard.

Maggie stirred the hot lard while Marthey added the lye and water. Both of them were concentrating on the task as Queen ran up the path from Emmy's house. She was yelling as loud as she could.

"Dora's having her baby. Ya'll come quick while I go get Lizzie and send for Nannie Taylor." As she made her announcement, she turned back toward Lizzie's house.

Marthey looked at the half-finished soap and frowned. "Dora always makes things complicated," she said under her breath. Then louder she said, "Maggie, go fetch Nancy from Emmy and when Lizzie gets here, bring Maurice and I'll tend the children and make dinner for the men." She went back to stirring her soap before it could separate.

It was only mid-morning so Queen was surprised to hear Jeff's voice when she stepped onto Lizzie's porch.

"You are being unreasonable and stubborn, Lizzie." She heard him say angrily. Queen had never heard Jeff raise his voice or speak harshly to anyone. Curious, she stood quietly to hear what the argument was about. A dirty work boot flew out the door and missed her head by mere inches.

"Jefferson Lafayette Taylor, I refuse to have those dirty boots in my clean kitchen. Get them out of here right this minute or I will burn them in the fire pit."

"Good heavens, woman," Jeff declared, "you would try the patience of Job."

He nearly knocked Queen off her feet as he stomped onto the porch in his stocking feet and hobbled over the rough ground toward the barn.

Queen stuck her head around the door facing and saw Lizzie holding a fireplace poker with the other one of Jeff's work boots dangling from the end.

"What are you doing, sister?" Queen asked irritably as she took the boot off the poker and set it on the porch next to its mate. "Dora's having her baby. You need to get over there. I'll take Maurice to Marthey. Dora's hollering something awful." She picked up the toddler and put him on her hip and headed to the barn as Lizzie grabbed her bonnet and rushed out of the kitchen.

Queen found Jeff in the barn brushing down one of the horses. "Go get your mama. Dora's having her baby and we need Nannie Taylor." Then over her shoulder, she said, "And your boots are on the porch ya might wanna put 'em on first."

When Lizzie arrived at Dora's cabin, they found Emmy and Aggie trying to calm a hysterical Dora. "Don't touch me!" She was screaming. "Get away from me."

She had been such a calming presence during Aggie and Marthey's deliveries and had been cheerful and good natured throughout her pregnancy.

But this woman was a stranger to all of them.

"I want my mother. Get out of my house. All of you. This is my house, and I don't want you here," she screamed.

Aggie quietly tried to settle her and Emmy spoke more sharply. "Now, Dora, you need to calm down. You aren't helping the baby when you act this way. Get up and walk around the room between the pains. Come on get up off that bed."

"You walk around the room. I'm not a brood mare. You can't lead me around the paddock. I'm not having this baby until my mother gets here..... ohhhhhhhhhhhhhh."

Lizzie set her mouth in a frown; took a deep breath and entered the room. Queen slipped in behind her.

"Madora Ann Turner Ownby, quit acting like a spoiled child. You are a woman grown, who is fixing to be a mother. Now hush up and breathe through the next pain."

Dora's eyes flashed, but before she could respond the women saw her swollen belly tighten into a hard knot and in unison all said, "Breathe, sweetheart."

Mrs. Turner and Nannie Taylor arrived simultaneously, and Elizabeth Turner stepped back to allow Nannie to precede her then went to her daughter's side and held her hand and spoke softly.

Nannie examined the hysterical and exhausted Dora and said to the room. "It's going to be soon. Is everything ready?"

"Yes, ma'am," Maggie said from the doorway.

"Ahhhhhhhhhh....." came the scream from the bed.

"Push hard, Dora!" Was the reply from the foot of the bed.

"It's a girl. You have a beautiful baby daughter." Nannie held the newborn high as the little girl let out a howl to rival her mother's earlier screams.

At the baby's cry, Craig tried to enter the house, but Lizzie stepped in front of him. "Wait. Let us get them both cleaned up then you can see your daughter and your wife." Then seeing her father on the porch, she said, "Pa, get him out of here for a while."

Eli laughed and said, "Come on, son, let's go to the barn. I got something to show you."

As Craig reluctantly followed his father, the women all knew that the "something" was some of Nannie's hard cider Eli kept just for such occasions.

When Lizzie, Emmy and Aggie went to retrieve their children from Marthey, they found her sitting on the porch; rocking A.C. while Debra and Maurice played in the dirt. She was surrounded by 100 drying cakes of lye soap and singing the "Bonnie White Flag."

CHAPTER 13

CENTENNIAL CELEBRATIONS, 1876

Another Double Wedding

January 1876 dawned with the promise of great things to come for the country. It was the beginning of the 100th year of American Independence.

On January 13, Ruthie gave birth to her ninth child. A baby girl they named Sarah Frances.

Six days later, Nannie and Anderson hosted another double wedding. Caledonia Ann Taylor married Benjamin Youngblood and Mary Elizabeth married John Lafayette Campbell.

The day was cold and snowing so only those close by attended, but it was a beautiful wedding and Callie and Betsy were both radiant as they joined their husbands in wedlock. The party after was a pleasant break from the dreary winter chores.

In mid-February, Eli received a letter from Joe:

Dear Eli,

I hope you are staying safe and well this winter.

Will and me have almost completed our winter repairs and are thinking about what to plant this spring.

K and Jane have a new son, born on the ninth. They named him John Wesley. K is still attending those KKK meetings and is all worked up about the Presidential election this year. He says the KKK are determined to see a Democrat in office next year.

Will and Minerva also have a new son, born two days after little John. They named him Guy William. That makes six children under the age of six here in the house.

Tabitha insisted we sell Papa's silver service to hire a housekeeper to help Minerva with household chores.

Brother, you were correct about our sister. She has been a blessing through these rough times. I believe her blindness has sharpened her other sensibilities. When I have troubles she always has a solution.

Eli, stay well and write your baby brother soon.

Love to all,

Joe

A Quilt for Eli

On a beautiful sunny day in March, Queen and Maggie were beating the bed quilts preparing to store them for the summer.

"This old quilt of Pa's is falling apart," Queen complained to her sister as another hole appeared in the quilt top. "All of our better quilts were destroyed or stolen during the war. Let's make Pa a special quilt for Christmas?"

Maggie smiled and said with excitement, "What a wonderful idea, Queen. We can use Emmy's quilt frame."

"A name quilt. We will embroider each family name on a block and Pa can sleep warm, surrounded by family every night."

"What names should we include?"

Queen cocked her head and started to count on her fingers with an intense look of concentration on her face. "How many grandchildren are there?"

Maggie was using her fingers to count also and said, "I count fifteen at the moment, but if you add us children there are twenty names. What about husbands and wives?"

Queen frowned, "This is getting complicated. Let's finish cleaning these quilts and then talk to Lizzie and the others to see what they think."

The women loved the idea and Marthey liked it so much she approached her sisters about making one for her mother and father. Since both Carol and Nannie had given birth to eleven children, they decided to make twelve blocks for each quilt. Each block would have a child's name, their spouse if they had one, and their children. In the center of the quilt would be a block with the parent's names. The blocks would be joined with scraps from their outgrown or worn clothing.

"I'll make the blocks for Mack and Henry. I can do yours too, Queen. Since it was your idea and you are so busy with the babies," Maggie commented one day.

"Oh, sister, you don't have to do that. I can make mine."

"But I enjoy embroidery much more than you do, and it won't take me long. Please let me do this for you."

"All right, if it will make you happy," Queen said as she headed into the kitchen to find something to eat.

Lizzie didn't realize she was holding her breath until it exploded out of her mouth.

Maggie looked over at her big sister and grinned. "I knew that would please you."

Lizzie had been concerned since the beginning. Between Queen's lack of needle skills and her quirky sense of humor, the Lord only knew what the girl would have done. "Polly and Ruthie both promise to have their blocks here in time to add them," Lizzie replied.

The Taylor women had a different perspective. Ellen had lost her young daughter last year and four of the eleven Taylor children were dead. Everyone wanted them included so it was decided to use black fabric embroidered in white thread on the blocks for, Fate, Virgil, and the two babies who had died.

Emmy offered to keep the makings at her house so Eli and the Taylors wouldn't see the pieces and ruin their surprise. Throughout the summer and early fall, the women spent every spare moment embroidering or piecing the quilts. Of course, Lizzie and Marthey made double blocks, one for each of the quilts.

4th of July

In July, every county seat had a special 4th of July celebration. A joint resolution of the House of Representatives, concurred by the Senate:

"Recommends on behalf of the Senate and House of Representatives that the people of the several States assemble in their several counties or towns, on the approaching Centennial Anniversary of our National Independence, and that they cause to have delivered on said day a historical sketch of such county or town from its formation, and that a copy of the sketch may be filed in print or manuscript in the Clerk's office of the county and an additional copy in print or manuscript in the office of the Librarian of Congress, to the intent that a complete record may thus be obtained of the progress of our institutions during the first centennial of their existence."

Chores were done early and the picnic baskets were loaded and packed. Dora sat impatiently in her buggy hitched to the prancing Lancelot. Queen sat beside her holding little Lela on her lap.

Emmy and Maggie were perched atop the buckboard seat. The bed was loaded with food for dinner; preserves and pickles for contest entries, and Marthey and Aggie holding their babies.

Billy and Andy at eight and seven years old sat proudly on their ponies waiting to ride to town with their father and uncles.

Craig and Mack had loaded the big wagon with pigs and chicks to sell at the livestock show and decided they would both go in the wagon. A string of colts and fillies was tied to the back.

Watt, Ed, Jack, and Henry were astride their horses and everyone was impatient to be off.

"Where's Pa?" Henry asked. "I saddled Storm for him and I thought he was right behind me."

"Go see what's keeping him, little brother," Watt said, but before Henry could turn his gelding toward the barn, Eli came galloping down the path waving his hat over his head.

"Happy Birthday, America!" he yelled and pulled the reins on Storm making him rear.

A collection of gasps came from his children but the horse settled back down, and Eli smiled like they hadn't seen him smile in years.

"Let's roll," he called as he turned Storm Cloud toward town.

"We are a band of brothers
Native to the soil..." he sang at the top of his lungs.

Watt and Ed exchanged a look and then shrugged, smiled, and joined in while Marthey frowned and held her baby close.

"Fighting for our liberty
With treasure, blood and toil
Hurrah for the Bonnie Blue Flag
That bears a single star."

Spirits were still high when they reached Woodbury. The town was crowded. Red, white, and blue bunting hung from every window. Tents and awnings were everywhere. Wagons, horses, and people filled every available space.

They had agreed to meet the Taylors near the square but needed to unload the livestock and food entries first.

Craig and Mack headed for the livestock sales barn and Emmy drove toward the tables set up for women's interest. Watt, Ed, and Jack went to enter the horse races.

Billy and Andy stayed close to their grandfather who went to the square after tying the horses to the back of Mack's wagon.

"Now don't you boys get so excited you sell our ride home." He laughed as Craig and Mack frowned.

Not surprising, Dora was already at the square and Lancelot was receiving his due in admiration. The noisy crowd was making the Walker jittery and the buggy kept rocking backwards and forwards.

"I'll take Lela and go find Lizzie," Queen said as her father helped her down from the unstable buggy. She looked pale, dazed, and a little queasy. The wild ride with Dora and Lancelot had frightened her more than she wanted to admit. Eli helped her settle on the lawn under a tree to wait for Lizzie or any of the Taylors.

He then took his grandsons to the mercantile. Young Wilbur was behind the counter and Eli handed him two pennies and chuckled. "Give these two boys anything they want. Up to a penny's worth."

Mrs. Turner approached Dora and scolded, "Get that animal out of this crowd before someone gets hurt. You should know better, young lady."

"Yes mama," Dora replied with contrition and slowly moved him forward.

"And don't try to enter him in the buggy race either. That's no sport for a young mother to participate in." Mrs. Turner yelled after her spirited daughter.

Lizzie found Queen under the tree just as Marthey and the others walked up.

Soon there was a large crowd of Ownby's, Taylors, Turners, and Knox's as Emmy's family joined them.

They all watched the races, which none of their party won. They watched the parade and listened to the military band. Friends and neighbors came and went all day for the various activities.

Eli purchased several farm journals with articles and advertisements from the Centennial Exposition being held in Philadelphia.

All of the livestock sold and so did the two litters of pups from Princess and Countess that Jeff brought to sell.

The men all paid close attention to the political speeches. The candidates had already been selected for the upcoming Presidential election. Democrat Samuel Tilden was opposing Republican Rutherford B. Hayes. If the response of the crowd at the July 4th celebration in Cannon County was an indicator, Tennessee would support Tilden.

The talk about town was of the massacre of General George A. Custer and his army out in Montana Territory. The news was on everyone's mind.

Watt was sitting under the tree with A.C. on his lap while Marthey packed away the leftovers from dinner. He was sipping lemonade and watching his baby boy sleep the sleep of the innocent.

Mack and Henry came up all excited about what they called the Little Big Horn.

"I wanna go fight those heathen Indians," Mack said. "Is there any chicken left?"

"I could go too. Couldn't I Watt?" Henry said with enthusiasm.

Swallowing his fear for one brother and the desire to laugh at the other, Watt took a sip of lemonade and slowly said, "Henry, the army doesn't allow fifteen-year-olds to join, and Mack, they don't serve fried chicken as rations out west."

Lizzie overheard the conversation and walked over. She stretched her arms up as high as possible and took both of her little brothers by the ear lobe.

"I will not hear any more nonsense about either of you joining that Yankee army for any reason. Now go find Pa. He's wandered off somewhere."

"Yes, ma'am," they replied in unison.

More from habit than consent.

Susan B. Anthony

"What in tarnation is this?" Eli said as he slammed a farm journal down on the parlor table. "Are these women hysterical? First, they took this country to war with their abolitionist nonsense, and now they want to vote. Don't they have better things to do than be rabble rouse and manufacture problems where there aren't any? It's not natural I tell you; it's just not natural."

Watt and Ed exchanged a look across the table; they had both seen the article and had hoped that their father would be more engrossed in the newest inventions and innovations like the new so called telephone. They were hoping he wouldn't see the article buried in the back section under women's news.

The article read in part:

"Those attending opening ceremonies of the Centennial Exposition in Philadelphia on July 4, were shocked after Richard Henry Lee read the Declaration of Independence for this 100th anniversary of our great country's independence. A congregation of determined women marched down the aisle. Miss Susan B. Anthony took the podium and began to speak.

"While the nation is buoyant with patriotism, and all hearts are attuned to praise, it is with sorrow we come to strike the one discordant note, on this 100th anniversary of our country's birth. When subjects of kings, emperors and czars from the old world join in our national jubilee, shall the women of the republic refuse to lay their hands with benedictions on the nation's head? Surveying America's exposition, surpassing in magnificence those of London, Paris and Vienna, shall we not rejoice at the success of the youngest rival among the nations of the earth? May not our hearts, in unison with all, swell with pride at her great achievements as a people: our free speech, free press, free schools, free church and the rapid progress we have made in material wealth, trade, commerce and the inventive arts? And we do rejoice in the success, thus far, of our experiment of self-government. Our faith is firm and unwavering in the broad principles of human rights proclaimed in 1776, not only as abstract truths but as the cornerstones of a republic. Yet we cannot forget, even in this glad hour, that while all men of every race and clime and condition, have been invested with the full rights of citizenship under our hospitable flag, all women still suffer the degradation of disfranchisement."

After listing several grievances Miss Anthony concluded,

"And now, at the close of a hundred years, as the hour hand of the great clock that marks the centuries points to 1876, we declare our faith in the principles of self-government; our full equality with man in natural rights; that woman was made first for her own happiness, with the absolute right to herself—to all the opportunities and advantages life affords for her complete development; and we deny that dogma of the centuries, incorporated in the codes of nations—that woman was made for man—her best interests, in all cases, to be sacrificed to his will. We ask of our rulers, at this hour, no special favors, no special privileges, no special legislation. We ask justice, we ask equality, we ask that all the civil and political rights that belong to citizens of the United States, be guaranteed to us and our daughters forever."

Miss Anthony preceded to hand Senator Thomas Ferry, a Republican from Michigan, the printed Declaration of Rights of the Women of the United States."

"Settle down, Pa," Ed said calmly. "Nothing will come of this. Miss Anthony will get married and have babies and will lose all interest in trying to vote and meddle in men's business."

"You're probably right, son. No right-thinking mother would want to neglect her children for men's work. I wonder what Marthey is fixing for supper."

The Election

On November 7, 1876, Eli and his sons went to town to vote. This was Craig's first presidential election and he recognized the responsibility.

The men had discussed how best to cast their votes. The Reconstruction policies in place all across the South were crippling the small farmer. Inflated prices for goods from up North coupled with low prices for local crops kept the small farmers from thriving.

Samuel Tilden a Democrat from New York seemed the most likely choice to break the Republican stranglehold on the South.

A few days after the election, Jack returned from town with a copy of the Nashville Tennessean. The front page declared Tilden the winner with 51 percent of the popular vote, which gave him 184 of the needed 185 electoral votes.

"It appears as though our man won," Craig told his brothers and father.

"If I was a bettin' man, I wouldn't bet the farm on it, son," Eli said despondently. "Those damn Yanks in Washington will try to find a way to stop Tilden from getting that last vote. You mark my words."

Eli was proven correct. The Republicans accused four states of using intimidation to discourage freeman of color from voting. The Democrats accused the Republicans of ignoring or destroying Tilden votes.

Florida, Louisiana, Oregon, and South Carolina each submitted two differing sets of returns. Congress was charged with making a final decision.

More Letters from Texas

Dear Eli and family,
December 15, 1876

Was so glad to get your letter and am happy to hear you all are in good health. I received a letter from Joe. He said the political climate in Tennessee is bad. I will tell you, Eli, we do not have those problems here in Texas. You should come down here and see for yourself. Land is plentiful and cheap.
Stay well cousin, and write soon.

Your own cousin
R. D.

"Ya know, Pa, we might look into moving. With the family growing and prices so low here in Tennessee there might be better opportunities in Texas," Watt told his father after reading the letter.

Land prices had fallen from 15 dollars an acre in 1868 to ten in 1876. Property value was decreasing and crop prices were at an all time low.

Eli told his eldest son, "Let's wait to see how this election turns out. If Tilden wins, things might get better."

Two days later another letter arrived from Texas.

Sgt. Watt Ownby   *17, Dec 1876*

I recently had conversation with a neighbor W.C. Reeves. When he told me he was from Cannon Co I mentioned your name from knowing you in the war. He tells me you sold him his roan stud from which he has built quite a reputation as a horse man. I remember that chestnut mare you had at Stones River as well as your brothers Appaloosa.

To get to the reason for this letter, another neighbor of ours is selling out and moving farther west. Reeves and me thought you or one of your brothers might be interested. We would both be proud to call you neighbor.

The land around here is selling for $4 an acre and there is plenty to be had.

Regards to you and yours
Zeke Skaggs

Naughty Anna Jane

December 23, Lizzie gave birth to David McAlister and just had time to add his name to her quilt blocks.

Christmas of 1876 was a truly merry occasion. Polly came with Roy and their children to stay a few days. Sam and Ruthie brought their children along with Tennessee and her children, Gracious now eight, and fifteen month old Martin. Watt and Marthey insisted on hosting this year and the parlor was overflowing with tables set up in the hallway and bedroom.

After dinner Eli, Anderson, and the other men were gathered on the porch smoking their pipes while the women cleared the table and the young mothers tended their babies.

Queen was trying to gather the older children together and was heard to mutter, "This is like trying to herd a bunch of chickens."

The men were sitting quietly smoking, rocking, and enjoying the peace and quiet of the glooming as big flakes of snow drifted down quietly. Suddenly a shower of small rocks pelted the men on the porch and they heard a little girl's giggle.

Without even looking up, the men yelled in unison, "Stop that," as she bent over and picked up another handful of small river rocks and threw them. She giggled again and ran away just as Queen came around the corner of the house and grabbed her.

"Anna Jane Ownby, what are you doing?" she scolded the three year old as Sam sighed and rose from his chair. In a stern voice he said, "Anna, you know better than to throw rocks. Come with me."

The child stuck her thumb in her mouth and hid in the folds of Queens's skirt. Sam repeated, "Anna. Come with me NOW, young lady." He stepped off the porch and scooped up his daughter and headed toward the side of the house.

The men on the porch smiled, glad it wasn't one of their children and happy to leave any punishment to Sam. Wails could be heard coming from the wood shed. Queen started in that direction ready to give her brother a tongue lashing when the cries were replaced with giggles. Realizing the punishment wasn't severe; Queen went into the house to find the rest of the children as Sam came out of the shed with his daughter in his arms. He deposited her on the porch and she primly stood there.

"Do you have something to say?" Sam, prompted little Anna.

"I apopalize," she said contritely and then turned and clasped her father's leg with her little arms.

Eli wanted to laugh but restrained himself and instead held out his arms to his granddaughter and said, "All is forgiven, Anna. Come give Papa Eli his Christmas hug." She ran to him and threw her arms around his neck. He stood and said, "Let's go see if we can find you some gingerbread."

Everyone moved into the crowded and overly-warm parlor. The children all had presents to open. Eli, Anderson, and Nannie were sitting by the fire with various grandchildren climbing in and out of their laps.

As the excitement started to die out, the children drifted off to play or nap in the corners. Marthey and Queen pulled out two large paper wrapped packages. Marthey handed her package to her mother and Queen laid hers on her father's lap.

The paper was removed revealing the quilts. Anderson stood and looked over her shoulder and placed his hand on her shoulder. Nannie ran her hand over the black squares of her gone but not forgotten children. Tears filled her eyes and she whispered, "Our babies William and Mariah."

She looked up at her husband and Anderson touched the quilt with a finger tip. "Our sons lost to war, Virgil and Fate."

Nannie placed her hand over his and squeezed tightly as tears flowed from both of their eyes.

Eli closed his eyes as he fingered the embroidery on the quilt. He placed the center block, to his lips and said, "I love you Nancy Carol Winstead Ownby."

A chill passed over Lizzie, replaced immediately by a warm glow, and she knew her mother was present and approved.

CHAPTER 14

TEXAS, 1877

John Murrell

In January, there was still no declared winner of the Presidential election held in November. Congress had established a special commission of five Republican senators, five Democratic US Representatives and five Supreme Court Justices, whose sole responsibility was to render a decision on the disputed electoral returns. The appointed Justices included two Republicans, two Democrats, and one non-political Republican.

The swing vote belonged to Justice Joseph Bradley whose final vote produced an eight-to-seven ruling to award the electoral votes to Rutherford B. Hayes.

Threats of a Democratic filibuster at the official count in Congress put both sides in fear of another Civil War.

Watt and Craig wanted to see for themselves the land in Texas. So in the midst of the political upheaval in the Capitol they prepared to leave.

"I should be home before the baby comes," Watt told Marthey as he kissed her and hugged A.C.

"Make sure there is a sturdy house and a good barn for Lancelot," Dora told Craig, "and don't you let anything happen to him, Watt Ownby," she addressed her brother-in-law without taking her eyes off her husband's face.

Everyone was gathered for the brother's departure and excited about what the outcome might be of the trip to Texas.

Ed slipped some extra ammunition into Belle's saddlebag and whispered to Watt, "Shoot straight if you have to shoot, ya sack-of-bones." Then he clapped Craig on the shoulder. "Mind our big brother out there. The Sarge always knows what to do."

The women were crying and anxious about the two men being gone for months but were trying to be brave. After all they were just going to Texas; they weren't going to war.

Eli was last to say good-bye. While Craig checked the packs on the mule, Eli told his eldest son, "Tell R.D. and John Smith that I hope to see them soon. You are as good a judge of land as Ed is horseflesh. Take your time and don't get horn swaggled. And get home in time for spring planting. God go with you, son."

Watt and Craig mounted Belle and Easter and waved goodbye to their family and led the pack mule down the road toward Texas.

They stopped the first night and stayed with Polly and Roy in Shelbyville and after a good hot breakfast left the next morning.

Late on the second day, they neared Lewisburg and Watt stopped on the road and sat looking at a farmhouse set back in the trees.

"Do you remember this place, little brother?" he asked.

"Can't say that I do, Watt. Why do you ask?"

"This is the house that Pa grew up in. All of us children, except Maggie and Henry, were born about a mile south of here."

"I barely remember when we moved but not much before."

The two-story log house was still standing and appeared to be occupied. Chickens scratched in the yard and laundry was flapping in the wind.

"Granpa Neddy always said he bought the place from one of the John Murrell gang."

Watt laughed and continued, "He used to scare us into behaving ourselves by pointing to a large bloodstain on the parlor wall. He said, a gang member got cocky with Murrell one night and Murrell shot him. He said the outlaw's ghost punished little children when they were bad. It used to scare Sam and Polly something awful."

"Did you ever see the ghost?" Craig asked reluctantly, a shiver running up his spine.

"No. I never did. But I was always well behaved," and he laughed long and hard.

Watt recovered his breath and took a sip of water from his canteen then started on down the road.

Craig glanced back over his shoulder; gave another shiver then pulled up beside his brother.

Watt started talking again. "It's said that Murrell's father was a travelling preacher and his mother took advantage of her husband's absence and helped her son become a thief."

"Really? How did she do that?"

"Well, the story I heard was, the preacher tried to tame her from her wild ways, but he couldn't break her from walking and dressing the way she did, with her breasts free; her hips swaying back and forth, and her skirts molding to her thighs as she moved. He couldn't change her so he took to the road preaching the gospel. He was afraid that if he stayed home he would waste all of his time on her constantly, like a boar in rut."

"I don't understand. How did her immodest ways make her son a thief?"

"When the preacher was away, she offered lodging to any passing strangers. It was easy for Murrell to steal from those who stayed the night. They would be worn out from the sport she gave them in her bed. It's said the men could sleep through an earthquake."

Natchez Trace

Two days later, the men turned south onto the Natchez Trace. Once called "The Devil's Backbone" the trace had been used for centuries as a path by animals, Native Americans, and later European explorers and traders. Used as a main thoroughfare until the steamboat traffic opened the Mississippi River, the trace was still the best road from Nashville to Natchez.

The brothers spent six days along the trace, crossing the Tennessee River by ferry and camping close to the "stands" or Inns that dotted the trail.

Twice they indulged in a hot supper at a stand but preferred to sleep under the trees instead of sharing a dirty bed with five or six strangers and any creepy varmits that might inhabit them.

At Maben they left the well-worn road and made their way due west to Greenville, Mississippi where they took another ferry across the Mississippi River.

"That's sure a lot of water," Craig commented in awe of the one mile expanse of rolling water.

"Yes it is. I had heard about it, but I never knew it could be bigger than the Tennessee at flood time. But I swan, it sure is," Watt said shaking his head.

"I hope we don't fall in. I don't think I could swim that, do you big brother?"

"No, Craig, I don't think I could and Belle couldn't either. Could ya, girl?"

He patted the horse's rump as she fidgeted when a steamboat blew it's whistle.

The men had been on the road for two weeks and decided they—the horses and the mule—could benefit from a night under a solid roof.

Greenville had been completely gutted by fire during the Siege of Vicksburg. When the city fired on a Union gunboat going down the river, the boat landed and retaliated by burning every building in town. Returning veterans and those citizens who survived, rebuilt the town and everything was new.

The men found a clean, inexpensive hotel with a good stable and enjoyed a hot meal while Belle, Easter, and the mule had oats for supper.

The ferry ride across the river was uneventful and almost boring. They landed safely on the Arkansas side and refreshed and optimistic, continued west across the southern part of the state. Making good time, they covered 200 miles in six days.

They arrived at the Red River a few miles east of Texarkana and took another ferry across. The river was down so the crossing was quick and much smoother than the other two had been.

Craig remarked how easy it was to the ferryman.

"That's so right now, boy. But you oughta see her during the spring rains. She swells and rolls like a woman in labor. And 'bout as predictable." The grizzled old man spat brown tobacco juice into the murky rust-colored water.

"How far is it to Paris?" Watt asked.

"Lemme see," the old man spat again. "Ya gotta go through New Boston...then Clarksville. That's after you cross the border at Texarkana. It's 'bout a three day ride. Problly clos' ta hunderdt miles."

Texas

The ferryman was correct. It took Watt and Craig three days to reach Paris, Texas. It was a bustling town of around 3,000 inhabitants. Building was going on everywhere they looked, but they found the Ownby Carpentry Shop with no problems.

Eli's cousins made them comfortable and welcomed them to Texas.

John Smith Ownby had five children and Robert Donald had three. John's wife cooked the men a delicious supper and R.D. gave them a bed to sleep in.

Talk at supper was about the election. Watt and Craig had no news and their cousins shared the latest newspapers, which stated Congress was still at a stalemate.

"Pa says the Republicans will find a way to declare Hayes the winner," Watt told the group.

"I'm afraid your wise father is right," R.D. said. "Joe writes that K is still riding with that KKK group. We don't have those problems down here. There hasn't been a need for it. Where is this land you boys are going to look at?"

"It's in the southeast corner of Grayson County. A place called Pilot Grove. A neighbor of ours moved there after the war and wrote to say there was some good land for sale cheap. Craig here is all ready and chomping at the bit to buy. If it suits."

The next morning, R.D.'s wife loaded their saddlebags with biscuits and bacon for the trip and Watt and Craig headed due west. They spent the night outside Bonham and made it to Pilot Grove late the next afternoon. They asked for directions to the Reeves place at the general store.

Arriving at dusk, Reeves was glad to see them and his wife fed them a hot meal. They bedded down in the barn.

"Your mama did throw some good stock," Watt told Belle the next morning as he looked over the roan stud and his various offspring. "But so do you." He patted her neck and added another scoop of oats to her feed.

Belle's dam was Watt's mount during the war. He had raised her from a foal and she had seemed to read his mind. Wounded in the Battle of Stones River, she had managed to carry Watt to safety through heavy shelling. Destroying the animal was one of the hardest things he had ever faced and he had never forgotten Molly.

Belle had the same characteristics as her mother and according to Reeves, so did the roan stud.

Lost in reminiscences, Watt jumped when Craig touched his arm.

"Breakfast is ready then Reeves wants to show us that farm that's for sale."

The farm was a nice piece of land and looked remarkably like their farm back in Tennessee, except the hills weren't as tall. There was a house with a well and an open barn out back. Pastures and fields had been cleared, and a shallow creek ran through the property, bordered by tall and stately pecan trees.

Watt and Craig walked over the fields and Watt dug his fingers in the dirt. He smelled the earth and nodded his head at Craig.

The white rock hills made a solid base for building stable homes and good blackland dirt for growing cotton, oats, and corn. He understood that tobacco wasn't grown much in this area, but there were other crops they could grow for cash.

It was a small holding of only eight acres, but the farmer was selling for $4.00 an acre.

"What do you think, big brother?" Craig asked Watt. They were riding around the surrounding countryside to get a feel for the area.

"I think it's good land and everyone we've met has been friendly. That farm is a good place to start if you think Dora would be happy here."

"Then let's go find the owner," Craig said. "I'll buy it, and maybe Reeves will look after it until me and Dora can get moved."

Craig bought the land, and paid Reeves two dollars to keep an eye out for squatters or outlaws, until Craig could return with his family.

Arbuckle Island

"We should take the northern route home, little brother, and stop in Arkansas to see John Christopher," Watt told Craig as they left Reeves' farm.

"Wouldn't that take us through Indian Territory?" Craig questioned.

"Reeves says there's been no hostility for a few years. At least not to the east, where we're going. If you think you can shoot straight, we shouldn't run into anything we can't handle."

They went north through Sherman and spent the night in a campground at the edge of Denison four miles south of the Red River.

The next morning, they crossed the river at Colbert's Ferry into the Indian Nation. They followed the newly constructed Missouri-Kansas-Texas railway, north to McAlester. They camped at night near jerkwater towns that had sprung up around the train water stops.

At McAlester, they left the rail bed and took the old Fort Smith Road east. This well traveled road took them through the valleys and around the Kiamichi mountains. The nine-day trip from Pilot Grove to Fort Smith was uneventful and enlightening.

Both men had envisioned the area as flat and dry. They were surprised to find it was anything but. Rivers and creeks wound through rocky hills and green valleys. They saw very few Native Americans and those they saw, were at the water stations.

When they arrived in Fort Smith, they stopped at the General Store to see if anyone knew John Christopher.

The proprietor knew John well and said he was highly regarded in the area.

"Go east along the river about four miles. When you come to a fork, follow the lower one. It joins back up with the river a little farther on, creating an island. You'll see a bridge crossing to the Christopher place. Tell him I got that calico his missus has been looking for and some pretty china buttons that match."

"Why don't I just take it to him? How much for the calico and the buttons?"

"Let's see. At seven cents a yard...there's twenty-two yards on the bolt...that's one dollar and fifty-four cents. And the buttons are fifty cents a card. But there's forty-eight buttons on the card. That's a total of two dollars and four cents, but since you fellers are friends of Christopher, I'll let you take the lot of two dollars even."

"That sounds like a good price," Watt said as Craig dug in his pocket to find some change. They paid the man and stashed the fabric and buttons on the mule and took the road out of town to the east.

They found the bridge easily and crossed to the island. It looked to be about fifty acres with cleared fields and pasture surrounded by towering pine trees. As they approached the house, John was leaving the barn.

He was surprised and delighted to see Watt, and he remembered Craig as a youngster. John and his wife had two little boys and another child on the way.

Watt and Craig gave a descriptive account of Grayson County Texas and the lieutenant was interested. He had been thinking about moving into Indian Territory where his wife had relatives, for a while now.

Craig presented Mrs. Christopher with the parcel of calico and John tried to pay him for the purchase.

Watt refused to accept payment. "It's small payment for all you did for our family during the war. Me and my brothers are much beholding to you for your help. Queen still speaks of you frequently."

"I didn't do anything any officer worth his salt would have done. But I'm sure Lucy is glad to get a new dress," John said and glanced at his wife who was smiling shyly.

She said, "Thank you very much, this will make up nicely for a new Sunday go to meeting dress and maybe a shirt for John, too." Then she turned back to the pot of stew on the fireplace hook.

The brothers slept in the barn where it was warm and snug, but they heard the wind howling outside. They planned to leave in the morning but when Watt opened the side barn door, the wind almost blew it out of his hand. Blowing snow, like he had not seen since Fort Donelson, hit him in the face. He shut the door quickly and told Craig, "Looks like we're caught in a blizzard, brother. I'll make my way to the house to see what we can do to help John. You saddle Belle and Easter so we're ready if he needs us to ride with him."

Head down to keep the pelting snow out of his eyes, Watt almost ran into John who was making his way to the barn. Yelling loudly to be heard over the wind, Watt asked, "What can we do to help, John? Craig is saddling our horses."

Once inside the barn, John hitched a team of mules to a sled and started piling it with hay. He told the brothers, "I need to feed, but there are three cows due to calf any time now, and we need to find them."

John drove the sled as Watt and Craig followed on their horses. He led them into a slight depression in the middle of the island. Surrounded by hills, it wasn't really a valley, but more of a shallow bowl that was somewhat protected from the wind. The snow was falling gentler there. "They should be here," John called out.

Craig spotted a cow surrounded by black specks in the snow close beside her. As the men proceeded toward the cow, an eagle swooped down from the sky and the crows flew away. The eagle didn't want to relinquish its find, but the presence of men and horses convinced him to abandon the newborn calf.

John stopped the sled by the cow. She was in obvious distress.

Watt checked on the calf. The little bull was fully formed but the membrane still covered his face except where the carrion birds had pecked out his eyes. The cow bawled louder and a tiny hoof could be seen under her tail.

"Twins!" said Craig.

The position of the protruding hoof alerted the men they must turn the calf or lose both mother and baby.

"Let's see if we can save this one" Watt commented as he threw a rope and caught the cow's back legs and dallied the rope to his saddle horn. As he backed Belle away the cow sank to her side in the snow.

"Craig sit on her head and hold it tight. John can you turn that calf?"

John had already removed his coat and was rolling up his shirtsleeves. He reached into the cow to reposition the calf.

The cow's loud bawls brought the other cows who encircled the birthing mother. They all bawled loudly as if giving moral support.

Craig struggled to hold her head down while Watt kept the rope taut.

After much slipping on the wet, frozen ground John got the calf positioned and with a final tug the little bull slipped into the cold snow.

Watt released the rope and Craig let go of the head and the cow stood and turned to sniff her baby.

John cleared the calf's snout and he bawled as his mother started to lick him all over. The little calf found his mother's milk and as he nursed the afterbirth delivered quickly.

The men threw out the rest of the hay in a wide circle to the waiting cattle and came back to the cow and calf.

John asked Craig, "Would you take the sled and the calf back to the barn so we can watch him for a day or two? If you don't mind I'll take your horse and me and Watt will go look for the other cows and herd 'em back into this bowl."

"I don't mind if Easter doesn't," Craig laughed. "What about this dead calf?"

"We'll drag it down to the bone yard behind that hill over there. Let the scavangers have it. Maybe that'll keep 'em occupied for a while."

Watt hogtied the newborn and laid him on the sled while John removed a long iron bar and a heavy axe from the front of the sled.

Craig headed back toward the barn and made quite a parade; two mules pulling the sled; a baby calf bawling loudly and a cow following behind, making her own noises.

Watt roped the dead calf and John mounted Easter. The iron bar stuck in his stirrup resembling the lance in a medieval tournament.

They deposited the calf in a hollow behind a hill. There were bones everywhere of other animals. The men knew that in a few days this little bull would be reduced to the same condition.

Watt and John found the other cattle quickly, all huddled together in a low spot down by the river. There were two newborns that were up and healthy and had mothered-up. The snow and wind was still blowing fiercely. The water was quite shallow at this watering spot and was frozen solid.

John took the axe and started chopping at the ice. Once he got it broken, Watt pried away chucks with a long metal bar. Soon the thirsty cattle were drinking their fill.

When Watt and John returned to the barn, they found the cow eating hay while the calf nursed.

Craig was lying in the corner of the stall unconscious. There was blood on his forehead and tricking from his mouth.

Watt bent over and shook him as Craig began to groan and tried to sit. "What happened, little brother?" Watt asked with alarm.

"The calf was lying down and I thought he was dead. I picked him up. I guess he was just sleeping and I scared him, 'cause he jumped out of my arms and startled me. I jumped back and must have hit my head on that low rafter. Damn! I think I bit my tongue off."

Lucy Christopher, was alarmed when the men entered the house supporting a blood-covered Craig. She put the baby in his cradle and cried out, "What happened?"

"He'll be alright as soon as the bleeding stops," Watt told her. "At least it will keep him quiet for a while."

Craig shot his brother a spiteful look and sat down hard in the kitchen chair. He was rolling his tongue around in his mouth trying to ease the pain, while his head dripped blood down his nose.

Lucy filled a basin with warm water and tore some rags to bind his head.

John turned to Watt and said, "I suspect he is in good hands now. Let's go finish unhitching the team."

"Supper will be ready when you men get back," Lucy told her husband.

She set the basin on the edge of the table. Lifting her skirts, she straddled Craig's lap and started to gently clean his bloody face and forehead.

He closed his eyes and tried not to wince when she wiped near the cut. The warm water felt good and was soothing. Lulled by her ministrations, he was starting to doze when he felt her breath on his neck.

Scooting up close to his chest, her full round belly pressed against his firm slim waist. She ran her fingers through his hair and down his jaw and neck toward the opening of his shirt.

He opened his eyes and her face was a fraction of an inch from his. As he looked into her dark brown eyes, he saw what could only be described as lust.

She wiggled in his lap suggestively and placed her hands on either side of his face and whispered, "Let me see your tongue. Ever since you gave me that material I've wanted to kiss you and say thank you."

Startled by her actions and by the growing warmth in his groin, he lifted her off his lap and held her at arms length. "Ma'am, John Christopher is like family to me and I think your stew is burning."

He stood her on her feet, and she looked at him with scorn as she picked up the basin and moved to the fireplace just as the door opened and John and Watt entered.

They both had to push the door closed against the wind and by the time they removed their coats and settled at the table, Lucy was dishing up the stew.

Neither man mentioned Craig's red face. Each assumed it was due to the bump on his head. Nor did they question his lack of appetite or conversation attributing those to his bitten tongue.

The storm lasted three days and three nights. Each morning Watt and Craig helped John feed the cattle and break the ice on the water hole. The other two newborns were strong and the cows had no complications.

On the fourth day, the wind died and the sun shone brightly. The men returned the penned up calf and cow to the herd and fed and watered the livestock. By noon, the ice was beginning to melt and the river was breaking up.

The brothers decided it was time to return home.

As they saddled to leave, John handed Watt a package wrapped in burlap and said, "Would you please give this to little Queen? I bought it right after the war and this is the first chance I've had to get it to her."

"I'll see that she gets it, John. Thank you for the hospitality and write us often."

As they crossed the still-snowy bridge, Watt looked back over his shoulder, grinned and told his brother, "At least we won't have to contend with blizzards in Texas. Come on, Bumpy, let's go home."

Homeward Bound

The brothers kept to a fast trot when they could and arrived in Memphis, Tennessee around noon on March 7. They had been on the road for nearly two months.

This time the Mississippi was rolling fast and furious and the ferry ride across was rough and long. Watt told his brother, "Let's get a hotel tonight and stable the horses so we can be fresh tomorrow for the long ride home."

"I'd rather get through town and just camp on the road. I want to get home and tell Dora about our new farm," Craig argued.

"A few hours won't make a difference. I want to find out if the election has been settled and Memphis has a good newspaper. Aren't you curious about what is happening in Washington?"

They found a hotel on Beale Street and stabled Belle, Easter, and the mule. Watt paid a few pennies extra to assure the animals got plenty of oats and a good grooming. Then they took much-needed baths and dressed in fresh clothes to go eat an early supper at the cafe on the corner.

The special of the day was pork with sweet potatoes and apple cobbler for desert.

It was a treat to have coffee that wasn't boiled over a campfire. As the men savored a last cup of coffee, the waitress cleared the table and Watt asked her, "Who's the President?"

"I guess I am, since I own this place. Did your supper not suit?" The middle-aged matronly woman replied with a puzzled expression.

Watt laughed and said, "I mean President of these United States. We've been on the road for months and haven't had any news."

"Oh," the woman frowned, "some Yankee scoundrel from Ohio. Names Hayes, I believe. Would you boys like another cup or coffee or some more pie?"

Patting his full belly, Watt looked questioningly at Craig, who shook his head.

"No, ma'am. I'm fuller than a tick on a redbone hound. That was an excellent meal. Thank you very much. But could you direct us to the newspaper office. I would like to read about this fella Hayes."

Following her directions, they found the Memphis Daily Appeal office. The clerk gave them copies of the last week's worth of papers and they took them back to the hotel to read.

"Well, little brother, it looks like Pa was right. The Republicans found a way to get Hayes declared the winner, but they had to give up Federal control of the south. They are recalling all US troops from the southern states and allowing the duly elected Democrats to assume the governors offices. So it appears to be a compromise," Watt stated.

"Go to sleep, Watt," a sleepy Craig grumbled. "I want to start early tomorrow morning. We need to get home."

"You're right, brother. I wanna get home before the baby is born." He rolled over and turned down the lamp and soon both brothers were snoring.

Riding hard with only short rests, the brothers covered the 275 mile trip from Memphis in seven days and arrived home late in the night of March 14.

The farm was dark and they stabled and fed the horses and the mule. Even the animals seemed to be glad to be home.

Craig bid his brother goodnight and said as an afterthought, "I hope Dora doesn't come after me with a skillet when I walk in."

Watt laughed. "Marthey might stick me with a knitting needle. See ya in the morning, Bumpy."

Watt quietly stepped up on the porch and opened the door to the foyer. His bedroom door was open and he could see Marthey lying in their bed. The light from the moon shone through the window and he could tell from her swollen silhouette that he was in time for the birth of his second child.

He closed the bedroom door and it squeaked softly. Marthey's gentle snoring stopped then resumed. A little head peeked up over her enormous mid-section.

"Papa?" little A.C. asked, still half-asleep.

"Yes, son. It's your Papa," he said as he crawled into the bed and snuggled with his still sleeping wife, his son, and his unborn child.

CHAPTER 15

TENNESSEE, 1877

Queen

The morning after Watt and Craig returned, Queen went down to the kitchen to find Marthey singing softly.

"Hurrah! Hurrah! for peace and home, hurrah!
Hurrah for the Bonnie White Flag
That ends this cruel war."

"When did Watt get back?" Queen asked, chuckling. She knew that was the only thing that would cause her sister-in-law to sing so early in the morning.

"Late last night." Marthey smiled her biggest smile. "Help me get breakfast finished. He's gone to help with the chores and then him and Craig want to talk to everyone about their trip." She continued to pat out biscuits as Maggie entered and grabbed an apron off the rack.

"Where's the milk pail?" Maggie asked.

"Watt's milking for you this morning," Marthey said.

"He's back?" the girl cried out.

"Yes. Came in late last night. He's sent Henry to fetch Lizzie. So you crack some eggs and let's get breakfast on the table.

Hurrah! Hurrah! For peace and home, hurrah!
Hurrah for the Bonnie White Flag
That ends this cruel war."

After breakfast was finished and the table cleared, everyone met in the parlor. The adults had settled in to hear about the journey to and from Texas while the children played in the corner. Lizzie and Jeff arrived and Watt grinned at his brother-in-law.

"I'm glad you are here, Jeff."

Jeff smiled and winked. "I was told I didn't have a choice."

Eli rocked slowly and when everyone quieted down he said, "Craig, do you have something to tell us?"

"Yes, sir," Craig stood, barely able to contain his excitement, "I bought an eight acre farm in Texas."

Gasps and whispers circulated through the assembled family. Most looked to Dora to see how she was responding. She was smiling broadly.

"I know it's small. But it was available and it will give us a base to build from in the area."

"When do you plan to leave?" Ed asked.

"Not until after harvest this fall. I figure we go in November and travel through the slow months, and get there in time for spring planting. And the sale of the crops will give us some cash for the journey and incidentals in our new home."

"Is there room for more of us?" Jack wondered as he took Aggie's hand.

Watt rose and Craig sat down.

"There is plenty of room. Grayson County is growing but is mostly rural down in the southeast corner. Pilot Grove borders Fannin and Collin counties and there should be no problem finding farms and homes for any who want to move. Reeves is on the look out for more property and once Craig is established he can look too." He paused then continued. "The land is good and the climate is warmer...and the politics are more to our liking. Texas isn't having the political problems that Tennessee is. The carpetbaggers haven't taken over like they have here."

"That's all I need to hear," Eli said. "I want to go as soon as possible. But, do tell us about your trip. Was it easy going and how long should it take with wagons and families?"

"We made pretty good time by going down the trace and there's good wagon roads across southern Arkansas. It took us less than thirty days so with wagons and the family it should take about three times that long. The weather wasn't bad for winter. I think Craig and Dora will be safe and have an easy trip."

Dora smiled again. She was excited about an adventure and starting a new life in a new place.

Watt continued, "We went the northern route through Indian Territory coming back. We stopped for a few days in Ft. Smith to visit John Christopher."

A loud gasp drew Watt's attention and he saw Lizzie take Queen's hand and squeeze it hard. Queen jerked her hand away from her sister and asked, "How is Lieutenant John? Is he happy?"

"He seems to be. He has a really nice place and two little boys and another on the way."

"What about his wife? What's she like?"

Watt didn't seem to know how to answer that question. He was more comfortable describing land quality and horse flesh. He looked at Craig for help and was surprised to see his brother blushing bright red.

Puzzled, he looked again at Queen. "She's nice. And pleasant. Seems to be a good mother. Makes a fine stew. John is fond of her."

"What does she look like, Watt?" Queen was getting impatient for answers.

"She's dark, with black hair and eyes. I think she has Indian blood. John mentioned she has relatives in the Nation."

"I knew it!" Queen burst out. "She's just some squaw he found in a tepee. He felt sorry for her and married her out of pity."

"Queen! That's enough," Lizzie snapped. "If you can't act like a lady, you are excused to the kitchen."

In a huff, Queen rose and exited the room leaving every mouth hanging open in shock.

Marthey rose and quietly commented, "I think I'll start dinner," and Emmy and the other women joined her, including Lizzie.

As they left, the men heard Dora whisper to Aggie, "What was that all about?"

Aggie shrugged. "I don't know."

Craig told Watt, "That reminds me. Where's John's present he sent Queen?"

197

"I'm not sure. It was in one of the packs on the mule. I don't know where it is. I guess we need to look for it."

The Storm

On April 3, Marthey delivered a beautiful baby girl they named Nancy Jane.

"There's too many Nancys, Nans and Nannies in this family already," Queen told the newborn as she cleaned her new niece with egg white and lard to make the baby healthy and to ward off evil spirits.

"I'm going to call you Jennie," she cooed with confidence then whispered, "and soon the others will call you Jennie too."

The crops had all been seeded, and the men were looking forward to a substantial harvest this year.

The tiny green sprouts were peeking through the soil when the sky darkened for two days. The clouds were so heavy and low, it appeared as though they would burst open if someone poked them with a stick.

On April 18, the rain started. Marble size hail beat down for ten minutes followed by sheets of water that the wind blew horizontal to the ground. Thunder and bright flashes made the animals skittish.

The men were moving the pig sty fences to keep the hogs on high ground, and Dora had moved Lancelot to the big barn so he could be secured safely. The creek was rising and for fear of being stranded, she took little Lela and went to the main house where the other women had gathered.

The men came for dinner at different times, ate, and went back to move stock or the many other chores to attend to in the storm.

Marthey was nursing two-week old Jennie.

Queen could be heard singing to the three toddlers in the loft, trying to get them to nap.

Emmy was explaining to her sons, once again, why they couldn't go outside and play in the swollen creek.

Maggie was quietly showing five-year-old Nancy how to hem a handkerchief for Emmy's birthday present.

The lamps were lit to brighten the gloom when a tremendous flash of lightening was followed by a loud clap of thunder.

Aggie screamed and collapsed on the floor.

Dora rushed in from the kitchen and bent over her prostrate sister-in-law.

"Aggie, darlin' are you all right?"

"Yes, Dora. I just fainted. But I do believe the baby is coming."

Dora sat back on her haunches and laughed loudly. "Well, at least we're all together. I'll go put some water on."

Emmy turned to her oldest son and told eight-year-old Billy, "You get your wish to go outside. Go find your Uncle Jack and tell him to go tell Mrs. Willis that it's time. Then you come straight back here. Don't stop for anything else. You hear me, Billy?"

"Yes, ma'am," and the boy took off out the door before his mother could change her mind or make him put on a coat.

Of course, Billy didn't come straight home. After he found Jack, he went to the barn and helped his uncle saddle Easter, then spent some time with the horses. Like his father, they were his favorite animal and he seemed to have Ed's eye for good stock.

Billy knew the women would be busy taking care of Aggie so he walked through the stalls patting and soothing the jittery horses. Talking to this one and giving that one a handful of oats.

As he was digging in the feed box near the mules stall, he spotted a piece of burlap behind the box. He pulled it out from between the wall and the box and could tell there was something hard and lumpy inside.

After he visited all of the animals, he thought he had better go to the house so he stuck the parcel under his shirt and ran through the rain for the porch.

He entered the parlor and he had been correct. The women were all busy with his Aunt Aggie, and his Aunt Queen was holding a squalling bundle in her arms.

The burlap package was scratching his little chest so he pulled it from under his shirt and laid it on a chair in the corner and went in search of his mother and something to eat.

At dark, the men all staggered in, exhausted, wet and despondent.

Mrs. Willis was in Marthey's bedroom with her daughter and new granddaughter, Mary Lou.

When supper was finished, the storm was suddenly over. The rain stopped and the sky was dark but sparkled with stars.

As Emmy and Ed left to take their children home, Watt told his brother, "we'll check for damages at first light. I hope the crops survived."

He turned to Craig. "The creeks still too high for you to get home. Ya'll can bed down here in the parlor."

Marthey tugged her husbands' sleeve. "Aggie is in our bed and doesn't need to move 'til morning."

Watt laughed and clapped his little brother on the shoulder. "Well then, Bumpy, looks like we're back in the loft. We'll let the women have the bed in the parlor."

Aftermath of the Storm

The next morning came early. Marthey and Dora had breakfast started well before dawn.

Mack came in with only four eggs in the egg pail. The hens had been too frightened by the storm to lay properly. "The hail beat holes in the hen house roof, and I'll need to fix it today and rake out all the wet hay," he grumbled to Watt.

"Did we loose any of the chickens?" Watt asked

"No, they are all there just still very broody."

"What are you doing out of bed?" Dora asked Aggie who stood in the doorway.

"I tried to get her to stay in bed, but she's stubborn," Queen said from behind Aggie.

The men were clustered at one end of the table in the parlor, discussing the storm damage and what needed to be done first.

Queen walked to the corner to retrieve a chair and saw the burlap parcel Billy had left there.

"What's this?" she asked.

Watt recognized it and said between a bite of sausage and biscuits, "We've been wondering where that package got off to. John sent you a present, but it ..."

Before he could finish his sentence, Queen cried out and ran from the room with the parcel clutched to her breast.

"...got misplaced." Watt finished and looked at his brothers for an explanation of his sister's behavior.

Eli seemed to be having one of his spells and didn't notice.

Mack was eating his breakfast like his belly had rubbed a blister on his backbone..

Henry just shrugged.

Jack and Craig exchanged a look and finally Jack replied, "We knew she was sweet on John when she was a little girl. But I thought she was over it." Then he turned to Mack, "I'll split those shingles for the hen house first thing after breakfast."

Aggie watched Queen run toward the woods. Confused and concerned, she left the table and went into the kitchen.

Mary Lou began to fret so she sat in the kitchen chair and nursed her new daughter as Maggie led the little ones into the room.

"Queen just did the strangest thing." Aggie said to her sisters-in-law. "That John Christopher fella sent her a present and she ran out the door crying."

"Oh, my!" Maggie gasped.

Marthey frowned as Dora and Aggie looked more confused.

Finally, Dora put her hands on her hips and scolded, "You must tell us the story. You know we are dying of curiosity."

"Not much of a story really," Marthey replied. "As a little girl Queen attached herself to the fantasy of Lieutenant John and obviously she hasn't outgrown it."

"It was more than a crush for Queen," Maggie said. "Lieutenant John was her hero on a big silver stallion. She would put me to sleep telling stories about how handsome and dashing he was. She convinced herself that one day he would come back for her and they would ride away on Shadow Dancer like in a fairy tale. To Queen, John Christopher was Robert E. Lee, Sir Galahad, and Jefferson Davis combined."

Once breakfast was cleared away, Aggie took her children and went back to her home.

The creek had receded so Dora moved Lancelot back to his stable and took Lela home.

Emmy came to see Marthey mid-morning and they walked through the orchard. Peach blossoms covered the ground. "I doubt if we get much fruit this year," Emmy observed.

The apples hadn't begun to bloom yet so there was hope for a good apple crop.

Ed walked through the orchard on his way to the ox barn. "We won't be home for dinner. Lightening felled a tree and killed one of the cows. Her calf is trapped in the branches and I'm taking Lester to help clear it." He shook his head sadly and kept walking.

Henry came to get some water to take to the other men and told them the crops were ruined. They had been either beaten down by the hail or washed out by the eight inches of rain.

Nannie Taylor stopped by to check on everyone and report that Lizzie was fine. No real damage to her place or the Taylors, but a rider had stopped and delivered the news of a big twister up in La Vergne. There were ten people dead and fifty others injured.

The two made a light dinner for themselves and their children and Emmy asked Maggie, "Where's Queen? I haven't seen her all morning."

"Watt forgot to give her a package from Lieutenant John and she ran out. She's just pouting somewhere. She'll be home for supper."

Queen had run off into the woods where she finally stopped. She was angry with her brothers for not giving her John's gift when they got home, but she was giddy with anticipation to see what her fantasy lover had sent.

She hugged the parcel one more time and sniffed it to see if she could catch his scent. But it just smelled like dirty leather and horse barn hay. Then laughing joyously, she sat on a stump and carefully peeled away the burlap covering. Inside was a pretty little doll with a painted china face. She had a red wig, big blue eyes, ruby red lips, and was dressed in the fashion of the war years. Pinned to her full hoop skirt was a note penned in ornate script handwriting, "To the little Queen of my heart."

When reality set in, it hit Queen hard. Her heart stopped beating for a second. She sat on the stump; filled her lungs with air and screamed. It didn't make her feel better. She stood; the doll falling to the ground. She took two steps forward; stopped; turned around and picked up the doll. She sat on the stump again, hugged the doll and cried.

No thoughts were in her head. Only pain and emptiness. She didn't know what to do. Her dreams were shattered.

Oxygen and blood started to flow again and she said out loud, "Lizzie was right. He sees me as a little girl in short skirts and pigtails."

Gasping again for breath she murmured, "I'm twenty-one years old. Almost an old maid. I don't need a silly doll."

She took the doll by the legs and raised it high over her head, intending to smash the smiling face. Instead she lowered the doll slowly and clasped it to her, then cried again.

Deep, agonizing sobs followed by huge gasps for air. The type of sobs that only come from the soul.

Dora

"It's going to be lonely in Texas until all of y'all get moved there. But I'm excited to see my new home." Dora told Queen as she chopped at the stubborn weeds invading the young twining tomato plants.

Ruthie had sent more seedlings to replace the ones ruined by the storm.

It was a hot June day, and Emmy was big with her fifth child and had begged off the hoeing for the day. She was helping Marthey in the main house so Queen took her place in the garden.

"Craig says our land is lovely with tall trees and a creek running through the pasture. He also says the house is solid, with a deep well and room to build. He says we can put up a picket fence and paint it white, and Lance has a barn and everything sounds beautiful."

Dora peeked out from under her bonnet to see if her sister-in-law was listening. She had been trying to get Queen enthused about Texas, but so far that hadn't happened.

Queens eyes were downcast and no emotion showed on her face. She just kept hoeing and chopping at the weeds.

"I swear, Queen Ann Matilda Ownby, what is the matter with you? Talking to you is like talking to a fence post, these days."

Queen raised her head but looked past Dora. "I wonder who that is riding so hard."

A cloud of dust was drifting away from the top of a hill in the distance. The rider came over the next hill and neither woman recognized him.

They simply stood waiting as the dogs came out from under the porch and started barking. There were several around the place but none had ever replaced Old Ned or Lady Blue in the family's heart.

As the rider approached, Dora squinted and said, "Why, that looks like Papa's stud, Hector. I'd know that white blaze anywhere."

The rider reined in next to the garden fence and the winded Hector pranced and whinnied.

"Miss Dora, It's me, Columbus Banks. I live next farm over from your Pap."

"Yes, Columbus. I remember you as a boy. You've grown a mite. But I'm sure you didn't get my Papa's horse all lathered up just to talk about old times. What's wrong?"

The youth removed his hat and clasped it to his belly, while trying to control the big stud. "Well, ma'am," he stammered. "There's been an accident over at your place. I mean your Pap's place. Ya see, I was helping your Pap cut a tree that was damaged by that storm from a while back and," he stopped and gulped. "Well, Miss Dora, ya see, he's dead."

Dora dropped her hoe and Queen reached out to catch her before she collapsed. Both women fell in the garden between the rows of tomatoes.

Emmy and Marthey had stepped out on the porch when the dogs started barking, and both ran to the garden, beating Aggie only by seconds.

"Get that horse some water over at the trough, young man. Then come back and tell us what has happened," The ever-practical Emmy ordered young Columbus.

Dora revived and sat up. "I've got to go to Mama. She needs me," and she jumped up and ran toward her house leaving the other women staring after her.

Aggie had already sent Billy to find his Uncle Craig. Soon Craig came running up to see what had happened.

"There's been an accident and Dora's father is dead. Go with her and we'll keep Lela until you get back." Emmy told him.

"Thank you Emmy, but I believe the baby will be good for Mrs. Turner. Come to Papa, sweetheart. Let's go find your mother."

Dora already had Lancelot hitched to the buggy and was moving toward the road when Craig stopped her. He placed the little girl in Dora's lap and climbed into the buggy.

"I'll drive. You will kill us all if you get the reins," he told his wife who was sobbing loudly into her daughter's hair.

Elizabeth Turner didn't need her daughter as much as Dora needed her mother.

On the two-mile buggy ride, Dora kept urging Craig to go faster. "Lancelot knows where he's going. Make him hurry."

"No, wife. I won't risk our lives or damage to this horse, just to get you there a few minutes faster."

Mrs. Turner waited for them on the porch as they came down the wide drive. Dry eyed and stoic, she took Lela and held her while Dora stumbled out of the buggy. "Take Lancelot around back and someone will unharness and water him, Craig. Then join us in the parlor, please."

"Oh, Mama!" Dora was crying again. "Is Papa all right? Did that boy exaggerate? You are so calm. Take me to Papa."

"Come inside, daughter. Your Papa is gone. We've laid him in the parlor. Your brothers are there and your sister has been sent for."

"We'll ask the Ownby men to be pallbearers," J.E. was saying to Rufus when Dora entered the room.

She saw her father laid out on the large table and immediately ran to him and fell across the body.

J.E. let her sob a few moments and then pulled her into his arms and held her tight. "Hush, little sister. Your tears won't bring him back."

Craig came into the room and J.E. turned his sister over to her husband and said, "We were discussing if you and your brothers would act as pallbearers for Papa."

"I'm sure they would. Pa and Jeff too."

"I want Jack to make his coffin," Dora declared.

"Now daughter, that's asking a lot of Jack," Mrs. Turner said, bouncing the baby so she wouldn't cry. It was obvious the toddler was getting tired and fussy.

They all turned to look out the front window at the sound of horses approaching.

"It's Pa!" Craig seemed surprised. "And Watt and Ed and Jack right behind him."

The four tall men entered the parlor after dusting off their hats on the porch. Eli approached Mrs. Turner while Watt and his brothers walked toward J.E. and Rufus.

"We've come to offer our condolences, Mrs. Turner. Your husband was a mighty fine man and he will be sorely missed. Is there anything me or my boys can do for you?"

"Thank you, Mr. Ownby. I appreciate your kind words. J.E. is handling the funeral arrangements."

J.E. stepped to his mother's side and said, "Why don't you and Dora take the baby into the kitchen, and I'll send Margaret in when she gets here."

"I'll put on some coffee for you boys. Come, Dora, let's leave the men to discus the details."

Two days later, the family and friends stood encircling the grave as the preacher prayed over Martin C. Turner. Eli and his sons lowered the coffin into the freshly dug hole a few yards south of Nancy Carol Winstead Ownby.

Dora and her sister, Margaret, were sobbing and supporting each other as the first clods of dirt resonated off the beautiful wooden box Jack had made.

Suddenly, Elizabeth Turner lost the tight control she had on her emotions. Her bottom lip trembled. Her eyes filled with tears. Her posture remained rigid, but her face seemed to melt. No sound came from her constricted throat.

J.E moved to his mother and bending low, kissed her forehead. For the first time in his memory, she looked old and weak.

Eli took notice. His heart tugged painfully. He knew well how it felt to have half of your existence suddenly ripped away.

Eli and Elizabeth

By the end of July, Mrs. Turner was a regular guest at the Ownby Sunday dinners. In the warmer months, the Ownby's and the Taylors alternated hosting both families for a large picnic.

Elizabeth Turner insisted on returning the hospitality one hot Sunday in mid August.

Sam and Ruthie had come for the weekend and brought the children as well as Tennessee, Gracious, and Tennessee's two-year-old son Martin.

After dinner the men were all grouped together under a large tree in the front yard. They were smoking their pipes and watching the older children play baseball while the younger ones chased a litter of kittens.

The men were discussing Craig's new farm in Texas and the subsequent move. Sam was saddened by the fact that Ruthie was tied to her property. The plantation was entailed to her son by Mr. Smith and she couldn't leave it until the boy came of age.

Emmy was sitting quietly in the parlor, nursing two-week-old Cynthia Delia when Lizzie stormed into the room and sat in a chair with her arms across her chest.

"What's wrong, dear?" Emmy asked as she put the baby on her shoulder and patted her back to burp.

"I don't understand Pa anymore. All he wants to do at Sunday dinners is talk to Dora's mother. He acts like a lovesick schoolboy. What is wrong with him?"

Emmy laughed and laid the baby down to button her bodice. "Maybe he's in love, Lizzie. Or maybe he just wants some womanly companionship."

"He's been meeting Mrs. Turner at Mama's grave every morning since Mr. Turner's funeral. I see them from my kitchen window." Lizzie started to sob.

Oh my goodness, Lizzie. That's the answer. He knows what it's like to mourn someone. He's just offering comfort to the widow. It's a bond they share and your Ma and Dora's father will rest side-by-side for eternity."

Wiping her eyes on the perpetual rag from her pocket, Lizzie sniffed. "He promised to get her a headstone when the war was over and she's still on that hill with a rotting wooden cross. And now he's courting another woman at her gravesite."

"I doubt he's courting Mrs. Turner, Lizzie. Here, hold little Dell while I go get us some lemonade."

In the kitchen, Emmy glanced out the window and saw Eli and Mrs. Turner sitting in the big white double swing hung from a sturdy Oak limb.

"With Martin gone there's nothing to keep me in Tennessee," Elizabeth said and looked out the corner of her eye.

Eli took a moment and asked, "What will you do?"

"Well, Margaret is married and Rufus has a mind to go to Colorado, of all places, and J.E. has been like a ship without a rudder ever since his wife and baby died. So I think I'll sell this place. I can give Rufus funds to chase his dream and Margaret's husband can pick up the acreage he's been coveting. Then J.E. and I will head to Texas with Craig and Dora."

Eli's heart jumped. He had been dreading leaving her, but it was too early to declare or even understand how he felt about her. He just knew he wanted to be with her. He hadn't felt that way in sixteen years and it confused and exhilarated him.

Scarlet Fever

Eli Ownby   *29 October, 1877*

Dear brother and family

We just returned from burying little Guy. That is the third baby Will and Minerva have burried in as many weeks.

All of the children have been stricken with the Scarlet Fever. The two older boys came down with it first and pulled through and are recovering now. The rash and fever was bad and both boys are peeling like a dried onion, but the doctor ways they will be normal soon.

The babies had it worse. The twins were too young to fight the fever and the infection spread to little Guy. They all cried so with the sore throats and there was nothing Minerva or Tabitha could do to entice them to eat.

Minerva is overcome with grief. She took to her bed after Tessa's funeral and hasn't left it since. Will couldn't even get her to attend Reed or Guy's burying.

There were three other buryings at the cemetery today. All of them friends and neighbors children under ten-years-old.

It is a sad time in Carroll County.

Will is ready to move to Texas as soon as Craig can get settled and find a place for him and Minerva. He thinks the change will help with her grief.

K and Jane's children escaped the fever and Tabitha is well and sends her love to all. She is deeply mourning the babies and doing her best to lift Minerva's spirits.

I hope you have a Happy Thanksgiving Day and are planning a festive All-Hallows Eve celebration.

Write soon big brother.

Yours,

Joe

When Watt read him Joe's letter, Eli cried.

"Those poor babies. How they must have suffered. Let's go visit. I need to see Tabitha."

"We can't get away right now, Pa. We have to get the crops in, and Craig wants to leave in a couple of weeks. Since Dora is expecting in the spring, they need to get to Texas before time for spring planting. We'll go after harvest. I promise."

CHAPTER 16

GOING TO TEXAS, 1877

Craig and Dora

"Haaww," Craig yelled as he snapped the reins to begin their journey to a new life. The procession made quite a sight as it wound down the road.

Dora was in the lead with her mother and two-year-old Lela. Lancelot pranced and stepped high, pulling the light covered buggy like he was leading a parade.

Elizabeth Turner had sold her property, and after gifts to Rufus and Margaret had purchased a large covered wagon and a team of six mules.

She and Eli had said their goodbyes with a promise from Eli that he would be in Texas as soon as he could.

John Ephriam Turner drove the covered wagon. Eighteen-feet long; eleven-feet high and four-feet wide, it was loaded with household goods and trunks of clothing. The sides rattled and clanked with buckets and tools and things needed each night for making camp.

Craig brought up the rear in a heavy freight wagon, loaded with farm equipment. The sides of the shallow wagon had been extended with the planks containing the names and birthday measurements of the eleven Ownby children.

Eli had removed them from the foyer walls and insisted Craig take them to their new home. The boards represented a talisman to draw the family together again..

Lester and Baxter needed little coaxing to plod along and keep the wagon and buggy in sight.

Lela's dog, Spot, was running back and forth between the wagons, barking at everything. Lizzie had given the child the puppy as a going away present.

Pleased that the weather was dry and moderate, Craig and J.E. had decided to follow the same route taken by Watt and Craig back in January.

The family had been together for Thanksgiving in October and Polly and Sam had said their goodbyes to the sojourners.

Eli stood on the porch watching his son drive off into the unknown with a portion of his heart. He wanted badly to be in that wagon train with them but knew he needed to stay to help get everything in order for the rest to move.

Watt watched the group leave with a different perspective. He had bought Craig's five acres and had given him some cash. He clapped his father on the back and said, "I better get to my chores if we want to sell those pigs at market on Saturday."

"Son," Eli looked at Watt, "what about going to see Will and Joe and them."

"I can't get away, Pa. With Craig gone, I've got to cover his chores too. If the pigs bring a good price Saturday, let's get you a train ticket to Huntingdon. You could take Queen. I think she's still angry with me and maybe a train trip will cheer her."

Shelbyville

The pigs sold for premium prices and Watt purchased two train tickets from Shelbyville to Huntingdon.

Ed wanted to take a look at some horse stock for sale in Shelbyville, so he drove his father and sister in the wagon. They planned to spend the night with Polly and Roy.

As Roy lead Ed and the team to the barn, Polly took Queen upstairs to Nancy's room to freshen up after the long wagon ride.

"Oh what a beautiful room!" Queen declared when she saw her fourteen-year-old niece's bedroom. She touched the white bedspread embroidered with birds and flowers in pretty colors. The windows had white ruffled curtains that fluttered where the window was open a few inches to allow fresh air in the room.

Nancy was a lovely young woman. She attended school every day and resembled her mother and her aunt Lizzie in looks and stature. Nancy proudly told her Aunt Queen, "I embroidered the spread," then added as an afterthought, "with some help from Eliza."

Queen raised her eyebrows and looked at her sister questioningly.

"Eliza is our cook. She belonged to Roy's father but stayed with us after the war. You'll meet her at supper along with..."

A child's laughter followed by "Git back here you wicked little girl," interrupted Polly's sentence.

A pretty little toddler with curls and a frilly dress burst into the room giggling. She ran and hid her face in Polly's skirts and was followed by a young skinny black girl

"I's sorry, Miz Polly, she done got away from me. Come here Miz Beulah. Yore mama done got company. Let's go get you some shoes on afore you ruin your stocking."

She reached for the child who ran from her mother to her sister and hid behind Nancy's skirts.

Polly smiled and said, "It's alright, Caroline, I'll tend my daughter. Go help your grandmother get supper ready."

Turning to Queen again, she plucked her youngest from behind Nancy's back and kissed the squirming little girl on the cheek. "Beulah, this is your Aunt Queen. I'll put you down but you best behave and mind your manners."

Queen held out her arms to take the girl and, ignoring Polly and Nancy, sat in the rocker and started telling the girl all about her cousins back on the farm.

In the barn, Ed was unhitching the team while Roy filled the feed trough and Eli watched young John remove their bags from the back.

"So, Craig is on his way to Texas?" Roy asked.

They left last week," Ed answered. "Him and Watt were excited about what they saw there and Craig bought a place before they left to come home. Me and Emmy plan to move after the first of the year. Do you want us to look for you some land out that a-way?"

"Polly and I discussed moving, but to be truthful, we're both happy here. The farm is doing well and I just can't see moving away from what we have."

Eli looked at his son-in-law and said, "I'd love to have you bring my daughter and grandchildren with us, but a man has to do what he thinks is best for his family. If you change your mind, just come on out to Texas."

He turned to his oldest grandchild. "How about you, John? Think you might like to go with us?"

At sixteen, John was a pleasant young man who helped his father work the farm. He smiled shyly but said clearly, "I'll stay and help Papa here on our place."

The next morning after a hot breakfast cooked by Eliza and served by Caroline, Ed and Polly drove their father and sister to the train depot and saw them aboard. They stood and watched until the train was well down the tracks.

"I'll walk back to the house so you can get on the road," Polly told her brother. Ed hugged her tight. "I'll be back in two weeks to pick them up. I need to go see about those horses and get back before the ole sack-of-bones comes looking for me."

Polly smiled and said, "Bring Emmy and the children next time, if you can. And have a safe journey, little brother."

Eli and Queen

Eli and Queen settled into their seats on the train and Eli dozed off to the clacking of the wheels. When he awoke, he looked over at Queen who was staring forlornly out the window. His once vibrant and spirited daughter was sad and despondent and he didn't know why.

"Why are you so sad, Queen?" he finally asked her.

"Do you remember when you started calling me Queen instead of Mattie?"

"No, daughter. I'm afraid I don't remember. When was it?"

"Lieutenant John gave me that name. I thought he was so handsome and gallant the first day he came to the farm. And when he came the day the wounded Yankee was found, he was a bright light in an otherwise dark world. I saw him as a knight on a big grey charger. All he saw was a silly little girl. I suppose I'm still a silly little girl. A silly little girl with no dreams left."

Eli took her hand in both of his and held it a few minutes, trying to think of something to ease her pain. "Is he the reason you have rejected the young men who have tried to come courting you?"

"Yes, Pa. I always thought he would come back for me. But he isn't. Is he?"

"No, Queen. I don't think he is. John Christopher was a fine example of a Confederate Cavalry officer. His sworn duty to protect the innocent combined with his chivalrous and loving nature drew him to you like a moth to a flame. I could see it when he looked at you." He stopped and thought for a moment.

"You were so young. If you had been a little older or if he had been a little younger, things might have worked out differently. You'll find someone else to share your life, my dear. Just be sure to keep your heart open."

Father and daughter sat holding hands quietly for a while as the train clicked and clacked its way into the sun. Queen broke the comfortable silence.

"Why didn't you marry after Mama died? I know there were widows in the county who would have been happy for your attention. It would have been much easier for Lizzie. She needed a woman to help with the babies."

Eli didn't speak but seemed to be lost in thought. Then, he smiled a wistful smile and said, "I was selfish. Your Mama was the only woman I ever loved, and I didn't want to share you children, who were the proof of that love. Was that a mistake?"

Overcome with emotion for her father, Queen squeezed his hand and said, "No, Pa. We survived, and perhaps we are stronger because of it."

She reached up and adjusted her hat and plumped her curls and gave her father a sideways look. "Are you gonna marry Mrs. Turner?"

Eli turned to look at his daughter and for the first time saw the stunning woman she had become. Instead of answering her, he simply began humming the "Bonnie Blue Flag".

Crossing the Tennessee River

"I haven't been this tired or dirty in my whole life," Dora complained to her mother as she hung wet clothes across a rope strung between two trees.

Two weeks of travel had brought them down the Natchez Trace to the Tennessee River near Florence, Alabama. They were camped at Colbert's Stand for a few days until they could secure ferry passage across the wide river.

"Hush up, daughter and wring that shirt tighter or it will never dry," Elizabeth Turner said.

The women were cleaning garments and readjusting their packing. Clothing took up the most space in the covered wagon and they were trying to make everything easier to get too on a daily basis.

Both women dressed in simple day dresses for the trip, foregoing corsets, bustles and beribboned bonnets, but they had brought their best dresses packed away in trunks.

Craig and J.E. had gone to the ferry landing to make arrangements for the river crossing and the women were taking advantage of the men's absence.

"Seventy-five cents for the wagon and mules. That seems like a steep price," J.E. grumbled as the men approached the campsite.

"And thirty-five cents for the wagon and oxen sounds cheap," Craig replied. "What the devil have those women done now?" he exclaimed as he saw the chaos in camp.

Trunks were open; the wash kettle was over the fire; clothes were hanging everywhere and Lela and Spot were hiding under the wagon afraid they were next for the wash pot.

"Is that my new rope, woman?" Craig yelled. He had bought it before they left home and now it was wet from the soggy laundry and knotted and wrapped around two trees.

"I couldn't very well use one of the old, dirty ropes for the laundry, now could I?" Dora yelled back and continued to hang Lela's bright dresses across the line.

J.E. laughed out loud and poked Craig in the ribs. "Glad she's my sister and not my wife."

Craig scowled and told his wife, "The ferryman says we can cross tomorrow if we start at first light. It might take two trips to get across. Get everything packed up, so we can be there before dawn."

"Our skirts aren't dry yet and I refuse to pack them away still wet," Dora stated adamantly. "Make arrangements for the next day," and she turned back to her laundry.

"NO! I don't care how you do it. But we are leaving in the morning. With or without your fancy dresses."

The ferry master rubbed his eyes in disbelief the next morning as the procession approached the landing. In the lead was a pretty young woman expertly handling a buggy and a prancing Tennessee Walking horse. Next were two oxen pulling a heavy freight wagon. But bringing up the rear was a covered wagon with the canvas rolled up on each side. Suspended between the ribs were ropes draped with men's shirts and colorful girls and women's dresses all flapping in the breeze.

The ferryman took a long look at everything and spat in tobacco on the ground and said, "That'll be one dollar and thirty-five cents, mister."

Craig grumbled but counted out the coins as J.E. lead the oxen and freight wagon aboard the big flat barge.

Next, Craig drove the mule team and covered wagon up the ramp and lined it up beside the other. There was just enough room to put Lancelot and the buggy behind the freight wagon.

Pleased that they could all go across together, Craig smiled as he stepped off to lead Dora's stud and buggy aboard.

Lancelot balked. He whinnied. He reared. He refused to step on the ramp.

Terrified, he wanted nothing to do with the rocking barge. Wild eyed and neighing loudly, neither J.E. nor Craig could coax the animal forward.

Dora dismounted and calmed the stud with a gentle whisper. She took one of Lela's dresses from the line and covered Lance's eyes and walked the horse onto the barge, giving her husband and her brother a smug look.

Spot ran back and forth along the dock, barking. He was afraid to follow but didn't want to be left behind.

"Do somethin' with that dog, mister. I gotta shove off now," the ferry master told Craig.

Lela was screaming, "Spot, Spot, Spot," and the dog was getting more frantic trying to get to the little girl.

Craig jumped off the barge, picked up the dog, and jumped back on the ferry. He barely made it. The puppy squealed during the jump and in his fright, he released his bladder. Craig put the trembling, wet animal in the wagon. He lifted Lela into the wagon and told the sobbing little girl, "Hold that damn dog, or next time I'll let him swim."

Mrs. Turner climbed into the wagon and held the little girl and the wiggling puppy for the long river crossing.

"How's Lance?" Craig asked Dora as he fanned his puppy-soaked shirt.

"He's calmer. As long as I keep his eyes covered and stay with him," she replied and giggled at her husband's wet shirt.

Craig moved toward the front of the barge. When he passed the wagon, he yanked a clean shirt loose from the wires. He removed his soaked one and threw it in the river.

The ferryman stood there watching their progress. "I'm sorry, mister, but I'm gonna need to charge you for that dog. It's another two and a half cents for extra animals."

Craig dug in his pocket and pulled out three copper pennies and handed them to the man. "How much would you charge to let me leave him behind?"

The ferry man laughed and said, "That would cost you a dollar," and he made his way back to the rear of the barge.

Craig patted Lester on the rump and pulled out his pipe, lit it, and exhaled. "I think I'd rather go through a blizzard than a repeat of this morning. Wouldn't you, boy?"

The ox just snorted. Craig took that as a sign of agreement.

Tabitha and Queen

"There's Joe," Eli told his daughter as they stepped off the train at the Huntingdon depot.

It had been four years since Joe's short visit but Queen would have known her uncle in any crowd. Tall, slender with the same dark hair, deep set blue eyes, and cheekbones as high as his brother's and nephews.

Eli hugged his youngest brother and smiled broadly.

"Do we need to wait for your luggage?" Joe asked.

"Pa wouldn't let me bring anything but these two cases," Queen pouted and pointed to two soft bags at her feet.

Joe picked the bags up and said, "I'm sure the ladies in my house can supply anything you might have forgotten. The buggy is just over there, and Tabby is waiting for you both at home."

Queen was once again charmed by her unassuming uncle, and she entertained him with chit-chat all the way to Joe's house.

Will was sitting on the porch waiting for them when they arrived and he helped Queen down from the buggy then took her bags to the porch.

Queen was delighted to see her uncle Will again. She remembered his visit ten years ago with his new bride Deliah but had never met his new wife, Minerva.

"Will, get Queen set up in the front bedroom while I unhitch the team."

Eli set his bag on the porch and turned to help Joe.

Will stopped him. "Tabby is waiting to see you in the parlor, big brother. Joe can unhitch the team."

The house was quiet and solemn. No children's voices could be heard nor any bustle from the kitchen. It was obviously a house of mourning.

Will led Queen upstairs to a large sunny room at the front of the house.

"This was Mother Laurie's room. We keep it for special guests now that she no longer lives here. Tabby wants you to come see her in the parlor as soon as you freshen up. Take your time. She and Eli will visit for a long while."

Meeting her Aunt Tabitha was a life changing experience.

Seated in the sunny front parlor, Eli's older sister was composed and immaculately dressed. At fifty-nine, she looked much younger. Still-dark hair was pulled back and fashionably coiffed. Tiny earrings sparkled in her ears, and a simple ring adorned her right hand. Quality materials clothed her trim body in the latest fashion. Her unlined face was pleasant and her sightless eyes were bright blue and wide open. Queen could see intelligence and curiosity in her expression.

"Come closer, niece. I want to see your face."

Puzzled, Queen hesitantly approached her aunt. Tabitha could sense her niece's confusion and extended her hand. The scent of lavender swept through the room. "Sit next to me so I can feel your face, Queen."

The younger woman sat patiently beside the older one as Tabitha ran her hands over Queen's face and hair. "Such a pretty girl you are. You must look like my mother, Mary Jane." Then she clasped the soft plump hands in her cool slim fingers and said, "Why are you so sad, child?"

Queen broke down in tears and spent the next hour pouring her heart out to this compassionate aunt who was really a stranger to her. She never shared what Tabitha said to console her, but from that moment on she always had a smile on her face.

A woman from town came daily and cooked and did light cleaning, but she didn't tend the children.

The two remaining children in the house, eight-year-old Geoffery and five-year-old Ernest stayed quietly in their room except at mealtime. They missed their little brothers and sister, but most of all they missed their mother's love and attention.

Minerva had taken to her bed, incapacitated with grief over the loss of her three babies. The boys were allowed to visit her twice a day in her darkened bedroom. She didn't laugh, or smile or tell them stories like she did before.

When Queen entered Minerva's dark room, the first thing she did was rip open the curtains and let the sunshine in. The sad woman in the bed cried out in pain as the light struck her red, tear-stained eyes.

"Who are you and how dare you intrude on my mourning."

"I'm your niece, Queen Ann Matilda Ownby, and you, Aunt Minerva, have children to take care of."

"My babies are dead. Leave me alone and close those drapes." Minerva screamed and pulled the covers over her head.

Queen sat on the edge of the bed and gently pulled the covers from her aunt's face and said in her sweetest voice, "I know you are sad, but you have two little boys who need their mother's love. They have lost their baby brothers and sister also. Now, sit up and let's dress your hair before they come visit."

At Queen's insistence, Tabitha and the children started to congregated in Minerva's bedroom, forcing her to be social. Queen entertained her aunts with stories about the family and all the children.

K brought Jane and their three children to visit one afternoon and Queen realized immediately what type of person her Uncle K was. She understood that anything he said was to be only half believed.

While the women and children visited with Minerva, the four brothers locked themselves in Joe's office with their pipes, and Eli shared Watt and Craig's trip to Texas and discussed their future plans.

Laurie came to visit with her nine-year-old daughter, Minnie.

The little girl took to Queen immediately and followed her around like a lost puppy dog. Minnie only left her side when Joe was in the room. She ran to her big brother for hugs and kisses.

For two weeks, Tabitha and Queen spent a private hour together every afternoon.

At the end of their visit, Minerva was out of bed and tending her children; Eli had established a better relationship with his much younger brothers whom he barely knew, and he had spent quality time with his beloved sister.

Eli noticed a change in his daughter and knew his sister had worked her special magic.

On the train ride back to Shelbyville, he asked, "Did you enjoy our visit with your Aunt Tabitha? Did she have anything special to impart?"

Queen just smiled and paraphrased 1 Corinthians 13:11

"When I was a child, I spake as a child, I understood as a child, I thought as a child:

but when I became an adult, I put away childish things....

"Mostly."

Queen once again had a spring in her step and color in her cheeks and a smart comeback to anyone who dared tease her.

Christmas in Mississippi

"Give me four of those blue candy sticks and let me see that baby doll on the top shelf, please," Dora told the clerk at the General Store in Greenville, Mississippi.

The girl behind the counter rolled an attached ladder over to the section and climbed up to retrieve the boxed doll. As she was descending, she stepped on her skirt, screamed, dropped the doll, and started to fall backwards toward the counter.

J.E. was standing next to his sister and rushed around the counter to rescue the girl. He caught her in his arms and just stood there holding her and gazing into her face.

Shaken by her near fall but amused by the man holding her tightly, she glanced at the very pregnant Dora and whispered, "Shouldn't you put me down before your wife gets angry?"

He let her go so quickly she barely landed upright while J.E. looked all round the store. His eyes met those of a smiling Dora.

"That's not my wife," he sputtered. "That's my little sister."

"And you_r_ little sister would like very much to see that doll, J.E. Turner. I want it for Lela's Christmas present. Since we're stuck in this one horse town for the holiday, I want her to be happy."

The clerk bent over and picked up the box and handed it to Dora without taking her eyes from J.E.

The bell on the front door tinkled and the clerk broke her gaze and J.E. jumped like he had been shot and moved from behind the counter when he saw his mother and Craig enter the store.

Mrs. Turner was carrying Lela and handed her to Dora as she said, "I secured us rooms at the hotel down the street. They have a very nice evergreen tree in the lobby and promise a lovely Christmas dinner tomorrow. Just think, daughter. A bath and a bed for two whole nights." Elizabeth Turner looked very satisfied with herself.

Craig looked irritated and went straight to his brother-in-law. "Your mother is as stubborn as her daughter. I tried to tell her we need to save the money and not waste it on a hotel. But she insisted on staying there until we can get the ferry across the river. She said Dora needs to rest. Humphffff. She's not sick; she's just having a baby. See if you can talk some sense into these women."

J.E. was still watching the young clerk. He had discovered her name was Malinda Weiss and her father owned the store. He glanced at Malinda and said, "A couple of days sleep in a real bed would be good for all of us. Let the women have their little luxury."

The bell tinkled again and three overdressed ladies entered the store, all of them talking at once.

Craig slapped his hat on his head and growled at J.E. "Let's get away from this hen house. I saw a saloon down the street."

He turned to Dora. "Don't buy out the store. We don't have room to carry it. I'll see you at the hotel for supper," and he stomped out with J.E. following, reluctantly.

Dora showed her mother the little doll and Mrs. Turner's practical side prevailed. "Lela will have a real baby to care for in a couple of months, so she doesn't need an imitation. Let's look at the yard goods. I doubt if we can get pretty calico in Texas."

That evening after supper, the little group was having a last cup of coffee in the dining room. Lela was asleep on her grandmother's lap. The hotel was decorated with greenery and bright ribbons and a large evergreen tree sparkled in the lobby. Tomorrow was Christmas Day.

Dora had taken a long warm bath and washed her hair in the hotel bathhouse. She was relaxed and comfortable for the first time in six weeks. She was also anticipating sleeping in a real bed instead of the back of a wagon.

"Are you gonna go calling on that girl from the mercantile?" she teased her brother. "She was very pretty in an exotic way. But kinda young though."

J.E. blushed and ducked his head. "I might. Although it's Christmas Eve, she's probably busy with her family."

"I doubt it, son," Mrs. Turner said.

"Why do you say that, Ma?"

"Because she is Jewish, John. Didn't you say her father owned the store? I saw several references to Morris Weiss and his son-in-law Nathan Goldstein in the newspaper. They are very prominent in the city and in the Jewish community. You had best forget little Malinda, son. There will be young women in Texas. God-fearin' Christian women."

Elizabeth sat back; stroked her granddaughter's hair and sipped her coffee as both her son and daughter sat with open mouths. Neither had ever met a Jewess before.

Christmas morning, Mrs. Turner insisted they all attend services at the Methodist Church and then they had a lovely dinner at the hotel.

The group was much refreshed after their stop for the holiday. Even Craig conceded it had been a worthwhile two days.

Early on the morning after Christmas, Craig and J.E. loaded the freight wagon and tied Lester and Baxter to the front railing. They secured the unruly Spot in the covered wagon with a rope and Mrs. Turner held Lela tightly in her lap as J.E. drove the team onboard with little effort.

Spot had spent the two-day stop over tied to the wagon wheel in the stable and was desperate to run and chase. Mrs. Turner kept him on a short rope and promised he could run later.

Dora covered Lancelot's eyes, fed him a sugar cube, and apologized profusely for ignoring him for two days. He seemed to understand and stepped high onto the big barge.

The party made a smooth trip across the Mississippi River to Arkansas.

The Natchez Trace

CHAPTER 17

A BRAVE NEW WORLD, 1878

Callie Taylor

"Please, come quick," Ben Youngblood begged. It was a bitter cold day in January of 1878. The wind was howling and blowing a light snow around the farmyard as he stepped up on the porch. "Callie's having her baby," he told Watt. "I stopped to tell Mrs. Taylor and Lizzie, but Callie is scared and wants all of her sisters with her and any other women folk available."

Watt hitched the team to the wagon while Marthey and Queen gathered rags and other supplies. Marthey would take eight-month-old Jennie with her, but Maggie would stay and watch over AC.

The wind and snow cut visibility so badly the three-mile trip took longer than normal. When they arrived, Nannie and Lizzie were already there. After getting his wife and sister in the house, he unhitched the team and put them in the barn and joined Ben and Anderson in the kitchen.

Lizzie's one-year-old Dave was playing by the fire. Jeff stayed home with four-year-old Maurice. The men settled in for what they hoped was a short wait.

Cold wet air followed Ellen and Betsy as they came in the door together, accompanied by Ellen's husband Joe Lance.

Betsy was carrying her eight-month-old daughter and put her down next to Dave, knowing the men would keep close watch on the little ones. The snow was falling harder and Joe told the men, "Looks like it might be a major blow. The snow's falling harder now than when we started out."

The women hurried into the bedroom and found their sister well on her way to delivering. Her contractions were very close together and Callie was pale and weak.

"Callie, you need to start pushing hard with the next pain," Nannie told her daughter. "I can see the baby's head and it looks like a big one." Marthey and Betsy flanked the laboring woman. They each held a hand and allowed her to squeeze as hard as she could. Callie's breath was raspy and her cries were getting weaker.

"The birth canal is tearing; this baby has broad shoulders," said Nannie to no one in particular.

"It's a big boy," cried Queen as the baby slipped into the world and into his grandmother's hands. Nannie swiftly handed him to Queen who blew in his face. He let out a loud yell, and Queen placed him on Callie's belly.

Nannie turned back to her daughter. She quickly and with confidence tied off the umbilical cord.

Lizzie and Queen rushed the baby into the kitchen to show his father.

Queen started breaking eggs and separating the whites into a bowl.

"What are you doing?" Lizzie snapped.

"I'm mixing egg white and lard to coat the baby in. What does it look like?"

"You aren't going to put that nasty concoction on this baby. Soap and warm water will keep him healthier. I'll tend to him. You go help Nannie Taylor. Go on."

Nannie had a very worried look on her face. She whispered to Ellen, "She is torn and bleeding and the afterbirth hasn't come yet. Rub her belly. We've got to get the afterbirth out."

Ellen started to knead her sister's abdomen. Callie screamed again and the contraction expelled the placenta.

Nannie let out a sigh of relief and began to clean her daughter and tried to stop the bleeding. The perineum tear was ragged and bleeding profusely. Nannie worked for an hour and Callie soaked one rag after another until the pile was high.

"Send the men for buckets of snow," Nannie told the room. "We have to get this bleeding stopped."

Lizzie stepped into the room with the baby. "Here's your son, Callie. He is beautiful and robust, with ten fingers, ten toes, and a full head of black hair," she said as she laid the swaddled baby at his mother's breast, but Callie didn't respond.

She had gone into a deep sleep.

Nannie placed the baby's mouth on Callie's nipple and he knew exactly what to do and started to suckle. All of the women smiled and for a few moments, they were content with the past few hours of work.

Ben came in followed by Watt. Each man carried two buckets brimming with snow.

"Thank you, boys, you may go now." Nannie shooed the men from the room. When they left, she started to pack snow around Callie's abdomen and on her genitals. "Now we wait," she said with resignation.

Nannie noticed Lizzie with an empty bucket in her hand, picking up the soiled linens from the floor. She was using a clean rag to gather the soiled ones. "You can put those in the pantry with the other soiled cloths. I'll clean them tomorrow," she told Lizzie.

"No, ma'am. I'll take them to the burn pile. We don't want to use these again," Lizzie informed her mother-in-law.

Marthey and her sisters exchanged a knowing look while Queen watched the baby nursing peacefully.

Close to midnight the snow finally stopped. Nannie tried to send everyone home.

Marthey refused to leave so Watt left his wife and baby daughter and took Queen home to get some rest. The other women left also, knowing they would be back to relieve Marthey and their mother later in the morning.

All through the night, Nannie and Marthey worked diligently changing and packing snow and trying to stop the bleeding. Toward morning, the blood flow had slowed, but Callie was burning up with a raging fever. She had not awakened since the baby was born. He was nursing and her milk had come so the women knew he was getting nourishment.

At noon, Watt came to take Marthey home and Nannie insisted that she go.

Crossing the Red

After crossing the Tennessee and the Mississippi rivers, the ferry crossing of the Red River was a non-event.

Craig and Mrs. Turner had both tried to convince Dora to ride in the covered wagon instead of driving the buggy. She was stubborn and insisted her pregnancy didn't hamper her handling of Lancelot. So far she had been correct. Spot was the animal who caused the most trouble on the trip.

Two days before they reached Paris, Texas, they were camped for the night. Mrs. Turner was making supper over a campfire while the men tended the animals and Dora mended one of Lela's dresses by the last light of the day.

Mrs. Turner glanced up from her task and looked around. "Where's the baby?" she asked her daughter.

"She's right over there playing with Spot," was the reply. Then Dora raised her head and didn't she her daughter. "Lela! Lela, come here baby. Lela, answer me. Where are you?"

All she heard was a faint dog howl and a far away, "Spot, Spot, Spot."

Dora dropped her mending and yelled, "Craig, J.E., Lela's gone chasing that blasted dog. Go find her." In her panic, she tripped over a piece of loose wood and fell.

Mrs. Turner rushed to her daughter and Craig and J.E. ran into camp.

"Go find my baby," Dora screamed at the men and stood then stumbled again.

Craig moved to offer his wife assistance. "Go, find Lela. I'm all right."

Mrs. Turner helped Dora to a stump and said, "Sit."

"I've got to go find her, Mama."

"I'll go look for her. You stay here in case she comes back," and she walked into the woods after the men.

Dora could hear the men yelling for little Lela. Not knowing what to do, she rose and a twinge of pain shot through her abdomen. In fear for her unborn child, she sat back down on the stump. She felt the baby shift. It was the type of movement the little one made every night before it settled down to sleep. Dora smiled and cradled her extended stomach.

Then she remembered. Where was Lela? She bent over and put her head in her hands and cried. She cried out of fear for her lost daughter; from exhaustion of the past two months, and finally she cried from fear of the unknown land they were going to.

"Mama. Mama. Spot is gone," Lela came running from the trees. Her father, uncle, and grandmother following.

"Lela, baby, where were you?" Dora grabbed her daughter and hugged her and kissed her face and hair. She held the girl at arms length and saw no wounds or damage, aside from a little extra dirt.

Dora wiped her eyes and hugged the girl again then turned her over her knee and swatted her bottom.

"You had us terrified."

She hugged the baby again as the girl started to cry. Then she shook her. "Don't ever wander off like that again. You hear me, young lady?" And she hugged the girl again and covered her in kisses.

The men just stood and watched. Neither of them had ever seen Dora so out of control.

Mrs. Turner knew. She understood a mother's anguish when her child is in danger. She took Lela's hand and tried to lead her away by saying, "Let's get you cleaned up for supper, sweetie."

"But Spot's still out there. I want Spot."

Craig stepped in, as he saw his wife tear up again. "He'll come back, let's eat supper." Under his breath, he whispered to J.E., "If we're lucky the damn dog will stay gone."

They left the campsite the next morning.

The buggy was tied behind the freight wagon, and Dora had consented to ride in the bed of the covered wagon and was holding her daughter to keep her from falling out. Lancelot was tied behind so Dora could keep an eye on her horse and Lela was hanging out the back of the covered wagon screaming, "Spot, Spot. Come here, Spot."

Joseph Franklin Youngblood

"Mama, where's my baby?"

Nannie Taylor was dozing in the chair by her daughter's bed and thought she was dreaming.

"Mama?" There it was again.

Nannie opened her eyes and saw Callie struggling to push back the heavy covers tucked around her feverish body.

Jumping up, she felt her daughter's forehead. The fever had broken.

"I'm thirsty," Callie whispered in a very weak voice.

"Oh, my sweet girl. I'll get you some fresh water and have Marthey bring you your son." Kissing the girl on the forehead, she hurried from the room.

"She's awake, thank the good lord, the fever has broke," Nannie cried out as she entered the kitchen.

It had been two weeks since the baby was born. Callie had nursed him that night but had lapsed into a feverish sleep the next morning, and Marthey and Betsy had been taking turns feeding the infant since then.

"Marthey, take the baby to his mother, and, Betsy, go find Ben and tell him his wife is awake. Ellen, take her some fresh well water. I'm going to warm some water to bathe her and get rid of the fever sweat."

Neither of the women had ever seen their normally stoic mother so flustered, and they all did as she said.

Betsy soon returned with an anxious Ben who barged through the house and rushed to his wife's bedside.

Callie was trying unsuccessfully to nurse the baby. She was pale and weak and crying. "He won't nurse. He doesn't like me." The distraught mother said as Ben entered the room.

"You're still weak, sister," Marthey said quietly. "Your milk needs to come back and it will with time. Let me feed the baby and you visit with your husband."

Ben looked at his frail wife and took her hand. "We have a fine big boy, Callie. But we can't keep calling him "baby". What would you like to name him?"

"Let's name him Joseph after your uncle and Ellen's husband. You choose the other name."

Ellen's husband Joseph Lance was Ben's uncle and it was through him that the couple had met.

"How does Joseph Franklin Youngblood sound? Would that please you, my sweet?"

Callie didn't answer. She had once again fallen into a fevered sleep.

Doctor McGrew had been to see her twice since her confinement and had told Nannie that treating the fever symptoms and prayer was the only course of action. The tear in her perineum was infected and he had no way to heal it. Her body had to fight off the infection or she would die.

On a cold but sunny February day, Caledonia Ann Taylor Youngblood was laid to rest in the Ivy Bluff Cemetery.

"What am I going to do with a baby?" Ben asked his sisters-in-law after the burial.

"Betsy and I both have milk. We've discussed it, and I have more help at home with Watt's sisters and his brother's wives," Marthey told the grief stricken widower. "I'll keep little Joseph with me until he's weaned and you can take him home."

Paris at Last

It was a long and arduous two days but Craig and J.E. pulled into the outskirts of Paris, Texas around noon. Lela had finally stopped calling for the lost Spot, and the hoarse little girl had stopped crying the night before.

Craig stopped at the livery stable to make arrangements for the wagons and horses for a few days.

J.E. hitched Lancelot to the buggy and Mrs. Turner followed the liveryman's directions and drove Dora and Lela to R.D. and Jane's house.

Craig and J.E. walked to the Ownby Carpentry Shop owned by R.D. and his brothers John and Bart.

A drunk had set a fire, which burned most of the downtown area a few months earlier and the carpenters were busy helping rebuild the town.

"I'll walk Craig and J.E. home," R.D. told his brothers. "Jane is expecting you all for supper tonight."

Supper was lively that night. Everyone caught up on news from Tennessee and the women shared stories of their children and various birthings.

Lela was the youngest of the children and cried herself to sleep in her grandmother's lap, missing the wayward Spot.

Craig told R.D and J.S. about Jack's talent for woodworking and the men discussed how the trait ran through the family.

Starting with Thomas who was born in 1728 in Essex, Virginia, who apprenticed as a millwright, there had been members in each generation who made their living working with wood.

Dora and her mother took advantage of Jane's hospitality the next day and laundered their clothing and repacked their trunks. It felt good to be a part of a household with a roof over their heads instead of canvas or the clear sky.

Craig and J.E. did some minor wagon repairs and picked up a few tools and supplies they would need to set up when they reached the farm.

The second morning of their stay in Paris, Craig told the women, "In another week we'll be in our new home."

"I can hardly wait to see it," Dora replied smiling. "First thing is to get the beds unloaded and set up, then the kitchen organized. Is there adequate barn space for Lance as well as Lester, Baxter, and the mules? We need to get a milk cow soon, and I know you want some pigs. And chickens, we will need eggs."

"Slow down, Dora; let's get there first," Craig reminded her. "There was a nice barn and a house when I left. I'm sure there will be repairs to make, but Skaggs and Reeves have already said they would help."

Breakfast was interrupted by a commotion of dogs barking and children hollering outside in the street. R.D. went to the door to see what was happening when he called for everyone to come see. Before they could all get up from the table, Lela took off running out the door yelling, "Spot."

Coming down the middle of the street was the blue tick hound with his nose to the dirt. He was totally focused on his trail and oblivious to the parade of mongrels and children following behind him.

He staggered up the porch steps and into Lela's outstretched arms and collapsed, breathing hard.

Lela threw her little body down next to him and started kissing his head and rubbing his ears.

His paws were bloody and his ribs were showing, but if a hound dog can look happy, Spot was content.

R.D. scratched his head and looked at Craig. "Your dog, I assume?"

Craig grumbled low so only R.D. could hear, "Yes. Dammit."

Delays

"Hush little baby
Don't say a word
Auntie's gonna buy

You a mockingbird
And if that mockingbird
don't sing
Auntie's gonna buy
You a golden ring"
Marthey crooned to baby Joseph.

It was two in the morning and the five-week-old infant was nursing loudly as she rocked him by the coals of the kitchen fireplace.

It was the third night since Callie's funeral, and the baby hadn't slept through the night yet. He shared the cradle with ten-month-old Jennie and Marthey was hoping he would soon be able to make it until morning so he didn't wake Jennie.

Marthey was exhausted but content. She was thankful for Queen and Maggie's help around the house and the support of Lizzie, Emmy, Aggie, and of course her own sisters, Betsy and Ellen.

Baby Joe was thriving and as Marthey burped him and placed him back in the cradle with his cousin, she smiled and adjusted the covers around both children and patted their backs gently.

As she crawled under the covers next to her husband, Watt said quietly, "We can't move just yet, can we?"

"No dear. Joe won't be weaned this year and I don't think Ben will allow us to take him to Texas."

She started sobbing softly. "I owe my little sister this much. To keep her baby safe and healthy until his father can care for him. I miss Callie so much."

Watt took her in his arms and held her until she stopped crying and fell into a restless sleep.

He laid awake the rest of the night rearranging his plans for getting everyone to Texas. He would write Craig a letter tomorrow, care of Reeves, and explain why their move would have to be delayed.

Home at Last

Craig thanked R.D. for his hospitality and help while Dora promised Jane she would write and try to visit soon.

Lancelot was once again tied to the covered wagon and the buggy was hauled behind the freight wagon as the group left Paris for the final leg of their long journey.

Spot's feet were still wounded and bloody from his hard travel, so he rode in the wagon with Lela and Dora.

Nine days later, on February 12, 1878 they neared Pilot Grove, Texas.

Dora insisted on driving the buggy with her Tennessee Walker, Lancelot, prancing in all his glory. She had dug around in the trunks until she found her best bonnet and prettiest day dress. She intended to make a favorable impression on any neighbors they might meet.

Craig was the only one who knew the way to their new home so he had the lead in the freight wagon pulled by Lester and Baxter.

J.E. followed the buggy with the canvas covered wagon.

The road to their new home was smooth and tree lined. The day was sunny and warm. Dora was giddy with expectations. She felt like Craig had chosen a lovely and serene place to raise their family.

Craig crawled to a stop throwing up a cloud of dust over the buggy, and when Dora and her mother stopped coughing, they saw a dilapidated house, which looked empty and forlorn.

Craig jumped down from the wagon and ran back to help his wife from the buggy.

"Are these our new neighbors?" Dora asked hopefully as her feet touched the ground. "The place looks abandoned."

"No, dear. This is our new home." Craig beamed proudly, sweeping his arm around the yard. He led her to a broken gate in a crumbling fence and as they stepped through, Spot ran between them and started baying at the one step to the front porch.

Lela screamed as an odd looking creature waddled out from under the porch.

Gun metal gray, it looked like an inverted cooking pot. It had short legs, a long snout, and long tail and was followed by four tiny replicas of itself.

Dora grabbed her daughter and screamed, "What in hell is that thing? What kind of primitive world have you brought us to, Eli Craig Ownby?"

Craig laughed. "It's called an Armadillo, Which is Spanish for little armored one. They are harmless and eat bugs and worms. That's a mother and her four babies. According to Reeves, they won't hurt you and Spot can't hurt them."

Elizabeth Turner and J.E. joined them in time to see the little family waddle off into the tall grass.

Both watched incredulously.

"Let's go look at the barn," Craig said cheerfully to J.E., "while the women decide where to put things in the house." Oblivious to his wife's distress, he walked off toward the building in back. The roof sagged and one door was completely missing.

Determined to remain cheerful and optimistic, Dora's face didn't register her dismay. She took a deep breath, put her hands to her massive midsection, and made a mental note to never again allow her husband to purchase a home without her prior approval.

She walked slowly toward the house, considering the potential and trying to ignore the negatives.

Lela took off chasing Spot who had given up on the armadillos and was trying to identify every new scent in the yard.

The two women stood in front of the house staring in amazement.

Built low to the ground, it had no cellar or loft. Large stone chimneys rose from each end and a wood enclosed well stood in the side yard next to a firepit with a collapsing tripod.

Shuttered windows flanked a central door and the porch sat almost on the ground with one corner missing several boards.

The walls were rough, irregular planks with daylight shining through the gaps.

Dora suddenly had a longing for her solid little one pen home back in Tennessee.

Mrs. Turner couldn't hide her disappointment.

"Let's look inside, Mama. I'm certain it just needs cleaning and a woman's hand. I'll write Marthey tomorrow and tell her to bring my curtains and rugs when she comes in a couple of months."

Lela ran up laughing and full of joy. She grabbed her mother around the knees and hugged tightly as Spot lay down at her feet.

The baby kicked violently and Dora put her hand on Lela's head as tears streamed down her face.

Mississippi Ferry

Ferry Fee Schedule

For man and horse... .10
For man or horse, either.. .05
For a carriage or wagon with four or more horses..................... .75
For a pleasure carriage with two horses................................... .50
For any one horse pleasure carriage or cart............................. .25
For an ox cart or wagon with two oxen..................................... .35
For an ox cart or wagon with more than two oxen..................... .62 1/2
For a dearborn or wagon with three horses or more.................. .35
For sheep, hogs, cattle, goats, etc. each................................... .02 1/2

Next in the Series
A TWIST OF TOBACCO

Heavens Promise-A Final Twist

Coming in the fall of 2016

On All-Hallows-Eve, Queen, Mack, and Maggie joined their single neighbors at a Snap-Apple-Party. The traditional autumn celebration was an opportunity for the young people to meet and choose a future mate.

Candlelit Jack-o-lanterns cast an eerie light along the walkways and the house was backlit by a large bon-fire burning in the fallow field out back.

Next to the fire, a big wooden tub of water contained floating apples. Each guest was given three tries to snatch an apple in their teeth. The first lucky boy or girl who managed to snag a bobbing apple would be the next one of the assembled group to marry.

Mack went first thinking this would be easy, but after nearly drowning on the third attempt, he gave up and went to check out the food tables.

Disdainfully, Queen refused to risk ruining her elaborate hairdo and walked past the tub toward the house.

Several other young men and women tried and all got wet for their trouble. Still no apple had been caught.

Henry pushed Maggie toward the front and sneered. "Go on, sister. It's the only way you'll ever get a beau—pure luck, or a blind man."

Furious, the normally shy Maggie walked up to the tub, bent down beside it, and to the shock of everyone watching, stuck her face in the water, and came up with an apple in her teeth. Not a hair on her head was wet. Reaching up she calmly took the apple from her mouth, pulled back her arm, and threw it as hard as she could, hitting Henry right square in the middle of his forehead. She grinned and with her head held high, walked away to find her sister.

In the parlor of the house, several young women were playing a different game. This test involved three shallow bowls. One was empty, one contained clear water, and the other held dirty dish water. The guest was blindfolded and the bowls were shuffled around. The blindfolded woman was led to the table, extended her left hand, and dipped it into one of the bowls. Whichever bowl she chose would determine the status of her future husband. If she chose the clear water, she would marry a single man. If she chose the dirty water, she would marry a widower. If she chose the empty bowl, there would be no marriage.

The crowd was quiet so as not to give any hints. Queen approached the table with blindfold in place. She stretched out her hand and took her time before she let it rest on the rim of a bowl. A gasp came from the other women circling the table. Wiggling her fingers her hand touched nothing but cool china. The bowl was empty.

She ripped the blindfold off and turned to leave the room just as Maggie came in.

"I got the apple, Queen. Henry goaded me into it, and I had to show him it could be done. Then I hit him with it."

Queen chuckled and sighed. "I'm proud for you, Maggie. It looks like I'll never get married."

"Oh these games are silly. They don't mean anything. They are just for fun," the younger girl tried to console her sister. "Look they are starting something else and I see Mack over in the corner, eating as usual."

The hostess was passing out slips of paper and pencils to all the young women. "Ladies, write your name on the paper," she announced to the room. "I'll place them in this bowl and whichever gentleman draws your name will be your escort for supper and the first dance."

Queen refused to participate and turned away, but Maggie wrote her sister's name on a paper and handed it to the hostess.

Queen was surprised to hear a deep masculine voice say, "Queen Ownby. I must meet this lady named Queen."

The crowd parted leaving Queen standing quite alone. She faced a tall, young man with dark brown hair and twinkling brown eyes. Her knees deemed to melt. She knew he wasn't John Christopher, but he could have been his brother.

The man walked toward her, took her hand, and kissed it. "Thomas Moore, at your service, Miss Queen," and he smiled.

Gulping air, she placed her hand on his extended arm and for the first time in her life, Queen Ann Matilda Ownby was at a loss for words.

Made in the USA
Middletown, DE
22 August 2016